Hell is
another place

by

David O'Neil

W & B Publishers
USA

W & B Publishers

For information:
W & B Publishers
Post Office Box 193
Colfax, NC 27235
www.a-argusbooks.com

ISBN: 978-0-6158894-6-7
ISBN: 0-6158894-6-8

Book Cover designed by Dubya

Printed in the United States of America

Chapter One

...Iraq 1991

The F15 landed, leaving a banner of dust in its trail. It was followed by the others in succession. Captain Mike Summers hauled himself out of the cockpit with the help of the ground crewman. He felt dehydrated and was looking tired as he made his way across the sandy ground to the concrete building the housed the flight office and debriefing centre.

Passing through the double doors into the air conditioned interior was like being slapped. The shock of the lower temperature was almost painful after the torrid heat outside.

He pulled on his flight jacket and walked through to the debrief area.

By the time he was seated his wingman had joined him in the next chair. Flight Lieutenant Sir Peter Hamilton-Davies was on detachment to the squadron from the RAF. His place as Mike's wingman had been resented by the others who thought that as an intruder he should have been relegated to a more junior place in the system.

After one flight Mike was quick to defend his wingman who was in danger of out-flying everyone else in the squadron, including Mike. Now after three weeks in the desert all resentment had gone and Peter was a valued member of the team.

The major from G2 came to the table and conducted the debriefing. It did not take long as the flight had been without incident and all aircraft had been brought home without damage.

In the mess hall the group gathered, the two women pilots who drove the big tankers hanging back until hauled into the group by Peter. Both women had qualified on F15's but the rules at the time did not allow women to fly in combat. As Peter was quick to point out, flying an unarmed refuelling tanker aircraft in the combat zone qualified as combat flying in his estimation, so they belonged in the club. Captain's Sarah O'Conner and Jessica Browning had each been in Iraq for three months before the arrival of the F15 squadron under Colonel Patterson. Major 'Stuffy' Smith, the second-in-command, had been lost in one of the early sorties. His F15 had flamed out and though his ejection seat had operated he had been out of contact from the call that he was ejecting. The beacon that should have located him had failed to operate. Though his approximate location had been recorded, searches by Special Forces teams in the area had failed to locate him after nearly three months. While he was recorded as missing in action, most presumed that he was dead.

Mike had been acting in his place in the interim and there was no surprise when the news of his official promotion to major came through.

The party in the mess hall was called to order by Peter, who stood on a chair and lifted his glass of Coke. "You are all invited to join me in celebrating the promotion of our beloved flight leader to the exalted rank of major, in fact now rather than assumed."

The cheer that followed this announcement attested to the popularity of the embarrassed man seated in the centre of the group.

A career member of USAF, Mike Summers loved to fly and to him the idea of being paid to do it was almost indecent. The party went on for just over an hour; they were all scheduled to fly in eight hours' time so there was a limit to the celebrations that all understood.

The squadron had been in country for three months and was anticipating rotation to Saudi Arabia for R&R in two weeks' time. They would be relocated at a recovered air-base in Kuwait after Saudi.

In the mess hall that evening, Mike and Peter were eating when a small group of dust-covered men in Army fatigues came in. They piled their gear in the corner and collected food from the commissary and sat at the same table to eat.

"SAS," said Peter quietly.

"How can you tell they're not Delta?" Mike said.

"SAS, they are all eating at the same table." Peter said confidently. "Officers and other ranks."

Another man dressed in the same way came in and looked around the room. He spotted Mike and Peter and came over. "Major Summers?"

Mike saw the tag with a cloth crown on it. "I'm Mike Summers, Major; what can I do for you?" He waved to a chair, "Have a seat. This is Flight Lieutenant Hamilton-Davies, RAF."

The Major nodded to Peter and took a seat. "Bill Chapman, SAS."

Having introduced himself he got down to business. "I understand that you have a Blackhawk here and that you two gentlemen are the only two people currently able to fly it. The normal crew I understand are all down with some infection.

Mike studied the Englishman with interest. "Can I ask why you need our Blackhawk?"

"I could tell you but I would have to kill you."

"In that case, I and my British friend here can fly the Blackhawk. Where and when would you like us to fly it?"

"We have a situation. We understand that you lost a Major Smith some time ago and he has been out of touch since. Well, we have managed to pick up a hint that he is being held with several others including two of my boys in a holding camp – that means an interrogation centre – in a desert location that we can get to; but it is a matter of time. If you could get us to the vicinity we would be able to reach the place, hopefully before it's too late.

Mike looked at the SAS major. "I'll need to get clearance from the boss; he doesn't like the helicopter to go beyond the boundary of Kuwait. It is mainly used for local search and rescue."

"I'll see your boss and find out if we can get to use it. If I can, are you game?"

Mike looked at Peter, who nodded. "Right, you get clearance and we're in. I'll need maps of the area and I'll also need to make arrangements with my flight leaders."

Bill Chapman rose and shook hands with Mike and Peter. "Thank you both, I'll get organised. We will need to get going by 02.00 hrs."

He left them and joined his men for a short talk, then left the mess.

Mike rose to his feet, "Peter, can you pre-flight the Blackhawk. I guess we will be going, that guy Chapman does not strike me as someone who will take no for an answer."

***

Mike called in to speak to Captain Sarah O'Connor and Lieutenant Jessica Browning in their shared quarters in the Bachelor Officers' Quarters. He told them what was happening and that the flights would be going out with the deputies. There was no actual reason for this except they had become good friends and he foresaw them joining the squadron as pilots in the near future.

Mike was married but things were not all they should be as his wife was unhappy with his career. This, despite the fact that he was already a career serviceman when they married.

There was nothing happening between Sarah and himself but he could not help thinking that he had possibly made a mistake marrying his high school sweetheart.

Sarah said "What sort of range will you need? Do you have fuel capacity in the Blackhawk?"

Mike said, "By carrying a blimp of extra fuel beneath the fuselage the 'Hawk can do the range and get back with a full load. It allows us to use the stub wings for the armament package. The boss, Colonel Patterson, is not happy with the situation but he has given approval for the mission.

The two men rose.

Sarah said "Come back Mike, we'll miss you."

"Piece of cake – quick in, quick out – no worries, as our Aussie friends say." Peter commented as they walked out.

"We'll worry about you, Mike!" Peter said, shaking h is head sadly. "Peter can go to hell, but we'll miss you, Mike."

"If I just happen to beat you with a two by four you will understand there would be nothing personal in it." Mike said. "For the thousandth time there is nothing going on between Sarah and me; were good friends that's all."

Peter grinned. "I believe you." But he didn't.

They studied the charts for the area, which were not particularly helpful, and Peter pointed out that most of Iraq appeared to be nothing, with huge areas where the only in-habitants seemed to be goatherds and camels. They would fly a course by GPS, using a dog-leg vector, stopping to refuel from the blimp at the turn. The return course would be direct, carrying the extra people and having lost the weight of the fuel blimp.

"All things being equal, you would be back in six hours, two and one-half hours out, one and one-half hours there and two hours back." The briefing officer sounded brisk and matter of fact.

"Since when have all things been equal?" Peter mut-tered.

"Any problems, Flight Lieutenant?" The major brief-ing them gave the impression that he regarded aircrew as a bunch of ill-disciplined schoolboys. He had little patience with their posturing and high spirits.

"Why no, Major, just a little dust in my throat."

As they walked out to do the walk-around inspection of the Blackhawk Mike said, "Dust in your throat?"

"Well, the man pisses me off. He hasn't even gotten his shoes dirty since he arrived here and he is always get-ting at the boys over their dress and horseplay in the mess-rooms."

Mike said nothing. It was true and it was also true that Peter used every opportunity to needle the Major, whose name was unfortunately Snelling, regularly abused by apparently accidental mispronunciation.

***

"Blacksheep 15, permission to hover?"

"Permission granted 15, you are clear to deploy when ready. You have a clear board, on your flight-path over a 30-mile radius. Good hunting!"

"Roger control, 15 out."

Mike turned to Major Chapman seated behind him. "Commencing 23.00hrs for the log."

Bill Chapman repeated, "Commencing the log 23.00."

The flight was boring but it demanded low level flying using the nap-of-the-Earth system to prevent radar detection. At that height there was no time for a SAM system to lock on before they were past and out of range. They landed on schedule and refuelled, leaving the blimp at the site as they lifted off on the new course for the vicinity of their destination.

The Blackhawk settled gently to the ground and the SAS deplaned. Chapman gave Mike a small radio. "It's encrypted and it jumps around the channels, I am told. It will send to and receive from my transmitter only. If anything goes wrong I'll call, and you can get the hell out of here. Okay?"

Mike shook hands. "Okay!"

The entire group disappeared into the darkness. The sounds of the night seemed to suddenly become heard, along with the creaks and squeaks of the cooling metalwork of the helicopter.

***

It was Peter who heard the faint sounds of gunfire about forty minutes later. The crewman of the helicopter came forward to report that he had heard the firing, too.

Mike said, "Get the guns mounted." He referred to the two 30mm Machine Guns that could be mounted both sides of the machine through the side doors.

The crewman said in a hurt voice, "They are already in position sir." Standing orders said that when in Indian country the guns would be mounted, so they were.

Mike was throwing switches and pressing the starter as he spoke and the rotor blades began to turn. The radio squawked, Peter answered.

Chapman spoke. "We got the men and a woman out but a platoon of reinforcements turned up, we're holding them off but it looks bad. You had best get out while you can."

Mike said, "Tell him to send up a white flare toward the opposition and a green from his position when he hears us arriving. Then take over the other door-gun."

Mike was lifting the helicopter into the sky as Peter relayed the message to Bill Chapman on the ground.

"Acknowledged!" Peter said laconically, and released his seat belt and went back to the starboard doorway. The crewman, Corporal Abbott, looked at him and grinned when he appeared. The gun was locked and loaded, ready for action. Peter seated himself and hooked on. He plugged in his intercom and reported ready.

Mike said, "When we see the white I intend going straight over. I'll turn beyond them and run back to our people. I'll pick up-on the hover. Tell Chapman, please."

Peter called Chapman and told him what was going to happen. "Acknowledged, sir; he'll be ready with cover when you hover."

Moving the control column, the helicopter moved forward, picking up speed and heading for the fire-fight that had developed at the scene of the rescue attempt. Flying very low, Mike used his night-vision headset until he closed the scene of the battle proper, then he pushed them up so as not to be dazzled by the flares and gun flashes. The white flare shot forward under them and out of the corner of his eye he saw the green shoot skyward from below.

"Ready?" he called to the door guns. At the same time he pushed the armament switch, allowing him access to the rocket pods mounted on the stub wings. The helicopter had been spotted by the enemy below and the flak was coming their way. The heads-up display allowed him to pick out the major concentration of fire and it was at that area that he aimed the first two missiles. He was rewarded with a bright explosion as he banked the big machine round to reverse his course. Both door guns were chattering away at targets on the ground. They were taking hits from some small arms, though there was no sign of the damage interfering with operations.

A second green flare indicated the location of the rescue party. He dropped down behind their position as immediately a group of four people came at a crouching run over to the doorway. Peter reported "There are three men and a girl here, Major Smith is rather worse for wear but the others seem quite mobile."

His next message was not so good. "Smith says that the others can't pull out without endangering the helicopter so we should just go and leave them to it."

Mike thought about it. "Peter come and take over, I'll have a word with Chapman."

Peter appeared and seated himself in the co-pilot's seat taking over the controls. "Mike, watch it outside; there is lead flying about like a gangbuster's convention."

"I'm wearing my vest." Mike said "I won't be long. Now take off and I'll shout when I need you." He held up a radio hand set. "Channel 6, right?"

At Peter's nod he left, collecting his personal H&K, smg and ammo vest as he passed out of the helicopter.

As Peter had said it was noisy and dangerous. In the door of the helicopter, Corporal Abbot fired bursts over the heads of the crouching SAS men. Mike slid down beside Chapman. "Can we break away from here?"

Chapman turned to him with a wry grin. "I don't think so."

Mike lifted the radio to his lips "Peter! Get out of here. I'll keep in touch, we will set out on foot."

"The boss is not going to like this." Peter said. "He didn't want you to come in the first place."

"Shit happens." Mike said "See you later."

They heard the helicopter rise and depart, the sound of the blades beating rising above the gunfire and explosions from the bitter conflict it left behind.

Five miles away the UH-60 Blackhawk settled to the ground gently and the rotor stopped spinning. Peter left his seat and turned to the others. "How are the wounded?"

Major Smith, United State Air Force, turned to him. "Nothing that would stop you popping back to pick up the others. If I take the other gun, have you any spares to refill the missile rack?"

"No but we still have four unused, and a box of grenades; all we need is someone to throw them."

One of the other men said "I can handle the door-gun if the Corporal can throw them."

Abbott grinned. "I've always fancied throwing grenades. They only let us throw one live one at training school; said we were Air Force, we leave the grenades to the Army. Here there, pilgrim, have you used one of these before?" He explained the workings of the 30mm while Peter and Major Smith worked out what they would do.

The woman, an Army nurse named Margaret Cross, having checked the dressings on the wounded man at the door gun, turned to Peter, "Have you another gun I can use?"

Peter looked at her for a few seconds, then he gave her his personal weapon, a H&K smg similar to Mike's, along with the ammo vest. "I do not have a Kevlar vest. I'm afraid though the ammo vest is a pre-Kevlar bullet proof, if you can get it on."

"Thanks. I'll manage."

They took off once more and made a wide circle to bring them up to the enemy line from the rear.

Peter aligned with the line of enemy indicated by the line of weapons firing at the SAS group. Arming the other missiles he dropped as low as possible for maximum results and fired; they skipped along the ground and exploded near the other end of the line.

As they flew along the line one door-gun fired aft while the other fired forward. Abbott threw grenades and Margaret fired at anything she saw move.

At the end of the line the firing had reduced considerably. The Blackhawk dropped to hover behind the SAS position and Abbott called, "All aboard!"

The party boarded in a rush and the helicopter sheared off, dodging a missile with a swing of the tail and making off at nought feet for the first waypoint on the journey back.

***

The board of enquiry was not sympathetic to the actions taken by Major Summers. Agreeing with the suggestion of the Brigadier General in command of the area that leaving the helicopter in the charge of an RAF Officer while under fire, even if said RAF Officer was on official attachment to the USAF, constituted neglect of duty. Their suggestion that this was desertion of his post in the face of the enemy could not be substantiated in view of the vigorous defence mounted by the British authorities who had in fact recommended the major for a decoration for his part in the rescue of the prisoners.

***

Brigadier General Wallace was not pleased. He delighted in a reputation of being a no-nonsense leader who would not tolerate inefficiency, and treated it ruthlessly where he found it. He had a long memory and having decided that Mike Summers did not fit his ideal of a USAF officer he used every opportunity thereafter to block any progress that he was in a position to block.

Over the next years Mike Summers and his wife worked at keeping together while Mary-Jo grew up. But by the time she got through high school it was all over.

General Wallace had been true to his word, transfers to the Aleutian Islands followed by attachment to Gann in the Indian Ocean, with a combined boredom factor to test a saint, was enough for Mike's wife Nancy to decide that the service life was not for her. She departed, taking Mary-Jo with her. It was no comfort to Mike to find she had already made arrangements for her future with a Washington suitor named Peterson. To be fair though, by that time Mike was no longer really bothered. As long as Mary-Jo was alright, and Peterson seemed to be a sensible sort of individual, then Mike was happy. There was never any problem over visitation or communication rights, and Mary-Jo got on well with her stepfather.

The general still managed to interfere though he was unable to block Mike's promotion to Lieutenant Colonel. His influence seemed to have diminished when the reductions in force came along, because Mike was transferred on retirement to the National Guard, maintaining his rank with seniority.

Chapter two

...Deployment

Mike Summers drove the pick-up truck along Roosevelt to his house. As he drew up into the driveway, he pressed the remote and raised the door of the double-car garage that stood next to the small building, and drove into the vacant slot next to the black Ford Galaxy. He had a routine for these occasions and as he swung out of the truck he reached for and lifted the heavy tool-bag from the truck bed. The ease of the action betrayed the fact that he was not only fit but there was strength hidden in the lean compact body. He turned as the door dropped and without stopping pushed a second remote button to pop the house door in front of him.

As he stepped through the door the house came alive and a female voice said, "Hi, Mike."

"Hi, Liz," he said. "Any calls?"

"Mary-Jo called, she is on rotation to Afghanistan this week. Give her a call tonight, nothing else."

"Right. Remind me in twenty," he was still moving; he dropped the tool-bag and hung his tool-belt in the closet in the utility room. As he passed the coffee maker in the kitchen he spoke again. "Coffee in fifteen." He stripped off the work boots, leaving them beside the stove.

He showered and returned to the kitchen in a soft white cotton shirt and jeans. The coffee maker had performed and all else was ready as he sat and hauled on his favourite low-heeled cowboy boots. They were tan and shined and as he stamped his feet into their depths he felt the familiar pleasure wearing them always seemed to bring. He was also reminded of the occasion when Nancy, his former wife, had bought them for him. Mary-Jo's mother was someone in Washington now. Not just a lobbyist, Mary-Jo had said, a 'Wheel!'

The house spoke, "Mary-Jo on the line, boss."

Thanks, Liz," he said. "Hi, Mary-Jo, what's happening?"

"Hi, Dad, thanks for the call back, I know you're on detachment for the next few weeks, I've got my orders for Afghanistan. I start staging out at the week end."

"Yeah, Liz said, but you've been expecting this for the last month. Is everything okay?"

Lieutenant Mary-Jo Peterson, United States Marine Corps, was an Apache driver and this would be her second deployment since she had qualified. Her stepfather had been sensibly supportive. A matter that had made his insistence on her becoming formally adopted when he had married Mike's divorced wife a little more bearable.

"True. I just thought it would be good to catch up before you and Uncle Peter hit the road to the Base."

"I'll let 'Uncle Peter' know you were asking for him. Maybe by the time you come back off rotation he'll have forgiven you for calling him that." Mike was laughing as he said it. His friend and colleague, Major Sir Peter Hamilton-Davies DFC, Bronze Star, former RAF and current reserve Major in the USAF, was rather sensitive about allusions to his approaching 'middle' years' as he put it.

They spoke for a few more minutes, the relaxed voice of her father reassuring to Mary-Jo, who was beginning to wind up a little in anticipation of the overseas rotation. She put the phone down reluctantly and turned away from the wall phone. She was in Quantico, where she was deployed for the initial briefing for the operations over the next few weeks.

***

Mike put the phone down, still a little troubled at the call from Mary-Jo. He stood for a few moments thinking, then he shook his head and got back into his routine, smoothly following a series of evolutions that culminated in his being at the door to the garage with his two rolling trunks of equipment and uniforms. As he always did, he swept his gaze round the area to see that nothing was out of place. Then, opening the door, he pushed the two trunks out and stacked them into the Galaxy. Back in the house he checked he had his cell phone and charger. Picking up the land-line phone, he called a number. When it was answered he said, "Leaving now!" Hearing a reply he grinned and said, "And you," put the phone down and turned, punched the alarm switch, saw red light come on, and left through the garage door.

As he locked it he looked around the garage, then, sure all was well, he climbed into the Galaxy and started up. The garage door was rising as he allowed the engine to warm up. He drove out onto the drive and the door closed once more behind him. The tell-tale on the remote went out proving the closure was complete. Only then did he swing out into Roosevelt and tool the Galaxy down to Notre Dame where he made a left down to the main road through Dearborn.

Mike didn't bother avoiding Detroit on his way to Selfridge USAF Base. He drove straight through to Lake St Claire. There he turned alongside the water northward to St Claire Shores to collect Peter Hamilton-Davis. At the Eleven Mile Road in the township he turned and rolled down past the football field. Checking the mirror he did a U-turn to the other carriageway reversing direction and after a few yards indicated and swung off into a private driveway lined with trees. The house lay back out of sight of the road; trees in the area scattered throughout the plot gave privacy to a low bungalow with a screened-in veranda. The building blended in with the landscape, and the wood shingles—faded to a natural soft silvery colour—seemed to create the illusion of a lack of care which, as Mike was well aware, was an illusion.

As he switched off the motor, the door opened and a figure appeared, towing two rolling trunks similar to Mike's. He took them to the nearside sliding door which rumbled quietly back on its runner while the trunks were loaded in. The door closed and the figure returned to the house, the interior lights came on and Mike finally shifted from the Galaxy and strolled into the house.

"'Lo, Pete." Mike offered

"Beer?" Was the reply

"Yeah, time for one." Mike said. "Things okay with you?"

"Nothing changed since yesterday, that is. How is Mary-Jo?"

"Just said hi, going to the big 'A'. I guess, she's maybe feeling a little wary after last time."

"Yes. Well, we all have to learn that experience doesn't cure fear, just lets us into a few tips on how to survive it."

As Mike listened to the clipped Englishness of his friend's voice he still marvelled at the fact that despite nearly twenty-five years in the new homeland, the accent had not altered or diminished in any way.

"The bottle drained, it's time to go." Peter said in an awful American accent.

"Promise me you will not do that again in this deployment!" Mike said in a pained voice. "I swear if you do you do you will spend the remainder regretting it."

"What did I do?" Said Peter with a grin, then, "Are we ready to go now, Sir?"

The pair were silent as they left the house and commenced the last few miles to Selfridge Air National Guard Base at Anchor Bay on the lakeshore.

***

As they checked in, they were both aware that all over the United States men, just like them. were doing the same thing. Since 9/11, it had become increasingly so. The US would not be caught out again.

At Selfridge the gate guard snapped to attention and saluted as he returned the two men's ID. "Welcome home, Colonel, Major."

Mike tapped his hat brim. "Thank you, son, carry on," and drove into the base, along Jefferson to the turn-off for the BOQ.

Both would normally have qualified for Quarters but neither had families, and though this was an extended deployment, did not need the inconvenience. Mike pulled up at the entrance of the accommodation and opened the door. The wind off the water was cool and he sucked a lung full noisily.

From the other seat Peter said, "Gung Ho, ho ho!" and leapt out of the Galaxy and slammed open the sliding door to retrieve his trunks. By the time Mike had hauled his own out, Peter had disappeared through the entrance. A young airman appeared as Mike closed the trunk of the vehicle.

He saluted. "I'm Oskar, sir, Tech Sgt Leman Oskar. I will take these to your room, sir. I will be attending to you during your stay, sir!"

Mike looked at the young man and nodded. "I'll put the Galaxy away then. What is my room number? "

"If you will, sir, one of the general's suite's has been reserved for you, sir."

Mike's eyebrows elevated at this information. He started to say something but changed his mind, they could sort it out in the morning. He climbed back in the car and drove to the flagged parking bays.

He parked without thinking too much, still preoccupied with the accommodation glitch. Then into the BOQ building where he was attended by a short, dapper airwoman with carefully contained dark hair and a spectacular figure. She escorted him to the end of the short eastern corridor and opened a door into a small suite of rooms. His trunks were in a room on the left, there was a second door into a bathroom, and to the right was a room containing a kitchen with cooking facilities and a refrigerator. This room had a settee and two easy chairs with a small desk in the corner. There was a wall-mounted flat-screen TV and the desk had fittings for the attachment of a laptop.

The airwoman coughed. "Would you like me to unpack, sir?"

"You'd better not, they'll realise the mistake in the morning and I'll have to move on. I am just a lowly Lt

Colonel and they don't give us this sort of accommodation."

The airwoman looked puzzled, then she opened her Blackberry and typed in some instructions. The cough was followed by, "Sir, may I?"

Mike who had seated himself, swung his head and nearly collided with the anxious bosom thrust in his direction; the blackberry was placed in front of him. The instruction was explicit. Dated July 2nd 2007, Brigadier General Hammond is replaced by Brigadier General Michael Summers. Accommodation to be arranged accordingly – Office of the Commanding General USAF- Reserve. The order was signed Wallace R.J. Beside the door was a package, and a separate letter addressed to Brigadier M. Summers USAF. The letter stated that Lt Col. Summers M. promoted, Brigadier General as from January 1, 2006. Pay and increments to be adjusted WEF that date. By order of the Commander-in-Chief United States Armed Forces. Signed once more by General Wallace .R.J.

The airwoman picked up the package that awaited collection on the small table inside the suite door. It was marked for the attention of Brig Summers. "Perhaps this might explain, sir?"

***

Later, alone once more, Mike now changed into shirt-sleeve order uniform, uncomfortable still with the loops showing the single star of his new rank. Pete had come in earlier, just to establish his envy officially at the quarters. He didn't stay and Mike did not blame him. Things were no longer the same. Earlier they were still two people who had never really grown up. Now, whether he liked it or not, he was officially an adult and expected to act like one. He sighed and put his old rank badges in the drawer. *I'll think about it tomorrow. First,* he wondered, *Wallace R.J.* It couldn't be, the man had dogged his career ever since the Gulf. Now, suddenly, he had overseen the promotion of the man he had victimised for years.

Neither Mike nor any who knew him believed the general had suffered a change of heart, so they gave serious thought to where the catch had been hidden.

***

Breakfast was in the roped off section in the mess dining area. He was joined at the table by Major Peter Hamilton-Davies and Major Jessica Browning. Still embarrassed by the new rank stars, he was relieved to discover that his friends were still friends, and neither held it against him. The fact was that both thought it was long overdue.

It was Jessica that brought up the inevitable question. "What about Hell Week? Will we be able to fit it in first or do we go as we are?"

Hell Week was the first period of a long deployment. Designed to bring the troops up to operational efficiency, it was a period of unremitting chasing by NCO's and drill instructors, PT, and forced marches. Everyone took part, and in Mike Summers' outfit, you had better be prepared.

"The troops will be waiting for the answer to that one." Peter said drily.

Mike sat back and pushed his plate away. "We have no time. The way I see it, we will be pushed to make the deadline anyway, so we just make sure everything is double checked as we do it. What I will do is insist all haircuts are cleared up today. No excuses. That way at least most will have some sort of look of the service, while we catch up on the rest in bits and pieces as we go. The deployment will be to a base in Turkey. I have never heard of it but I believe it's on the GPS." Mike grinned and both the others smiled. It was good to laugh, especially in the circumstances.

Peter stopped him before he left the table. "I gather your promotion was signed by General Wallace R.J."

Mike nodded. "I wondered, too. I can only conclude that whatever we are down to do in Turkey will be tough. That man would never do something like this." He tapped the star on his shoulder. "Without good reason. So it's eyes open and keep your powder dry!"

They parted, each deep in thought.

***

The wind from the mountains of the Georgian Republic was cold, a biting thing of dust and desolation. Here in the northeast of the Turkish Republic there was not a great deal to be done about it. As Mike turned, pushing the collar of his parka higher round his ears, his survey of the bleak landscape found little to make the vista feel more welcoming. A movement far away against the slope of the mountain caught his eye. He lifted the binoculars hanging round his neck and focussed them on the spot. He could just make out the figure, a man with a camel beside him. The figure was looking at him. For a second he stood frozen, then to the astonishment of the driver of the Humvee, he dropped to the ground flat.

The crack of the passing bullet was loud and shocking. It hit the newly restored corner marker of the Airbase with a thud.

Mike lifted his glasses from his position on the ground, focussing carefully he established that the sniper had gone. He clicked the rangefinder on the binoculars, 3870 yards registered.

He stood and looked for and found the bullet hole in the corner post. With his pocket knife he dug the bullet out.

***

The Turkish Air Force Base they had been allocated was serviced to full NATO specification, but apart from Colonel Pava Kemal and Master Sergeant Ali Baranka, there were no Turkish Air Force personnel on the base. There were however one hundred 'sweepers and carriers' as Peter put it. Maintenance and serving staff who were there to help the visiting US units to settle in.

In his office Mike was contemplating the spent bullet that he had dug out of the marker; he was still finding it difficult to believe that the shot had been aimed at him.

The knock at the door interrupted the train of thought and he called "Come in, it's open."

Lt Col. Chuck Hartog stepped through the door and snapped to attention at the salute. "Congratulations, Sir, a promotion long overdue."

"Aw hell, Chuck, sit down and brief me. How is the set up going?"

As base defence security commander, it was Chuck's job to make sure that they could not be jumped, and if they were there were sufficient trained assets to bloody the nose of anyone who tried.

"All the Patriot sites are mounted and manned, in fact we have been issued with more than I would have expected. In addition my manpower requirements have been exceeded by twenty-five percent.

"Luckily this base was built to accommodate a much greater deployment of men and equipment. Our hangar space is to spare, and once more I hear from Jessica that she is over manned by twenty-five percent, also. What is going on, boss?"

"Tell me about the radar and satellite cover. Is it all up and running?"

Chuck Hartog sat back and looked directly at Mike. "So what?"

"If I told you, I would have to kill you." Mike smiled faintly at the famous 'spook' quotation. "Until tomorrow, I can say nothing. For your personal information, expect visitors tonight, covert air arrivals, special vigilance overnight from everybody." He picked up the bullet and turned it in his fingers.

Chuck reached forward and took the bullet from Mike. "What is this?"

"It was fired at me last evening at the corner post overlooking the border with Georgia. Range at least 1.5 miles."

".303 Lee Enfield possibly sniper set-up. They always have had remarkable accuracy over long range, the sniper versions normal kill expected at 1.25 miles with sights." He studied the bullet closely. My guess is this came from a standard rifle."

Mike shook his head in amazement and retrieved the bullet. "We have a lot to do with the security of this place. How are you getting on with Colonel Kemal?"

After a few moments Chuck said, "I would say not too well. My feeling is that I can trust him less than my next door neighbour's cat. On the other hand, Master Sergeant, Ali Baranka comes across as an asset, provided we keep Kemal out of the loop."

Mike opened the file in front of him. "I will be flying off Combat Air Patrols through the night, there will be arrivals. I am advising you of this but only to confirm that the empty hangers will have occupants by the morning.

"Peter and Jessica should be here about now, could you send them in? Tomorrow all will be made clear." He smiled as Chuck grimaced, saluted and left the office.

Peter and Jessica were both waiting to be called when he went out. He nodded them in and kept going out of the office complex.

"Ruffled feathers?" Jessica suggested as they turned to enter the office of their Commander.

Peter shrugged, "He's a former 'leatherneck' (Marine) they are borne ruffled and trained to stay that way!"

The two officers stopped and saluted. "Sit and listen, this is critical tonight."

Mike's voice was clear and matter of fact. "Tonight, as you know, you will be running a continuous series of CAP's. Your aircraft will use the opportunity to do touch and go's as well as maintaining continual air cover. During the performance other aircraft will be joining us and parking in hanger number three which has been set up to receive them, The two C130's scheduled for 18.00 arrival will go straight into hanger two to unload, and immediately return to the hard standing in bays 4 and 5, both of which have been set up already for refuelling and servicing.

"These activities will not under any circumstances be revealed to Colonel Kemal."

Mike paused and looked intently at them both. "During the night we will be acquiring three Dassault Rafale jets from the Israeli Air Force, three F111's from Nevada, and possibly three Euro-fighters from UK. In addition, there may be some extra punch from USMC with their latest jump-jets. They will arrive in traditional circumstances during the day if they come at all. I stress that this base must appear a normal rotation training session under NATO protocols. Training will to some extent continue on a normal programme. But at all times I stress this base must be able to defend itself against infiltration or attack."

Jessica said it. "You say attack?"

"That's what I said and that is what I mean. No games, no get up and dust off for the after-war analysis. This could be a massacre, or not. The base will be on Defcon 3 from the time you leave this office. Now, are your aircraft ready?"

Peter and Jessica immediately responded, "Ready with a full list."

"I will take a look around in the P51, but just in case, perhaps you would both like to join me for the look around. This place makes me feel I am being watched all the time."

***

The three aircraft lined up on the main runway, the spinning disk of the propeller on the Mustang tracing a silver trail down the runway for a short distance before it rose in the air in a graceful climb, the wheels retracting as it left the ground. The two F15's followed, making short work of the runway before lifting sharply skyward in a more brutal climb that that of the Mustang.

Mike sat at the controls of the Mustang, at peace with himself, comfortable with the roar of the Rolls Royce Merlin engine effortlessly driving the aircraft through the broken clouds to just over ten thousand feet where he levelled off and gently banked round to the right in a wide circle that would cover the area around the airbase below. He ignored the two F15's they would establish their own protective envelope around him. He clicked on his radio "Mustang, calling gun test!"

The others acknowledged, "Dan dare 1, confirmed."

"Calamity J, confirmed!"

Mike slipped the cover off the gun button and fired a short burst from guns and cannon. Then he concentrated on observing what he could of the ground below. The tracks of the old roads and paths across the mountain slopes were visible on both sides of the border, many showing little sign of any barrier between countries. He was aware that the country below on both sides of the line was ruled over by the Kurdish tribesmen, who claimed allegiance to neither Government.

The flash was caught in the corner of his eye as he tightened the bank to go back over a piece of the ground below. His first thought was a ground-fired missile. He picked up the trail of the missile, waited for a count of five then slammed on the airbrakes. The P51 seemed to stop on the spot. The missile flashed past and buried itself in the mountain slope. The nose of the P51 dropped as Mike re-leased the airbrakes and pushed the stick forward. The Flanker flashed past, causing the Mustang to rock. Mike thrust the throttle wide open and turned to keep the intruder in sight. The radio burst into life and Peter's calm voice spoke. "I have him."

Jessica said "Where did his friend go?"

Mike lined his plane up as the second Flanker came out of a tight turn to line up on him.

When he pressed the gun and cannon buttons the plane shuddered with the force of the discharge. The nose of the Flanker disintegrated under the impact of the cone of fire from the Mustang.

There was an explosion followed by a series of others as the Flanker blew apart. In a screaming climbing turn, Mike kept his plane out of trouble.

Jessica said laconically "Scratch one Flanker."

Peter said "Scratch number two." The other intruder hit the mountainside in a ball of flame that dribbled down the rocky slopes.

"Home time." Mike called and descended downward in a series of controlled turns, eyes keeping the terrain under surveillance in case of any other attack.

All three landed safely and the first of the CAP's took off to establish security for the base.

"So what just happened?" Mike was curious. He had absolute faith in Peter and Jessica but he needed to know.

Jessica said "I spoke with our radar. They came through a window created while we were setting up the system. It has been identified and closed."

"Where did they come from? I saw no markings." Peter sounded thoughtful.

"All radar could tell us was that they approached from the north-east at ground level. That was pretty fancy shooting by the way." Jessica said "They are painting it up on the P51 as we speak. The legend endures!"

Mike looked up sharply at this. Jessica shrugged. Like it or not, Mike Summers was a legend among his contemporaries.

The intercom buzzed. "Master Sergeant Baranka asks for a word, sir."

"Send him in." Mike sat back waving the others to remain seated.

The Turkish NCO came through the door, his uniform immaculate and snapped to attention at the salute in front of Mike's desk. Mike returned the salute "At ease, Master Sergeant; what can I do for you?"

Ali Baranka relaxed and said, "Sir, I have received information from a local source that the attack this morning was not from local people."

"Explain, please. Ah, sit down, Master Sergeant."

"Sir I have friends in the area among the Kurdish peoples. This morning they reported that the attacking aircraft came from the Iran, based on the Caspian Sea. They were staged through a Russian base in Georgia."

"How do they know all this?" Peter asked.

"The Kurds have been oppressed by all the nations in this part of the world, even here in Turkey. Although things have improved somewhat, there is still very strong feeling against them as they are regarded as a threat to local livelihood and land holdings, all because of the efforts of the Kurds to establish their own homeland."

Jessica looked keenly at Ali. "Tell me, Ali, are you a Kurd?"

"No, Madam, I am not, but I am Armenian. My people have been driven from their homes for centuries just as the Kurds have, so I confess to have, how you say, a fellow feeling for them."

"What do they think of our being here?" Mike studied Ali's reaction to the question.

"They resent it, but they know that you, by being here, prevent any actions by the Turkish authorities against them. They also do not like interference from Georgia, Iran, Iraq or Russia."

"Do they know why we are here?"

"They believe it is NATO manoeuvres."

The roar of landing and take-off of the various patrols was intruding into the conversation and Mike decided to end things for now. "Master Sergeant, you have been honest with me and I will be honest with you within these four walls. What is going on here will in no way cause harm for the Kurds, and I welcome any intelligence they care to pass on to us, Politically I can do nothing, but otherwise I will see what can be done to compensate for our interference."

"Thank you, sir," Ali Baranka sprang to his feet and saluted. "Within these walls sir!"

He turned and left the office.

Mike turned to the others, "Let us take a stroll to hanger 3, I need to stretch my legs after that trip in the Mustang."

Collecting their hats all three officers stepped out into the pool of light outside the office complex. Instinct made Mike say sharply, "Move fast," and the three of them quickly crossed into the darkness.

Chapter three

...The task.

Under the cover of darkness, they made their way to hanger 3. At the side entry Mike swiped the card reader entry lock. They stepped through into a dark room. When the door behind them closed the light came on and they were able to enter the main hanger through the access door. The huge area of the hanger floor was busy with people making preparations. On the far side three aircraft were being attended to by mechanics.

It was Jessica that commented. "They are not American!"

"Look at the aircraft." Mike suggested drily.

Peter said "Dassault Rafales, Israeli at a guess."

As they reached the aircrew, all straightened to attention and saluted.

"Colonel Adam Smith and party, reporting as instructed, sir."

"Carry on, Colonel, welcome to Ciranu Base. There are quarters over there already arranged. Please keep your people inside the hanger until otherwise ordered; we would prefer that your presence remains secret for just now. Please introduce your party."

Smith introduced the five other members of his party, three female officers and two men, all of whom had the look of experienced fliers. Adam Smith greeted Peter like an old friend. They had, Peter explained, been on several joint exercises together.

While they were still talking a siren sounded and the lights of the hanger went out. The doors opened and one by one three F111 fighter/ bombers taxied in. The doors closed and the lights came on again as the three massive aircraft rolled to their parking spots and turned to face the doors once more.

The cockpit canopies rose almost as one and the crews clambered down, still stiff in their pressure suits. The group gathered together then turned to Mike and saluted. The shorter of the aircrew pulled off the flying helmet revealing copper-coloured hair and the attractive features of Lt. Colonel Sarah O'Connor, USAF Reserve, Officer in command of 14th Illinois air wing of National Guard, the only remaining unit to be still equipped with the F111.

Mike said, "I should have guessed it would be you."

She smiled. "Who else could it be? So it's the old team back together again." She nodded at Peter and Jessica. "Hi, Pete; hi, Jess; god, you look younger than ever, have you got a picture in the attic?"

Jessica laughed. "You can talk, you look like an advert for Pan Am. So who's your friend?"

The pilot who had walked up to join them was six feet of Texas named Major Charlie Walker, USAF, Sarah's wingman. As he was introduced around Peter observed with a wry smile that Jessica seemed his main focus of interest. An interest that seemed to reciprocated.

The voice at his elbow startled him for a moment. It was husky and warm and sort of coffee coloured. "Pardon me, but are you the Peter Hamilton-Davies, who flew with the RAF?"

"Who wants to know?"

"I am Captain Shelly Seabrook, I trained in UK on the Harrier, they mentioned your name while I was there. I admit I was curious, I was expecting someone at least seven foot tall with armour and a sword and buckler, whatever that is, with a dead dragon at his feet."

Peter turned round fully and looked at the smiling slightly anxious face looking up at him.

"A buckler is a small round shield worn on the other arm when two knights are in swordplay."

"Thank you, sir," she said.

"That dragon was eaten for lunch, I'm sorry we seem to be a bit short of dragons here." He grinned, "Hate to spoil the illusion but, yes, I am the Peter Hamilton-Davies, one time RAF Pilot."

Mike interrupted. "Gather round all of you, there is only one unit still to join and they will play a different role in our little exercise. With all nine of the new aircrews plus Jessica and Peter closed up around him, Mike gave the first indication of what they were all here for.

"We wait for word on the result of inquiries about the production of weapons-grade uranium in the Middle East. After the debacle over the so-called weapons of mass destruction not found in Iraq, the powers have decided that they will only move after positive evidence is produced of the existence of the material. This is not, nor will it be, the sort of cowboy operation that was carried out in Desert Storm. Our current major problem is that we are known to be here and I anticipate efforts to be made against each and every one of you.

"That means that while you are in country you will carry arms at all times. Do not step out into the light without previously checking the immediate area. Incidentally, I was targeted at 1.5 miles this morning. If I had not moved at the right time, Peter would be doing the briefing."

He turned to Peter, "Disperse the group to their quarters. No contact with the local colonel, please. I believe he is one of them, as opposed to one of us."

Peter called to the group "When we dismiss, split into two's and we will take the scenic route to quarters. Jess please look after five, I'll take the rest."

He moved off while Mike was still looking at Sarah.

"Shall we?" he said.

"Why not." Sarah smiled "Why ever not."

***

The lecture hall in MIT was full. *As it should be,* thought Hazel Cantrell as she completed the lecture. "And so ladies and gentlemen, that is the reason why it is necessary to always ensure that whatever you write down in your dissertation is written in readable English. You can always expect at least ten marks just for the fact that the examiner can actually understand what you have written. Right or wrong. Good day and good-by, people. My particular input is now complete. For the next semester you will be treated to the honeyed phraseology of Professor Gillian Freeman PhD."

Hazel departed the lecture hall to applause, her particular brand of lecture being universally popular.

"Sorry you have to go," Peter Townsend said, as he fell in beside her. "We will miss you here."

"Peter, you have been trying to get into my pants for the past year. Do you not get the message. It's Gloria Swift that fancies you, not me. You have wasted all this time chasing after me when you could have been canoodling with Gloria to your heart's content. Now I'm gone you can share together what you both obviously need. Bye, Peter."

She swept out of the building and down to her car, a sleek Green Jaguar XJS, a present from her guardian Avo Rankin.

Looking at the car reminded her that she was expected to join him in Kars in Turkey. For the past two years she had spent all her spare time on the mercy run in Africa, now she was needed to work on the Kurdish refugee problem. She shrugged, *One day I will get a life, maybe?*

***

Elmore Heard was CIA director in place in Georgia. He was a slim, wiry man in neat dark suit and white formal shirt, blue tie; a dapper man.

He was currently wrestling with a problem that was as yet unresolved. He did not really like the solution that seemed to be the only one with merit.

Having arranged and set up the CIA operation which could only be described as jet black, he was still struggling with his conscience over the final details involved in keeping the entire business out of the public eye. He knew the Iranians would be the last to admit that their vaunted nuclear labs had been destroyed. Heard's problem was ensuring that the United States did not get the blame. He was not happy with the people he was working with at present. His FSB counterpart Igor Zorin was a brutal vodka swilling pig, in his estimation, and appeared to have no vestige of humanity left. His appearance belied his habits and nature. A handsome, smiling, fair-haired man with a ready smile, and it was only when you looked into the eyes did you realise the depravity of the man. The dead, pale blue eyes where the smile never reached were, as always, covered with aviator sunglasses.

Heard's decision had to be made, and it was typical of the man that he would grasp the nettle and damn the consequences.

The phone in the office of the base commander was a direct line to Langley, installed specially for the current operation. He picked it up and quoted a number. The Director answered. Heard was succinct. "We go for clean sweep. Win or lose, repeat Clean Sweep. Confirm?"

There was a pause and finally the answer came back. "Clean Sweep confirmed, repeat confirmed." The phone went down at the Langley end. While the hand set was still at his ear He heard an automated voice say, "In 30 seconds this telephone will be no longer operative. Caution! Please replace the receiver there may be collateral damage to your hearing."

With a grim smile he replaced the handset and waited for the hiss that would signal the demise of that particular connection.

His next action was to call his associate Igor Zorin.

Igor Zorin was aware that Heard disliked him, but he didn't care, his own loyalties were to himself, there was no misplaced feeling for Mother Russia. Igor Zorin was the centre of his world. It was convenient at this time to humour the American whose interests were in line with Russian interests, and anyway, who cared?

Heard looked up as Zorin came in. "Clean Sweep!" he said.

Zorin nodded "I will speak with the colonel so that they will be ready to act as soon as the job is done. He left the office and Heard was once again alone with his thoughts. As he sat there he realised that this was his swansong as far as CIA was concerned. Getting away with things had, up to now, been the prerogative of the CIA, but after the debacle of the Bay of Pigs, the belief in the CIA had deteriorated year by year as disaster followed disaster and crass errors had come to light in increasing numbers. If this operation was ever made public there would be no going back for him as local director or for the Director of the CIA himself. One way and another, if the clear up operation was not completely successful heads would roll, and someone somewhere would be aware of what happened so there would always be the threat like the sword of Damocles hanging over their heads. It seemed that Zorin was right, it was time to start preparing his escape. Luckily he had no wife to concern him; she had divorced him within a year of their wedding. So he would have a chat with Zorin who seemed fairly well connected and certainly not bothered by conscience.

***

In Mike's quarters Sarah—now out of the flying suit and in undress uniform—sat across from Mike in the lounge area, there was a coffee cup on the table in front of her. She was just bringing Mike up to date on what had been going on since they last met. After leaving the regular Air Force the grapevine that kept everyone aware of the location of friends ceased.

The National Guard, they discovered, was more parochial. What they might know about the local state area was about the limit. The next state was another world.

Mike and Sarah had history. Sarah had a crippled husband, who died just over a year ago.

When she and Mike had hovered around the realisation that there was something between them that might be worth exploring, her husband and his ex-wife had made that impossible.

Both now realised that all bets were off. Both were aware of the tension between them, Under the current circumstances it was still tricky. Mike, as Brigadier General, was in charge of the entire unit. Sarah was a member of his staff. The whole situation was fraught with danger for them both if they wished to keep involved in their Air Force. Interest, as well as any suggestion of a relationship, would be a complete no-no.

Mike stood up and stepped across to Sarah, he took her hands and she rose to her feet facing him. He said "I want to see if we can have something between us, but once again there are things happening. What I would like to know is do you feel the same? Will you wait until this is over so that we can find out if we will be together?"

"Oh, Mike, of course I will." And for the first time they kissed. When they finally parted both knew it was the beginning they had both sought.

***

Sarah entered her quarters to find Jessica waiting. They had known each other for a long time. Jessica took a look at Sarah's face, then said, "Good/ I guessed it would happen and I am delighted for you both. See you in the morning, Sarah.

As she left, Sarah sank down on the bed, still a little stunned at the realisation that things were happening at last. She slept that night content for the first time in a long time.

Between midnight and three am six Apache attack helicopters took their place in Hanger 3.

Brigadier General Summers paced the length of Hanger 3, eyeing the Apache's sitting there, looking menacing with their armament dolly sitting waiting beside each aircraft.

The Marine lieutenant concentrating on the contents of the raised locker in the body of the second Apache jerked back and swore as she hit her head on the raised panel.

"Problems, Lieutenant?" Mike stopped to speak, then as the lieutenant turned, he realised he was looking at his daughter Mary-Jo. She snapped to attention and saluted. Mike returned the salute and grinned "Come here." He said and took her in his arms and they hugged. "Hell, it's been a year at least, you look good."

"You look pretty good yourself for an old man." Mary-Jo said. "Hey, Dad, what is this? When I saw the name of the Commander of this operation, I thought there must be another Summers on the list. Congratulations, it's long overdue. Have you met the skipper yet?"

"No, I was just making my rounds before breakfast, I was not here when you arrived last night and I thought I would check that everything was okay."

"Well, the skipper is in number one, I'll introduce you." The pair walked along the line of helicopters to another where a Marine major was talking to his ground mech. At their approach he glanced up and straightened at the salute. Mike returned the salute, "Major Shelby?"

"Sir!"

Mary-Jo spoke, "Sir, may I introduce my father, Brigadier General Summers, USAF."

Selby looked sharply at the female lieutenant as he shook the extended hand of the General. "I'm sorry, sir, I did not realise…"

"For your information, Major, neither did I. Last week I was Colonel Summers, now I'm a general, 'sic transit Gloria'. I also did not realise my daughter would be on this detachment. Though I am delighted to see her it was still a shock."

***

The satellite pictures were coming in regularly. The geostationary orbit was keyed into the zone of interest. The team of analysts were working shifts to pick up the slightest nuance of alteration in the area covered. The various wave cameras were gleaning temperature variations and people movements both on the ground and to some extent below it.

The AWAC flying over Saudi caught a glimpse of the missile, but could not capture it for targeting purposes. The warning was too late to save the satellite, its loss signalled by a picture of the targeting missile just before it exploded. The picture made it easy to identify the missile, which was still clearly marked with the Russian logo and the model number/ batch number.

The details were immediately despatched to Washington. There the life history of that missile was catalogued from its manufacture to the day it was transferred to a storage base in Georgia where it was destroyed in 1993, clearly certified by the UN inspector on site: a Major Sherman Leman, US Army Engineers, deceased. Reported drowned while scuba diving in Acapulco Bay 1994.

"Well, whatever is going on at that site, it is obviously not something they wish to share with the world." Peter commented to the group around the table.

Adam Smith looked up from the pictures of the missile taken moments before the impact.

"This is not a Russian missile."

For a moment nobody spoke, then everyone was talking at once.

"Ladies and gentlemen, please! This is a conference, not a debating society. Colonel Smith, explain, please."

Adam Smith stood and walked over to the big viewing screen. He clicked up the picture of the missile just before impact. "Please study this picture carefully while I find a library picture of the same class missile." He punched buttons and onto the screen beside the original picture appeared a second missile. He manipulated the image so that the two pictures were parallel at the same attitude. Then using the laser pointer he began, pointing out the crude welding on the library picture and the projecting bolt heads on the arming panel. Even the Russian logo compared badly with the work on the attacking missile.

"This missile was produced in a prototype lab at worst. The meticulous workmanship compared with the crude, brutal production from the factory model. They are allegedly from the same batch but all indications are custom build. My guess is that," he tapped the library picture, "this version would not have the range to reach the satellite. My guess would be that the killer missile was made of lighter materials with enhanced power/weight ratio, specifically to reach a satellite when the time came."

The session was interrupted by the arrival of an Air Force colonel with a briefcase and three Army officers. The colonel introduced himself as commanding the 2nd Insertion Group 12 modified Blackhawk helicopters. The Army units were commanded by a Delta Force major, the others were captains from SAS (UK) and Israeli Special Forces.

The general introduced them to the assembly, adding that the military section comprised one hundred and twenty men in three sections.

He sat down to a buzz of conversation among the assembled group.

The tapping on the table brought the group back to business.

"Yes, sir." Mike looked around the table. He tapped the earpiece in his right ear. "I have to inform you that Operation Earthquake is up and running." He held up his hand to stop questions then continued. "Tonight the Blackhawks fly, they leave at 0200, they drop and rendezvous in Dhahran. The F111's and the Dassault Rafales fly tomorrow evening, 2100 departure. They will be joined by six carrier-based Warthog Radar killers, liaising with ground resources who will laser the main targets and as many of the hidden AA units as they can cover. Between the Warthogs and the Special Forces they hope to keep heads down, but as you all know, nobody is perfect.

"Extraction will be by Blackhawks, and interdiction by the Apaches. Your individual packages are prepared and will be distributed after this meeting. Overall cover will be flown by F15s, My call sign is Mustang and I'll be on the designated channel for the entire operation. The Black-hawks will regroup here.

"Now just to get things straight. The target is on the border between Russian-controlled Georgia and Iran. We believe that the forces against us are an unattributable group, deniable by both Russia and Iran. They have power-ful forces at their disposal, and I expect reaction to our efforts to be immediate and lethal. All fast movers will return, refuel and rearm for immediate take-off in defence of the base. Apaches will concentrate on attack by ground troops. Hopefully we will have warning of their approach. Blackhawks will return here, leave their Special Forces and get the hell out, to bases deeper in Turkey. Returning troops will cooperate with Col. Hartog in the base defence. I do not expect outside help in this operation. We are not here!"

He stood and looked around the table "Ladies and gentlemen, to your duties." He saluted them and left the room.

***

Mike sat and worried in his quarters later that night. He had covered every angle that he could think of but he still could not get over the feeling that he might be missing something.

There was a knock at the door. He opened it to find Peter, Jessica and Sarah standing there.

He shrugged and stood aside to let them in.

They all settled down on the various seats in the room. Jessica opened the ball. "Sorry boss, we all felt that there was something we were missing. As you know we have known you and each other for some years. I guess, looking at you and the fact that you are still dressed that you, like us, think we might have missed something."

Mike smiled slowly, "Well, since you put it that way, what can I say. I was just thinking that since I know where we are, and I have guessed what we are doing here, what would be the best move I could make to, as Peter might put it, 'bugger things up' for the lot of us. Idea's?"

Sarah said. "Kill the aircraft!" She said it and put her hand to her mouth. "Of course, I could not think what it was that was worrying me. All the attack aircraft are in hanger 3."

The simplicity of the suggestion struck the group all at once.

Then "Yes..s..s..s..." Mike hissed. "Of course, I should have thought of that. The attack today proved that they knew we were here and the obvious next move is to target our assets.

"Sarah. There are hard-point dispersal sites all down the north side of the airfield, get your aircraft out now and net them in bays 1-3. Peter, get the Dassault Rafales out and the aircrews, Jess, let's get the Apaches airborne and nosing about." He picked up the phone and pressed a speed-dial number. The phone was answered immediately. "Chuck, we may have problems!"

The answer was short and the knock at the door came as Sarah, Jessica and Peter were about to leave. They passed Col. Hartog without comment, leaving the two men alone.

Mike wasted no time. "Chuck we have just realised, hopefully in time, that Hanger 3 is vulnerable to attack by our unknown opponents. The others are just going to shift and disperse the aircraft because I did not think of it sooner. Meanwhile we need to extend out base defences to try at least to prevent a concentrated missile attack from ground forces. Both Iran and dissident Russia have Special Forces just as we have. If I were them, I would make the effort, and tonight would be my time of choice."

Chuck smiled a tight twitch of his facial muscles. "Beat you to it, boss. I have active patrols out to a three mile radius. Mounted and foot sections basically briefed to observe and report, but to act if needed to prevent interdiction of the base resources."

Mike sat back "I should have guessed. Sorry, Chuck, good work. You can brief your troops that the Apaches are coming up, if directed action is needed. They should be airborne within 30 minutes, tops."

***

As the last of the Dassault Rafales was reversed into its hard-dispersal point Jessica sighed with relief. The dolly train with the armaments for this aircraft rolled between the barrier walls as the camouflage nets rose to cover the area.

The first missile arrived two hours six minutes later. It was badly aimed because it bounced on the runway scattering sparks and then went out with a pop.

The man who fired the missile hurled the launcher at the ground with fury, "Russian shit" were the last words he spoke as the sniper, a Kurdish tribesman, carefully shot him; the bullet burst his head apart. The rest of the body collapsed, revealing the uniform beneath the Armenian shirt that hung to his knees.

***

Three more missiles were in the air within moments of the failed first effort. The Gatling gun burst into action, shredding all three before they came within a half mile of the boundary fence. The voice over the radio said "Group gathered round mobile launcher!" There followed a GPS, reference. The first mortar bomb missed the centre of the group, falling into the vehicle beside them, but the second that was in the air two seconds later was in time to catch the bulk of the people, and more importantly the actual launcher with devastating results. The observer who had designated the target died along with the enemy, killed by a piece of shrapnel ricocheting from the body of the vehicle.

The instruction to move in came from Colonel Hartog as soon as the launcher blew up. His men rose from their ambush positions and directed withering fire into the ranks of the enemy. They took casualties but the result was that the enemy who were apparently mainly Iranian were very hard hit by the base defence force. The eventual casualties figure was the result of attempting to thread their way out of the area through the Kurdish people who resented their interference in the land they claimed as their own.

The CAP were warned of an approaching wave of aircraft, once again coming at low altitude. Without ado, the other nine F15s took off in pairs and joined the CAP in their patrol formation above the base.

In the radar control room Mike watched the approaching aircraft, obviously flying along the contours of the ground below. He had the suspicion that they were unaware of being discovered. This was quite possible as the sophisticated radar set-up used by the base was still very much a secret. The look-down radar of the AWACS linked to the horizontal sweep of the ground sets gave a picture seldom seen outside computer games. Watching the screens Mike could see what they meant.

As he watched a shadow appeared in the path of the approaching aircraft. It seemed to hover for a moment, and then one of the close formation of approaching aircraft disappeared from the radar. "What happened there?" He pointed to the screen.

The operator said, "Son of a Bitch!" Then realised he had been asked the question. "I guess we saw an Apache come out of the boondocks and ice one of the intruders."

Mike said "An Apache?"

The radar officer said. "That Gatling chin-gun is lethal. I guess he bushwhacked that guy before he knew what was happening. By the time they realised what was happening they were gone to hell past the scene. Too late to react."

"One down, eleven to go."

The F15's extended into line abreast and concentrated on locking on to the intruder aircraft. The first flight of missiles were on their way. Six of the intruders disappeared from the screen and on the main radar it was possible to see three others suddenly amalgamate into one blip before vanishing from the screen in their turn.

To Mike the comparison with a computer game was almost total. Then he saw the hint of movement at the south eastern side of the screen.

The radar officer was on the ball. He called the Peter and Jessica to warn them of the new threat, Jessica nominated two aircraft to finish the surviving level group members and the other ten F15's turned to face the new threat.

The British voice called in on a subsidiary channel, "This is Blacksheep 27 with my flock of 12 Euro-fighters loaded for bear. Can we join the fun?"

The radar controller called back on the other frequency checking the credentials of the RAF Unit. Then he called Peter. "Selfridge one, I have 12 Blacksheep offering to fly top cover while you scrabble in the boondocks. Are you interested?"

"Base, this is Selfridge one, delighted they could come, welcome to the party."

Mike looked at the radar officer, "Well?"

"Major Hamilton asked me to see if there were any friendlies in the area, for just this situation. The British Euros were training locally and they really are faster and better armed than anything we had so I hinted there might be some action in the area. I also said we were not here."

Mike turned back to the big screen, the F15s were really mixing it with unidentified fighters. Peter reported that they were facing what he thought were Mig 25s.

As they watched two of the Mig's got through the screen and were approaching the base at Mach speed. Two of the RAF planes appeared on screen and caught up with the Russian aircraft. The Mig's suddenly lost interest in whatever target they were attacking and started desperate manoeuvres to escape from their shadows. Both pulled into a vertical climb then they disappeared from the screen, one then the other. The two RAF aircraft climbed and rejoined their squadron.

On the field the runway lights came on and the first of the F15s came in to refuel and rearm, Overhead the RAF flew CAP whilst the F15s rotated. When the screen was clear of intruders the Euro-fighters came in pairs and refuelled. The squadron commander watched the last of his aircraft away and reported to Mike.

Wing Commander David Sheldon stood in front of Mike and saluted. "Pardon me, General," he said. "We get very little chance to practice anywhere apart from Afghanistan. That is a bad place to play games. This did seem like a good opportunity to give my boys some practice and to help out our friends at the same time."

Mike looked at the man in front of him. "Since we are not here, and since we are friends, I am happy that we were able to provide you with some practice. Thanks for the help, My lips are sealed and I would appreciate it if yours were, too."

"No problem, sir."

Mike watched the RAF plane take off. He noticed with approval that despite the apparent dispatch of the squadron earlier, in fact, three of the aircraft had remained at extreme altitude ready to join their leader when he left.

The ground units were returning to the Base and the Apache gun-ships were starting to land for refuelling. Chuck Hartog found him and reported that the ground attack units had either been eliminated or had withdrawn. He was bringing his patrols in and depending once more on the electronic warning devices for the rest of this night.

Mike hit the sack, finding that sleep, normally not that easy to find, took over before his head hit the pillow.

***

The following morning was marked by the activity in the servicing areas. Master Sergeant Ali Baranka reported to Mike that the local Kurds were taking over the security of the area surrounding the base. They had decided that on this occasion their interests and those of the NATO force coincided.

Apparently the attacking force had been arbitrary in their approach to the local people and the prompt removal of that threat by Chuck's base force had impressed them sufficiently to join their side.

This took pressure off the base defence units and gave the colonel a certain relief from the threat of long range sniping.

***

The briefing for the attack was comprehensive. There was no time wasted and the series of instructions were given clearly and concisely. Each of the attack group had their own instructions. The Special Forces had checked in with confirmed laser designations for the smart bombs. The F111 were armed with earthquake missiles. The sequenced series of explosions created by this missile was capable of penetrating four floors below ground level, and collapsing them on whatever lay below.

The Dassault Rafales' weapon load was designed to open the way by penetrating at least four stories underground, paving the way for the earthquake missiles to follow.

All identifying marks and emblems had already been removed from the aircraft as had those of the F15s of the escort squadron, all the aircraft had been fitted with self-destruct devices in the event they came to earth in a recoverable condition.

Night fell at 18.15 and the anti-radar aircraft took off to entice as many units into life as possible. Between the known sites targeted by the Special Forces and those fried by the anti-radar aircraft, the situation was going to be as clear as possible for the attacking flights.

The target near Shahin Dezh was just over 400 miles southeast of the base. Over rough semi-inhabited hills and desert, the final run in would be nap of the Earth until the final climb to ensure the radar could see the target before the attack followed by the mad scramble back to base.

No one had any illusions about the reactions to such an attack and the base was prepared to fight for its life in the aftermath.

"It does add a certain spice to the operation." Peter Hamilton-Davies was holding forth in the crew room while they sat around waiting for the orders to man their aircraft.

Lt Colonel Sarah O'Connor zipped up the patch pocket on her flying overalls, making sure that her issue automatic was secure in place.

"Ten shun!" The room was called to attention as the Brigadier came in . Mike was in flying gear just as were all the others present. "At ease" he called, and the room relaxed once more.

Mike had a word with Peter and Jessica then came over to Sarah and smiled at her. "This is possibly the last chance we get to play with real weapons."

"Yeah, well, maybe we will not need to any more, after this little excursion."

Mike turned to the room. "Listen up, we will be taking off in a few minutes, all I'm going to say is get in get out and get back. I'll be on high with my group dusting off any interference. Good luck, good hunting."

Chapter four

...The Raid

The buzzer sounded as he finished and a voice came over the system "Aircrews, man your aircraft."

The room emptied as the personnel went out to their waiting aircraft. Mike waited and as the others left he turned to Sarah. "Later!" He said and kissed her lightly on the lips. They left the room together, separating to walk to their respective aircraft.

Above them the tanker was climbing to the rendezvous point high over northern Iran, the escort F15s weaving a pattern around the big Boeing.

The other F15s were airborne now as the French trio took off on formation. All three had the penetrating missile on their centre line mount. The wing racks were all loaded, though in the event their use before the target would mean they had failed. The F111s now followed the other attack group into the air and settled on their course to the target 35minutes away.

***

In the target area Colonel Khyami swore at the son of a camel driver's whore who had arranged the set-up of the Sam missile site. Not only were the missile racks mounted on crumbling rock foundations, but the radar unit was not even functioning, and until he had arrived nobody had thought to check it out.

He turned to the Captain with the fair skin, from the north. "Is the radar on line yet?"

Captain Rissio, turned wearily to his hated commanding officer. "Ready to test now, sir."

"So what are we waiting for, do the test!"

"But, sir, I will first have to check with the other batteries that there are no intruders in the area."

"Who are you expecting, Captain, 'Superman'? Of course there are no intruders in the area. Look where we are. We are standing in the arsehole of Iran. It is so hot I would be sweating if I had any sweat left in me. Test the bloody equipment and let us get inside once more out of this cursed sunlight."

The Captain turned to his operator seated on the chassis of the mobile radar set. "Search pattern, switch on!"

There was a whining sound then a humming noise, gradually the screen in front of him lit up. As the screen cleared several images appeared, but before he could get an accurate assessment of the picture the screen exploded dramatically showering the unfortunate operator with shards of thick glass that turned his front from khaki to red in seconds as he died, still seated at his instrument.

"What the devil is that? What happened?" The colonel shouted. As the captain turned he realised the danger and hit the ground in a hurry, "Radar attack!" The captain called as the first missile came into the site.

Within minutes the whole area had been blanketed in high explosives. When the captain raised his head, amazed to be still alive, it was evident that he was the only one.

The colonel had taken a direct hit. His head, still wearing his cap, was on the other side of the wrecked missile battery. Eyes open, he looked thoroughly annoyed at something. The captain giggled. Perhaps he was having an 'out of body' experience. He laughed aloud, then with an effort stopped the developing hysteria, and wondered what to do. Eventually he gathered several water bottles that had survived the attack and walked over to the vehicle park safely located behind the rocky hillock which had been the site of the missile unit.

He chose the motorcycle, loading the bottles of water into one of the panniers. In the other he squeezed a can of petrol. Then he kicked the bike into life and rode off northward, back to the Caspian Sea and home. He had had enough of this war business. It was time to go back to the family and let the politicians start taking the risks.

The lonely dust cloud traced a path across the desert. The sergeant in charge of the Delta team who had carried out the assault on the battery watched the lone survivor ride off to the north-east. He considered finishing the job, then shrugged and started off to another target location.

***

The Dassault trio shivered and danced in the hot air rising from the parched ground flashing past at eight hundred knots just one hundred feet below them. As they approached the target area the ground levelled off and the aircraft sank to fifty feet and started trailing a dust cloud in their wake.

Colonel Adam Smith smiled grimly as the target area became clear in his heads-up display. He felt no sympathy for the people involved in the death and destruction he was about to initiate. His own family had been killed by a so-called Palestinian raid on the Kibbutz they were visiting two years ago. The alleged Palestinians were actually an

Iranian raiding party tasked with sabotage of the Israeli nuclear power laboratory which was mistakenly presumed to
be in the locality. Everyone in the kibbutz had died in a
storm of ordinance. In the orchard were three children and
one adult. By keeping silent and hugging the ground they
had survived. The adult said they spoke a strange dialect.
One of the children was autistic. When they were rescued
the child spoke in the voice of the raiders reproducing
words and accent perfectly. She spoke in Farsi, and dictated
the conversation between two of the raiders.

Adam Smith had waited for the opportunity to punish
the people who had caused the enormous void in his life
with the loss of his wife and daughter, mother and sister, in
that terrible massacre.

"Attack 1 climb!"

The three aircraft rose as one and formed line-ahead
following Colonel Smith to the designated height for the
launch of their missiles.

Adam switched on the tracker beam and immediately
picked up the location marker. He called the other two aircraft. "Target acquired, missile launched."

One by one the other aircraft launched in their turn.
Without waiting the three aircraft went into a fast climb and
circled the target area,

Mike contacted Colonel Smith and acknowledged their
place in the cover force.

The first explosions were signalled by the plumes of
smoke and dust that rose from the collection of low level
buildings that was the objective.

The three F111 appeared below and as Mike watched
they separated and rose up climbing to over one thousand
feet before levelling off and one by one releasing the mis-

sile from their centre-line rack, then climbing once more and joining the top cover aircraft for the return trip to base.

The first opposition came from an assortment of ground bases missiles that in many cases could not reach the aircraft above. The shower of materials dropped to mislead and fool the seeking systems of the AA missiles trapped all but three of the weapons. One managed to wound an F15 causing it to lose fuel from one of its wing tanks. A second was fried by a Warthog's anti-radar which was aimed at one of the attack radar sets below. The missile went haywire and fell to earth where it exploded harmlessly. The third could not be evaded in time. The port wing of the F111 disintegrated and the pilot and her back seat ejected, in time to avoid the explosion of the stricken aircraft.

Mike called the nearest Blackhawk and as he carefully circled down he was able to see the two figures land safely and gather their chutes together. He called them on the dedicated rescue band.

Sarah answered confirming that they were all right. He was able to direct them to the vehicle park where several vehicles still stood undamaged after the AA unit had been destroyed by the radar killer's missiles at the beginning of the raid.

Mike called two other F15s to take over protection while he refuelled from the tanker.

When he returned it was to see the vehicle racing across the desert floor in the right direction, and to hear that they had picked up one of the Special Forces teams. They were currently making for a rendezvous with the Blackhawk for the trip home.

Elsewhere the news was not so good as a squadron of Flogger fighters had appeared and were currently engaging the returning aircraft. A second group of enemy aircraft had appeared on radar approaching the fighting. Mike called Sarah. "We are going to leave you just now but we will keep in touch."

Sarah said, "Thanks, Mike, go and kick ass. We have been asked to pick up another team on our way so don't worry too much. I'm surrounded by a bunch of the most lethal lads in this hemisphere. I'll see you soon."

The three F15s rose to take their part in the engagement with the others fighting their way back to base.

***

The battle had continued most of the way back and only ceased at the Turkish border. The Apaches had gone searching for trouble and were currently bringing the Blackhawks home.

To Mike's relief Sarah strode wearily into his office at 22.00 that same night. Without hesitation he rose to his feet and collected her into his arms. Holding her close he whispered, "I love you. Sarah. Don't ever let me go."

"I have no intention of losing you now I've found you." Sarah breathed.

The thump of missiles being launched brought them back to earth with a crash. The phone rang, and the door opened as Chuck Hartog came in to report that the base was being brought under major attack.

The ground units were already deployed and the preparation that they had been able to make beforehand was now proving its worth. In addition the Kurds were making an impact on the invaders causing casualties despite the body armour worn by the invading troops.

***

The fact that the base was on Turkish territory, appeared to have no effect on the attacking force. They seemed to be confident that the base was not going to be reinforced by official sources and their advance was without inhibition and with complete disregard for Turkish sovereignty.

On the other hand they were by no means having things their own way. The Kurdish tribesmen were using their rifles effectively, causing the invaders serious casualties among the skirmishers.

On the base itself Colonel Hartog was in his element. He had seriously believed that his active operational career was over after his second year in the National Guard. Being stationed in the backwoods of Illinois was not in his opinion actually a cutting edge posting. His current situation was by no means ideal but if the truth be known he was in his element, doing what he was designed to do with a force that he considered as good as you get. The majority of his force was experienced, mainly veterans of the second Gulf war and the Iraqi-Afghanistan conflicts.

He had set up his control operation in the electronic centre of the base which had, apart from a satellite view of the base and its surrounds, also had comm links with all the outlying units and their cover weapons squads. In addition he had Micro comms with the Special Ops troops who had deployed as soon as they had returned to base and rearmed.

Brigadier General Mike Summers was in the bunker sizing up the situation. There were patrols in the air keeping an eye on the aircraft movements, until now keeping beyond the Turkish border, in the airspace nominally controlled by Georgian assets.

Mike had spoken to a contact in the Georgian Air Force. He was aware that their hands were tied at present.

The current forces flying, and ground, were unattributable. He was well aware however, that they operated with the tacit approval of the Russian Government.

The fact that they were, in effect, on their own, made Mike's job easier and more difficult at the same time. There was plenty of evidence from past campaigns to show how the stance of the powers that be, can alter, in the name of political expediency.

The pressure was on therefore to get this over as quickly and quietly as possible.

***

The situation changed abruptly when the patrolling aircraft reported that the enemy had crossed the border with three squadrons of aircraft. The sirens on the base wailed their warning and the dispersed aircraft started to take off and form in a defensive formation above the base. Jessica, leading the attack group called "Arm your weapons." And the nine F15s went into action, the first missiles flaring from their racks.

The ranks of the enemy broke up as the F15s went into action, though one group kept cohesion and bored onward toward the base. Even as Mike keyed the radio to warn of the danger a squadron of aircraft appeared from the west, the IFF signals were friendly, and the Typhoon, Eurofighters tore into the group ripping the tight formation apart and sending seven to immediate oblivion with their first salvo of missiles.

The initial air assault was stopped. The surviving enemy aircraft turned and returned to their bases beyond the Turkish border.

The cultured English voice of Wing Commander David Sheldon RAF came over the radio as the British aircraft reformed to return to their base. "My apologies for the interference, we have been ordered to stand down and restrict our practice manoeuvring to the western end of the country, I'm afraid with regret that I can no longer take part in your most realistic war games."

Mike answered the call himself. "You're welcome contribution to the realism of our exercise has been timely and valuable I would be proud to receive you into my Air Force at any time. Thank you, and your bandits, your contribution was appreciated. This is the '*Nowhere*' base signing off."

The Typhoon squadron did a pass, in formation, over the base and disappeared to the west once more. The two men stepped outside to watch the departing aircraft.

Chuck Hartog commented "I'll be damned, that guy stuck his neck way out for us. Where do they find men like that?"

"Read your history Chuck, he follows a tradition established two thousand years ago, and probably before that. Whenever and wherever there is a war, guys like that appear. As soon as the war is over, the politicians come along and smother them, condemn them, vilify them.

"This operation we are involved with doesn't exist. That is the reason that the forces ranged against us can fight and kill us, just as we can fight and kill them. We cannot depend on support from our government or in fact any other government in NATO. If we don't exist we are deniable. What would upset our people would be finding that we had failed with our assigned mission. What will also upset them would be our survival and serious damage to the forces attacking us at present. That they will feel is an unfair outcome of what should be a successful operation without loose ends."

Colonel Chuck Hartog looked at his Commanding Officer in disbelief. "No way, they would not send us out on a suicide mission like that?"

"Think about it, Chuck. We are an obscure unit of National Guard from nowheresville. You are a passed-over Lieutenant Colonel, promoted to take part in this operation. I am a passed over Lt Colonel promoted to one star General. Why me? Why not our existing One Star?

"We are expendable. We are given three F111s, for God's sake. Forty year old aircraft led by a female colonel who should be a three star general, with a record like hers. And three untried Israeli Dassault Rafale jets led by another politically incorrect colonel, who's wingmen are just as expendable as he is.

"And here we are in the middle of nowhere. Unloved, unwanted, with twelve obsolete F15s, two obsolete F111s, one obsolete Mustang, three 'state of the art' but untried French aircraft. The Apaches are a bonus that we did not anticipate, nor do I think did our masters. You are aware that the Blackhawks are all gone?"

Chuck stood clenching his fists, white-faced, facing the Brigadier. Then through his clenched teeth he said "Bastards!"

He stood staring into the gloom across the base that did not exist. Then he turned to Mike. "If we are going to embarrass our lords and masters then I think we have some planning to do."

***

Master Sergeant Baranka stood at ease in front of Mike's desk. "I can try sir," he said "I will change my clothes and go immediately to contact Ali Khan."

The voice of Colonel Pava Kemal interrupted the proceedings. "You will what? Sergeant."

"I go to contact the Kurd Chieftain in this area sir."

"On who's orders?"

"Mine." Mike interrupted.

The colonel turned and said icily, " I am under the impression that the sergeant is a member of the Turkish Armed Forces and thus is under my orders."

"This base is under my command. As NATO Oi/c I give the orders to NATO personnel."

"I forbid any contact with insurgent Kurdish people." The colonel was furious.

"And I outrank you, and if you attempt in any way to interfere with my running of this base, I will have you arrested and confined until a Court Martial can be convened. Am I making myself clear, Colonel?"

The red-faced colonel was furious "I will contact my superiors and have you removed from your post," he said. "My brother is the Minister for War; your career is over, General, do you hear me? Finished. And you, Sergeant, are under arrest."

Mike turned to Chuck and nodded, Chuck called two men in who took the furious colonel out and locked him in to a windowless cell in the rear of the building. The colonel's cell phone was confiscated and it was with interest that Chuck observed that the colonel had been in regular touch with an Ankara number.

Ali Baranka was on his way before the colonel reached his new quarters. The three Special Operations commanders were in conference with Chuck.

Sergeant Major Bill Battersby, SAS, was speaking. "I notice, sir, that most of the equipment supplied is rather old."

Captain Bruce Charles, Delta Force, was less polite. "Obsolete! Damn, we are expected to use equipment that is twenty years out of date. There are boxes of Claymore mines. I last saw those used in a movie about Viet Nam."

Battersby said, "There is one thing that is to our advantage. If we use the claymores properly, they are still bloody lethal. Also anyone we are facing during the next few days will be expecting state of the art weaponry. I know we use top line personal weapons, but I can tell you I would not enjoy facing some of the goods in our arsenal."

"I have asked the Kurdish leader to come and see us, I have the feeling that they will be happy to use what we don't need, and I think also that they will be a great help in disposing of our current problem over the border."

Bruce Charles asked, "Just how long will we be expected to hold our ground?"

Chuck looked at the grim faces of the men around the table. The Iranian rebel commander wore the tabs of a colonel. Chuck was aware that he had been an officer in the Iranian army before the Ayatollah took command. He did not seem to be bothered that he was working alongside junior ranks in the SAS and Delta Force men. To be fair the others accepted him equally so he guessed they respected his group in return.

"To answer your question, I have no idea how long we will be expected to hang on. It was pointed out to me that the results of the bombing raid may not be known for some time. It was also pointed out that we had been selected because we were expendable. In my considered opinion, gentlemen, it is anticipated that we will be eliminated by the opposition over the border. We will then cease to be a possible embarrassment to the people who sent us to this summer camp. My reaction to the news was to start planning to win this little war while our enemies are still gearing up to wipe us out. With your cooperation I intend to be as embarrassing as I can, and by so doing save my life and the lives of as many of my men as I can. If we play it right I believe we can spoil their day for them, then the next few days, too.

"First we need to establish exactly what resources they have, then either take them to use against them, or destroy them so that they cannot be used against us."

He looked around the table, all three men were nodding in agreement.

He produced the satellite picture of the enemy encampment. He indicated the group of containers in the corner of the site. "I am guessing that this is their weapons stores. But what does interest me at present is the vehicle park. They appear to have forty troop carriers. APCs in the vehicle park. What would the effect be if there was a claymore in each one and a call for reinforcements?"

The three men looked at him and the Iranian smiled.

***

In the encampment Colonel Grigor Volkov was enjoying a long lunch. His guests were two contractors from St Petersburg. Their presence was caused by the need for some weaponry of a more sophisticated nature. The overrunning of the base by brute force seemed to have been a slight error of judgement on the part of these who had planned the operation in the first place.

The colonel was curious. Despite his impeccable Russian, one of the guests was not Russian. He was certain of it. If he had been asked he would have said the man was American. *What is more the missile, though marked with Russian markings is not Russian.* He guessed it was American. He was now really curious about why an American, probably CIA should be involved in wiping out an American unit.

The Air attack force allocated to the colonel's strike force was in disarray, they had lost half their numbers in the last attack. The intervention of the bloody British had been unexpected and disastrous for his force. The morale was way down as even though the bulk of the opposing aircraft had been obsolescent, flown by reserve crews, they had demonstrated that they had not forgotten how to survive in an air battle.

The colonel's men had only ever been in action against poorly armed ground forces, their confidence had been shattered by the encounter with the Americans.

Chapter five

...The Alliance

The colonel had discovered the reason for the establishment of the base over the border. The removal of the Iranian Nuclear Plant was, as far as he knew, in the interests of both East and West.

It saddened him to realise that he was being asked to clean the slate for some politicians who wanted to show that their hands were clean.

He rose from his place at the table and walked slightly unsteadily from the room, he felt he needed some air, possibly because he was sickened by the duplicity of his employers and of the American still seated at the table that he had just left.

Outside his head steadied and his legs began to feel part of his body once more. He looked around the campsite. The dusk was confusing, light and shadow created by the moving men and the tents and containers. The swinging mobile rocket launchers added to a scene that was suddenly lit by gunfire from the hills that rose to the west of the camp. The whistles and shouted orders added to the confusion, and he saw men carrying weapons rushing to form up and embus into the row of APCs standing with their door open beside the parade area.

He shrugged, it was good to see the men responding to the training. The vehicles started their engines and as the men boarded the rear doors slammed shut, he shuddered. Twelve men crammed into the uncomfortable vehicles. All fifteen APC's were loaded now and they started to move off.

It was odd the first seemed to bulge and it stopped and was hit by the second which also seemed to bulge. He looked down the row of vehicles they were all bulging and the last vehicle door could not have been quite shut as it sprang open and a blizzard of blood and pieces of body blew out in a spray onto the dry dusty ground.

While the shock of the slaughter was still sinking in, the colonel realised that there was activity at the containers. He saw men running in all directions, gunfire lashed back and forth across the encampment. Men fell and died in front of him and still he had not managed to take it all in. He turned and jammed his hand on the siren, calling the camp to arm, signalling that an attack was under way.

The bullet took him in the back as he still struggled to clear his head and decide what to do. He spun round and collapsed in the doorway. The two guests appeared, took one look and retreated inside the mess once more. The sergeant caterer pulled the colonel inside out of the line of fire and slapped a dressing on the wound.

The roar of the explosion at the missile store seemed to fill the world and the walls of the temporary building that was the mess leaned, not quite collapsing under the blast.

So much for the new missile, thought the colonel, and the wry smile that appeared on his face was taken as a grimace of pain by the sergeant who had found a capsule of morphine and injected his commanding officer in line with the instruction he had received at training school.

***

The morning after the raid the Colonel sat in the straightened up mess listening to the reports and assessing the damage to his strike force.

Out of one thousand men remaining in service after the abortive attack three days ago they had lost two hundred and six dead and forty-four injured and ineffective from the mobile infantry alone. They had already lost twenty-two aircraft destroyed and fourteen damaged but repairable though not on site. The destruction of the container used for missile storage had effectively disarmed the remaining aircraft after one flight. The only missiles still remaining were those loaded already on the serviceable aircraft.

It was already obvious that the Mig 23 aircraft were no match for the F15s used by the Americans.

Colonel Volkov was unhappy. He was full of admiration for the force using the base, who, having destroyed their target, had in effect been abandoned. For himself he was aware that he would be receiving a visit from some of the friends of his two visitors from St Petersburg. They would not be coming to congratulate him on his narrow escape.

He realised that his current predicament was the result of their underestimation of the force required to sweep up the US strike force, his own comments on the subject had been ignored.

It was then that it occurred to him. Why should he take the blame for failing to carry out the instructions of what were probably rogue elements of two of the most powerful nations on Earth?

He picked up the phone beside him and spoke to the operator, a man that had served with him in Afghanistan, and Chechnya. "Can you connect me with the commander of the US Base we have been attacking in Turkey?"

"Sorry, boss; did you say the US base?"

"Yes, Boris, I did."

"Five minutes, boss!"

Colonel Gregor Volkov sat wondering if he had gone completely mad. Then suddenly he calmed down and looked at himself. He was 55 years old, his wife and son were dead, killed in a school attack by dissidents. Senselessly slaughtered because the authorities refused to negotiate. All his adult life he had been a soldier, loyally serving the state. Here he was carrying out a task for a bunch of crooks who would probably shoot him for failing to do what they wanted.

The phone rang "I've got Brigadier General Summers on the line, boss; are you sure you want to speak to him?"

"Put him on."

"Good morning Brigadier General Summers, this is Colonel Gregor Volkov of the 14th Mobile Infantry, Russian Army. "

"Good morning, Colonel. What can I do for you?"

"General, first I would like to congratulate you on the effectiveness of your troops and aircraft. But it is on another matter I would like to get together with you about. I believe a meeting would be a good idea if we can somehow arrange it. In the interim if I could suggest a truce while we meet?"

Mike looked at the phone blankly. Chuck, Peter and Sarah, all listening to the speakerphone, looked back dumbstruck.

"Colonel." Mike said, "Did you have somewhere in mind?"

"I thought of several places until I realised that the obvious place would be your base. It would answer your questions about my sincerity and when I explain what I have in mind it would allow us to make plans accordingly."

"Would you like me to arrange transport?"

"I have a twin Cessna if you would like to provide an escort. My party would be two of us, plus the pilot."

"Come immediately. An escort will be provided."

They both put the phone down. The colonel lifted his again and said to the operator, "Call Katerina. Have the plane prepared immediately. You had better come, too, just in case."

He put the phone down and called his deputy through to the room he was using.

"Petrov. The bastards are using us and expect to get rid of us as soon as this pantomime is over. We are an embarrassment to them and we will be the only witnesses to their nasty little plot made with the CIA; that is us and the people they brought us here to destroy. Are you getting the message?"

"Yes, sir."

"I am going to call on the American general in the base. I have decided that I will not waste the lives of any more men to play political games for the benefit of spooks. Do you agree?"

"I agree, sir."

"Most of the men here are the rag-tag and bobtail of the army selected for easy disposal with the minimum of fuss, am I right?"

"Certainly, sir."

" Right. This is what I want you to do. I expect a delegation to arrive from St Petersburg. They will, in effect be a hit squad. Now, regardless of their apparent rank I want them arrested and placed in cells. If it includes Putin, he joins them. I do not trust the people who sent us here, and I'm damn sure he is aware of what is to happen here. This phone is already linked to the base. I will instruct you when I have made arrangements with the Americans, but I want the men loaded into their vehicles—inspect them first this time, please—ready to travel across to the base. The aircraft will fly over, wheels down. Got that?"

"Understood, sir."

"If there are any dissidents they are to be locked up with the visitors."

"Very good, sir."

"Petrov, good luck, and I'll see you later today."

"Good luck to you, sir."

The jeep pulled up outside the mess and the colonel got in, Boris drove over to the airstrip. The twin Cessna was sitting, engines running, waiting. The colonel and Boris, carrying the colonel's briefcase, boarded. The pilot Major Katerina Shukov opened the throttles and took off immediately. As they climbed she said, "The escort awaits." She nodded at the lone silver Mustang that circled above them.

The two aircraft landed and taxied over to dispersal. Colonel Chuck Hartog greeted the Russian colonel and the major. Boris followed, still carrying his colonel's briefcase. The pilot of the Mustang climbed out of his aircraft and strolled over to the group, pulling the helmet off as he walked.

Noticing the star on the pilot's collar, Colonel Volkov called his party to attention and saluted Brigadier General Summers.

"Come into the office please. Let us get some coffee and find out what we need to discuss."

In the office when all were seated and served, Colonel Volkov began. "Ladies and gentlemen, 'We who are about to die, salute you.' I think I have that right. It took me a little time but I realised in the end that we have all been condemned to death. It would not be in the interest of the people who arranged your episode in the desert and our attack on your installation, to allow us to live to tell the tale. My conclusions were confirmed when we were visited by two gentlemen from St Petersburg who brought us a missile, especially designed to remove your entire base. The missile was marked in Russian, but it was not made in Russia. Added to that, one of the visitors spoke perfect Russian but I swear he was American, I guess CIA.

"Your raid disposed of the missile; blown up with the others in our store. It also cost us over two hundred men. Neither of my visitors showed any interest in the losses. They were only concerned about the missile." He turned to Boris. "Have I missed anything?"

"Just one thing, boss. Neither spook returned to St Petersburg."

"And why is that?"

"I shot them both and buried them with the other dead, I did apologise to the other dead at the time."

The colonel nodded, "I should have thought of that. Thank you, Boris; still looking after my ass as usual,"

He turned to the general. "That's it, General. Can we join you? I'm pretty sure my people would sooner chance dying fighting beside you for something rather than on their own for nothing."

Mike Summers looked at the others sitting round the room, then he nodded. "Bring them in."

Boris picked up the phone and dialled. He spoke briefly and replaced the instrument.

"They are on their way. They are bringing the prisoners with them. Petrov says you may wish to speak to them. The aircraft will come across, wheels down; the rest are in the APC's that survived."

***

The column of vehicles pulled up alongside the perimeter track and the men debussed. The wounded were directed to the medical centre. The others fell in and marched to the empty hanger where they were fed and given places to sleep.

***

In his office Mike discussed the situation with Chuck, Sarah, Peter and Jessica.

"The only real problem we are facing is that there has been no official recognition of our situation. As we have seen, the world news reports are of an attack on Iran's nuclear development facility, causing several deaths, by rogue forces. No mention of identity of aircraft or of attackers. We have had no communication from our side since zero day.

"Attempts to use the dedicated channels to communicate with our people fail. We are specifically ordered not to use open source comms. We have food and resources for three weeks now we have guests. Whatever we decide we have to move by that time."

Peter said, "The Brits know we are here, David Sheldon has saved our necks twice."

"Try contacting David now, Peter; he and his unit are long gone. My guess is that there is a cover notice on them all. We have disappeared from the official horizon."

"But what about our people who have families at home, how do they explain the one thousand National Guard personnel who have fallen off the radar?"

Mike turned to Sarah. "Sarah, how many of your squadron have still got F111s?"

"As far as I am aware there is only one flight of three remaining, the unit is re-equipping with F18s."

"And staff, have you any replacements being made in the base staff over the past six months?"

"Close on 100%. The new aircraft came with dedicated pilots so the F111 pilots were rotated to other units for re-training."

"In my case, along with Peter, we have both been shifted three times in the past six months. My promotion to Brigadier General was on transfer to this posting. Jess, you have your laptop, boot up internet and go to the staff list. Take a look at my name under Brigadier General."

"Interesting. You are listed as promotion backdated to one year ago, currently missing in action (BD) that means believed dead? Next of kin informed."

"Please look up my daughter Lieutenant Mary-Jo Peterson USMC?"

"MIA (BD) Afghanistan."

"If you go through the list I believe you will find that we are all gone, so this is what I suggest we do."

***

Colonel Volkov sat smoking a thin black cigar, listening to the report from the Kurds that was received through the good offices of Ali Baranka.

The Antonov arrived with an escort of four Hind-type Helicopters. As it landed, the tailgate opened and vehicles came out swiftly surrounding the remains of the encampment. The troops in the vehicles, from the description, are Spetnatz. There appear to be in region of 300 people including the crew and maintenance for the helicopters. They also appear to have brought missiles with them. Scouting patrols have been sent in this direction, presumably to confirm their satellite imagery."

Volkov looked at Chuck with a raised eyebrow?

Chuck drew his finger across his throat. "They stumbled into the wrong place and disappeared."

At Volkov's question, "Disappeared?"

Chuck said "That area is honey-combed with blowholes from old volcanic action, the patrols all seemed to make the same mistake. It is something to do with their training, I suppose."

"Who is in charge of the group, do we know?" The colonel enquired.

"A General Spassky I believe," Chuck said. "At least that was the name given by the last man to fall down a blowhole."

"Bastard! That was the man who briefed me on this entire operation, I will enjoy killing him."

"You may have to join the queue. They captured a Kurd and tortured him. He said nothing so they skinned him alive. His father had to shoot him to save him the agony. There is a bullet with his name on it waiting until suitable punishment has been exacted."

"Are we going to visit?"

"We plan to. The Kurds have the place surrounded. Nobody in, nobody out. The Apaches are going in nap of the earth to take out their Hinds. Then we go in."

***

Lieutenant Mary-Jo Peterson lifted the Apache over the ridgeline enough to bring the encampment into view. The Antonov loomed huge in the dawn light. Beside it stood the four Hind helicopters in a row. There were men working around the helicopters, and elsewhere the encampment was stirring. The signal came as she was about to drop down behind the hill ridge once more. Three beeps on the interphone. With sights set on the Hind nearest the Antonov, she pressed the missile release. The slight jerk indicated that the missile had separated, then the Hind exploded. She moved the control to her right and pressed the release for a second missile. This flew straight into the huge aircraft and obviously impacted near the control cabin. The far end of the aircraft crumpled and it sagged onto its wheels. The other Apaches had disposed of the other Hinds and were now targeting the buildings. Mary-Jo selected the mobile missile launcher and fired her third missile. The launcher and the three men working it into position disappeared in one noisy explosion. Mary-Jo was already shifting target to a second launcher which was swinging to target the Apaches. Her fourth missile hit the chassis of the launcher and blew it over on top of the operator and his crew. As it fell three of its missiles shot from their tubes drawing a swath of death through the men running to their positions to repel the attack. As the return fire built up Mary-Jo lowered her Apache and retreated behind the hill, following the contour of the earth until she was out of range of the ground fire. She joined the other three Apaches to return to base, the crackle of small arms fire rising as the troops in the encampment fought for their lives.

Colonel Volkov remarked, "I do not like the killing of fellow Russians, but if we don't kill them they will kill us."

The communications major came in to report to Chuck. "Sir, the encampment started to transmit, but no signal went out. I did record three cell phone calls." He turned a switch on a small box that was hooked to his belt. The excited voice of a Russian came from the box.

"Do we know who he was talking to?" The colonel asked.

"A number in Moscow." The engineer reeled off a number and the Colonel took it down.

The second call was someone else with a very calm voice, speaking to St Petersburg, to a Headquarters of some sort. "Attacked by local Kurds with missiles and small arms. All aircraft disabled. Caller terminated, I think."

The third call, also to St Petersburg, was in English. "For God's sake get me out of here. The locals have gone mad; they are skinning the general in the centre of camp. I am making for the rendezvous, collect me quickly. No, there was nobody here when we arrived, all the target forces had gone. There was evidence of severe casualties and at least 14 APCs destroyed . Tracks indicated that they had left in the direction of the base camp, target two. How do I know why, maybe they went to finish the job. Where is my ride? You promised it would be here. Bastard!"

The one sided conversation terminated after the final Bastard.

"I have no idea whether that man got away or not. No sign of an extra helicopter, but it may have been masked by the hills."

"Well done, Major." Chuck sent the man back to his equipment and turned to Colonel Volkov. "It sounds as if the attack was a success. I will keep up the patrols anyway."

***

Mike Summers finished copying the entire instruction brief. He made 12 copies and had them each placed in separate envelopes. He addressed two to opposing Senators and two to Congressmen, one of whom was the representative of the Illinois district where many of his men originated. The message he placed in each envelope was that on a given day and date he had found his record stating that he was believed killed in action as had his entire command. In addition that he had record of a unit of the Russian army that had been tasked to wipe out his command to save embarrassing questions of the origin of the raid on Iranian territory. The Russian force had also been targeted for destruction after they had removed the US force.

His final comments were that he intended bringing his entire unit home, and if any attempt was made to impede the progress of his unit or the Russians accompanying, they would respond with extreme prejudice and what is more they would place copies of these instructions and the orders for the force's destruction in the hands of the United Nations.

***

The arrival of the civilian aircraft from Georgia was monitored from its first appearance on the radar screen. The Georgian pilot had requested permission to land as an emergency and permission had been granted.

The passenger had requested an interview with the Brigadier General and she was brought to Mike's office. Colonel Volkov and his pilot Major Katerina Shukov were also present.

The middle-aged lady passenger was neatly dressed in a grey suit and she carried a brief case. The passport she produced named her Rosa and she freely admitted that was not her real name but it would do. Her purpose was to invite Colonel Volkov and his entire force to come to Georgia and become part of the Georgian defence force.

The sheer effrontery of the offer took Mike's breath away. On the other hand, Volkov seemed quite flattered at the offer.

While Rosa was being entertained by Katrina and Jesse, Mike and Volkov discussed the offer.

"How do you know this is a genuine offer?" Mike said.

Volkov laughed, "You Americans, you see spies under the bed. Here in this part of the world we have a practical way of viewing things. First I know who this lady is. She is a very senior government figure in Georgia.

"Georgia is suffering from interference from Russia, an example of which is the base where we were operating. We were not given the base, we took it.

"Taking our aircraft and eight hundred men into the Georgian army would reinforce them considerably, and our presence would guarantee that Russia would in the future stay out of Georgian affairs. I thank you my friend for your help and assistance and the sanctuary you offered when we needed it. I will speak to my people and tell them of the Georgian offer. I believe they will accept. I will become a general and you will always be welcome in my country and my house." He then grabbed Mike and kissed him on both cheeks.

***

The meeting in the hanger was a great success and the entire contingent saw things the same way that Volkov had. The Mig 23's were all anonymous so it was a simple matter to paint the Georgian colours on the plain silver aircraft.

The APC's also received the treatment and by the time the move was scheduled all the equipment was suitably signed. The US contingent paraded and gave them a ceremonial send off. Rosa departed with an escort of jet fighters, whilst the APC's used the road. Having escorted the APC convoy to the border, the US Apaches returned to their base to re-fuel and prepare for their own departure.

***

The SOS came within an hour. The convoy of APCs had been ambushed in Georgia by Russian troops smuggled in overnight.

At the head of the F15s Mike went into action, followed up by the Apache ground support assets. Chuck took two hundred men, including all the Special Forces, and cut the ambushers off from their transport before starting to mop up the surviving attackers. Between the APCs and the ground troops from the Base they collected nearly one hundred prisoners. It was an unbelieving Chuck Hartog who was told that the prisoners had agreed to join Volkov's men in Georgia.

The explanation from Mike when they returned to base convinced him, but he was still amazed at the pragmatism that drove such men.

***

Mike's conversation with the US four-star general in command of the NATO forces in Adana was not recorded. The convoy of troops was airlifted home and the aircraft staged home with tanker service, while the Israeli three made the Mediterranean jump back to their base on their own.

Back in Selfridge Air base an interesting situation arose when Brigadier General Hammond found he was outranked by Brigadier General Summers whose promotion had been back-dated one year for political reasons. The reasons aside, it meant that Hammond was surplus to requirements and he was posted elsewhere, to make way for Mike.

Lt Col. Sarah O'Conner transferred to Selfridge to enable her to marry General Summers, which she duly did.

The documents that guaranteed the safety and security of what became known as the Turkish Incident were securely held against any repercussion from CIA or political sources.

The covert deployment to Turkey had become part of the history of the National Guard in Illinois/Michigan area and, as is the way of the service, it was not too surprising that they were soon once more deployed to Turkey, albeit a far more populated area in a more traditional manner.

Now armed with F18's, under the direct command of Colonel Jesse Browning. Mike's deputy was Col. Sir Peter Hamilton-Davies, still happily a bachelor, though seriously under siege it had to be said.

Chapter six

...The Return

...Turkey

The convoys in that part of Europe were actually little different from those in Africa. The main difference was in the people. The actual convoy route was across reasonable roads with surfaces that, at the moment anyway, were in quite good condition. The people were intelligent and willing, and the supply of goods was available without the ever present bunch of human vultures always ready to take a share that should be for the refugees.

In Jesse's destination at Jolfa, she found the encampment was outside a civilised city with an infrastructure and paved roads. There were restaurants and shops which were all were divorced from the camp itself even though many of the refugees had found jobs within the area.

The border guards were helpful and their searches perfunctory. The commander of the guards met her on her first convoy, and they found common ground in that first conversation that both were willing to explore, on her second trip she accepted an invitation to dinner in a public restaurant in the city.

From then on they dined every time she came to Jolfa.

***

The arrival of the deployment in Turkey was not concealed nor was it particularly publicised. It was at least two hours after they arrived that the phone rang in the general's quarters and the call from General Volkov was announced.

The call was not long nor did Volkov mention anything specific. It was enough for Mike to plan a trip to Eastern Turkey to enable the two men to meet without being observed.

The result was that when Mike returned to Adana, he was able to brief the others on events that they had not been made aware of whilst in the United States.

Volkov had caught two CIA agents as they set a trap for him. On interrogation the agents had confessed that they had been charged with the removal of the general and his senior staff, a matter of 'face' apparently. They also commented that the US members were to be targeted by their Russian counterparts. Volkov said they were supremely confident that they would succeed and settle the matter once and for all. "It appears they are prepared to take a chance on the production of the documents now that the initial hue and cry has died down."

***

Serge Karloff had already formed a plan of action for the arrival of the US deployment.

Unfortunately, his plan was not working as it should due to the absence of the CIA man who was supposed to be his way into the base. He was unaware that his contact was currently a guest of General Volkov, in Tbilisi.

Karloff's partner was, in his eyes, an amateur. Product of the new school for spies in Moscow, he knew it all. Michael Popof was top of his class and he regarded Karloff as a dinosaur.

When Serge mentioned that the CIA contact was not in touch Popof had scoffed that they did not need the help of the Westerner; he would get them into the camp without any problems.

***

The discomforted Russian stood in front of Colonel Hartog, defiant but worried.

"Of course," Chuck said, "There is no record of you entering our camp so officially you do not exist. This makes it easy for us though it could be difficult for you. For example, if you tripped and fell down the steps outside, you would probably get hurt. If you broke your neck it could kill you. Either way there would be no repercussions as you are not here. You do understand that, do you not?"

"But I told my friends that I would be coming in here."

"I have tried to get through to you, Popof, or whatever your name is, whatever you said you were going to do was just talk. As far as we are concerned you didn't make it, and If you are found floating in the Black Sea, there would be no connection to us in any way."

Popof was now looking worried. The fact was that he would have had no problems with doing what the Colonel suggested might be done, so he was beginning to believe that this could be the end of the line for him. And after all he had only just started.

The cell he occupied was cold and stark. He sat there for two days; the food came, he ate and they took the dishes away without speaking to him.

On the third day he asked to speak to the colonel. On the fourth day the colonel sent for him.

Seated, this time in front of the colonel's desk, he was a different person to the arrogant spy who had appeared in front of the colonel before.

"So, you asked to see me. What do you wish to see me about?"

"Sir, it occurred to me that if I was able to give you some news of importance, you could perhaps consider some more equitable arrangement for me."

"Why should I consider anything you say? You lied to me before, how would I know you were not lying to me now?"

"I am telling the truth now, I know that there are people who wish to harm your General Summers as well as General Volkov of the Georgian Air Force.

"I am sure there are enemies of both men to be found, so what is so special about your information?"

"These people have discovered that the two men were responsible for the destruction of the Iranian Nuclear Power Laboratories. It seems that the death toll there included an Ayatollah and his family who were visiting at the time.

"Who was involved in the attack on General Volkov? Was that the FSB? Was that you?"

"I am not FSB, I am a private contractor, like the operatives that attacked General Volkov. They are private contractors."

"So who do you work for?"

"I cannot tell you; it would be death for me to tell."

"Very well," the colonel reached for the phone saying "This conversation is over."

Popof looked appalled, he lifted his hand, "No, No. You must not, please!"

The phone went down. "So, tell me!"

"I am contracted by the FSB, and the others by the CIA."

"What the hell goes on? CIA are supposed to be on our side. And you? Why are you involved for the FSB?"

"For us it is a question of 'face'. What the two generals did by surviving when they should have all died cost the CIA and the FSB credibility."

"How did the Iranians get to know?"

"I believe they were told by FSB, perhaps the CIA. When they realised that the job was more difficult than they thought, they decided it was easier to leave it to the Iranians. So now they will forget the insults and see what happens."

"I want you to write all this down, so that I can have the people concerned chastised."

"But sir I have no proof."

"Forget proof, just write it down so that I have a record of it. I will release you then to go back to doing whatever you do. If you step into my path again I will kill you. Do you understand?"

"Yes sir, I understand."

In the general's office Chuck reported his conversation with Popof. Mike and Peter were both present, Jessie came in halfway through and Chuck backed up to ensure that they were all working from the same page.

"So we have the Iranians after us because either the FSB or the CIA told them of our part in the removal of their nuclear lab. That is sick."

Jessie said, "Remind me to kill the next sonofabitch CIA man I come across."

Mike merely said, "I find it hard to believe that our fellow Americans would stoop that low. I think it may be time to convince our government that betrayal can be a two-way street."

"What do you have in mind?" Chuck said, though he could think of a few possibilities himself.

"First, a telephone call on the secure line, to Washington, then we will act on the results."

From the drawer of his desk he retrieved the red telephone linking him direct to the Chairman of the Joint Chiefs of Staff.

"General Abernethy, please, this is General Summers." There was a pause then Mike said, "He what? Is the Assistant Chief available?" There was a pause, then Mike slammed the phone down. "Would you believe there is no-one in the office of the Joint Chiefs."

The others looked at him in amazement. There was always someone in the office of the Joint Chief. Hell, wars started whenever.

"What does that mean?" Jessie asked.

"It means that the brass are letting the Iranians get rid of us, or not, if you see what I mean." Chuck sounded bitter.

"I do not see what you mean, actually. Would someone like to explain in simple language what is going on here?"

Peter said. "We have been thrown to the wolves. Our government has decided to take the chance on our exposing their little exercise to wipe out the Iranian nuclear plant and get rid of the evidence, i.e. us and the Russians under General Volkov."

"Ah, I understand, so what do we do? Go public!"

"Not yet." Mike said tiredly. He picked up the ordinary telephone and called General Volkov at the number the general had given him.

"Gregor! We have been shafted as you indicated any suggestions?"

He listened for a few moments, and then he said, "Okay. Gregor, I'll get back to you later."

He put the phone down and turned to the others in the room. "We need to get together on this."

Mike spent the next hour passing on the suggestions made by Volkov and his own proposals for their own independent action.

Relations between Georgia and NATO had improved to the point that discussions were under way over possible membership. Volkov would be visiting tomorrow.

Colonel Sarah Summers arrived from Selfridge with the final group of support staff in time join the meeting. After greeting the party in Mike's office she said, "Hey, guys, remember that Master Sergeant Ali Baranka." She looked around the group eyebrow raised. "Well, he is outside waiting to say hello, but he is a major now!"

Mike turned and pressed the intercom switch on his desk. "Is Major Baranka there?"

"Yes sir!"

"Send him in, please, and organise coffee and cookies or something for six."

"Yes sir."

The door was opened by Peter, who grinned at Ali Baranka and stuck his hand out. "Congratulations Ali, a major now, come in and say hello."

A beaming Ali came into the office and snapped to attention, saluting the people within.

"I am happy to see you all, sirs and ladies, because of you I am now a major and Colonel Pava Kemal has retired."

"So what is happening now in the area?" Sarah asked.

Ali's face became serious. "We have a problem I am afraid and in some ways it would have been better if you were not here. The Iranians have issued a 'Fatwa' on you all and General Volkov and his people. My people have been identifying Iranian agents here in Adana. Their activity has increased since your arrival. I thought at first it was because of Colonel Kemal, but now I am ashamed to tell you that your betrayal was by your own people. It seems that politics corrode loyalty and self-interest is more important than National Security."

"So we have been informed of the problem, Ali, by our friend General Volkov, who is also betrayed and threatened. He will be calling on us tomorrow, but how did you get involved?"

"I am in our own intelligence branch, and I am on the list as are you all. My people are keeping a close eye on the movements of the Iranians, who are being controlled by General Parvis for the purpose of this operation."

At the mention of the name Parvis Mike felt a shiver go down his spine. The man was a mad dog. His reputation had been gained over his deliberate elimination of the Kurds from a traditional part of the Kurdish homeland on the shores of the Caspian Sea. His particular brutality extended to the introduction of toxic chemicals that resulted in the agonizing deaths of approximately one thousand seven hundred Kurds and other local people living in the area. The area will be uninhabitable for at least another 48 years according to present calculations. The actual number of deaths is still unknown and according to rumour, Parvis could care less.

Ali spoke again, "His survival so far has been partly because he has avoided being photographed and thus remains anonymous to all but his loyal staff; passing through areas unnoticed and unsuspected. He has no wife, he uses women occasionally apparently, but such usage is normally a death sentence to whoever it is."

"So we have no idea who we are up against?"

"Oh no, that is not true. We are well armed against this man on individual terms. We know the group that includes him. Though with which of the groups he actually is we still don't know. We have a wide network of agents watching and protecting targets of the group, the Kurdish people have not forgotten him nor will they ever. The memory of the massacre lives and the fate of the man Parvis is certain in the minds of the Kurdish people.

"Meanwhile my people are watching and I am here today to let you know that they will cooperate with Colonel Chuck and his base security in any way they can, including vetting local staff employed on the base.

When Ali left Mike turned to the others, "Well I don't know about you, but I feel a lot better than I did before Ali came."

***

Volkov arrived in a two-seater jet trainer that bore a remarkable similarity to the Hawk jet used by the RAF. It turned out that it was actually a variant of the Hawk sold to the Georgian government as a training aircraft.

When the meeting and greeting was over the two former protagonists sat down to discuss matters.

For Volkov the suggestion that the Kurds were looking out for the Iranians was good news indeed and in fact his plans were advanced for retribution against the people of the FSB that had initiated his problems in the first place. There was no question in his mind that the issue would only be settled finally with a bullet. He tapped the holster under his arm to emphasise his point.

***

General Parvis sat and watched as his team discussed their plans for the approach to the assault on the Americans in their base.

The task Parvis had set was to destroy the base, regardless of any collateral damage that may result from the destruction. In the eyes of Parvis anyone who assists a target deserves whatever they get.

Most people who came into contact with Parvis could not understand why he was so ruthless.

There is always a reason, even if it is only that the man is a sadist. In the case of Anwa Parvis it was a misunderstanding. He was of the opinion that the death of his sister and parents was a result of action by a rogue section of the CIA/and the US Navy. In fact, they had died as a result of a misplaced bomb from an Iranian aircraft. The pilot decided not to go on the raid as ordered and dumped his bomb before he had gone feet wet. When he returned to base he reported mission accomplished. When the death of Parvis's family was discovered it was reported to be a sneak raid from US Carrier aircraft.

The man himself had a pathological hatred of USA and her allies. The fact that the Turkish were mainly Muslim did not absolve them from blame. Thus they would suffer for their association with Satan's representatives just as would anyone else who got in Parvis's way.

The team leader of the Georgian group tasked with the destruction of Volkov and his traitorous Russians turned to Parvis "We have to be aware of the Kurds in this part of the world. Do you have any suggestions, sir?"

Parvis turned his cold dark eyes on the man. After a few moments he said, "If they interfere kill them, in fact if the chance occurs kill them anyway, they are vermin, and we kill all vermin."

***

The efforts of Major Ali Baranka had borne fruit. Apart from the undoubted unpopularity of the Iranian administration with the Turkish people, the number of Kurds living within the community in the country areas of Turkey had increased considerably over the years. Despite the efforts of the leadership to find and develop a homeland, many families decided to make the best of things until that day arrived, and actually got on with their lives. The area of the NATO base close to the Mediterranean had its share of minorities in the community. There a serious communion had developed between the various peoples. A willingness to befriend neighbours be they, Armenian, Kurd, or Turk had come from working together in the workplace expanded markedly by the establishment of Incirlik NATO base, the biggest employer in the Adama area. The relationship between the different ethnic groups had become closer by shared interests at a social level, a situation unheard of elsewhere in Asia-Minor.

It was thus that the transmission of information on the movements of strangers into and through the area became an important feature among people who all shared the uncertainty of government acceptance.

Unlike in other areas in the Muslim world, the NATO forces stationed in the Incirlik base enjoyed a friendly relationship with the local people. The suggestion of a possible threat to the lives of the Americans therefore was regarded by the locals as a personal insult to themselves.

When the advance scouts of General Parvis's assassination team arrived, their presence was reported immediately to Major Baranka. They were all kept under surveillance and the community closed ranks, watching for any sign of a follow-up party posing a threat to the base.

For Brigadier Mike Summers, happily now back in contact with the Chief-of-Staff, having ordered all personnel to carry side-arms at all times there was little more he could do. The sheer size of the base prohibited the sort of security that would counter all but a missile attack from space. Thus it was what Chuck referred to as the 'watchful-eye' method that depended on the threatened people keeping an eye out for the unusual, the odd and the different.

The aircraft maintained their normal flight patterns, the AWACS eye in the sky reported no variation in the patterns of activity in the surrounding border areas.

***

In Georgia there was a slightly different situation. The relationship between General Volkov and the local Kurdish Chieftain was friendly and when the infiltrating group of Iranians made their presence felt, the report was immediately transmitted to the general. He warned Mike that things had begun in Georgia and suggested that the watch in Turkey be stepped up.

***

In consultation with Mike. Ali decided to lift the advance party of Iranians and keep them incommunicado until others came out of the woodwork.

The shock of capture was evident on the faces of the Iranian infiltrators. They could not understand how they had been detected and the leader was convinced that there had been at least a defection that had involved the revelation of the whereabouts of the entire group.

Ali allowed no disclosure to them as it would reveal that the people who had given the spies up were the ordinary people of the area.

From one of the advance party he found the name of the leader of the Turkish assassination group. He passed the information over to Chuck Hartog who revealed it to Mike. "Sir, this General Parvis is a fanatic and to my mind a pathological murderer. His erasure of the Kurds on the Caspian Shore was brutal and unnecessary. He is reputed to have toured the area after his men had been through. shooting any survivor he found with his pistol.

"Ali reckons he will be coming to supervise the execution of the people involved in our raid on Iran. This man does not trouble himself over collateral damage. Anyone that gets in his way will be killed offhand."

"Then we will have to make sure that he does not get the chance."

The troubled Iranian assassins working for General Parvis found life difficult to the extent that Colonel Khourosh, who commanded the advance guard though he had not accompanied them, actually spoke to the General, pointing out that his men had all dropped from sight. Before he had the chance to mention reports of arrests made, the general accused him of commanding traitors and shot him. While he did not actually kill, his bullet did remove the colonel from the active list for sufficient time for him to avoid the debacle that followed.

It had been a mistake to allow the operation to be left to the general however fearsome his reputation. Savage he may have been but in this operation he displayed a level of stubborn stupidity that defied belief.

He actually managed to get his team in without detection. They took over the estate of an absent millionaire. Moving in quietly they had the house occupied and the outbuildings in use commendably quickly.

The setting up of the missile launchers was straightforward as the Airbase was in plain sight of the house.

The first hint for the Americans that there was a problem on their doorstep was when a trigger man in the General's party inadvertently fired a missile into the airbase. He had tripped and fallen and in reaching out to break his fall he had grabbed the firing mechanism of one of the launchers and set one off.

At the base they did a reciprocal on the track of the missile, and sent a salvo in return. The explosion of the missile launcher and its weapons was sufficient to turn the building in which the raiding party were sleeping into an inferno. The two F18's that followed up the missile attack with two carpet bombs that prepared the area for a rebuilding program that the owner found extremely gratifying. The olive grove that was destroyed in the process was subject of compensation that more than adequately repaid the owner for the scrawny worn-out trees that burned so spectacularly.

The Georgian base was less fortunate since there were no accidental discharges nor were they hampered by the presence of a fanatical general. The raiders actually got as far as the perimeter fence of the base before they were stopped. There they were given the option of continuing and dying or surrendering and living. The problem for the Iranians was that returning home having failed would cost them their lives and those of their families. Death for the cause would confer martyrdom. Failure was therefore not an option. The fact that they were all trained soldiers who were actually pretty good at what they did had not been enough against the country craft of the Kurds. They had been surviving against multiple enemies for the past hundred years give or take. In the circumstances, after being informed of the demise of the general and his entire party, the Georgian assassins decided that surrender was the best option.

With the assurance that they would all be reported dead, thus lifting the threat from their families, the entire business became feasible. The forty man contingent joined the Georgian service under the direct control of General Volkov, having assumed good Georgian names of course. The graveyard outside the wire of the establishment listed the names of the entire assault party, and the date of their death. The photograph of the mass grave was sent through to Iran by post with a note of warning on the subject of warfare by stealth.

Chapter seven

...Escape

The unidentified patient in the Adana Hospital recovered consciousness during the night.

He had sustained a few cuts and bruises and concussion, the concussion had induced the limited coma and for a week the injured man had lain in hospital. His cuts and bruises healed mostly so that when he regained consciousness he was recovered sufficiently to operate once more apart from the odd twinge. He looked around the room. The other bed was occupied by an old man who was snoring quietly. Anwa Parvis uncoupled the drip from his arm and slid out of bed He was unsteady on his feet and stood for a moment recovering his balance. There was a pile of clothing on the chair in the corner of the room. He made his way over and dressed himself. He was still tired but he drove himself to his feet once more and cautiously tried the door. There was no lock and the door opened silently. There was no one about when he made his unsteady way down the silent corridor to the double doors leading out to the car park.

There were few cars scattered about in the parking area at this time of the early morning.

A police cruiser parked in the corner in the shadow of a copse of trees attracted his attention. There was no sign of activity around it, and when he approached it he saw the officer was lying across the front seat with his eyes closed, a girl in a trainee nurses uniform was performing an age old dance on his body. She was looking disgusted. The man with eyes closed was not interested in anything but the act the girl was performing.

Anwar went around the car to the side where the drivers head was laying. The girl saw him through the window He held up his finger to his lips and she smiled. He grasped the door handle carefully then yanked it open and slammed the edge of his hand down across the throat of the policeman.

The man's eyes sprang open as he gasped trying to breathe, his body jerking violently, throwing the small girl off as he reached for the gun at his hip. Anwar beat him to it and watched with the girl as the man died of suffocation in front of them. He pulled the body from the car and stripped him of his uniform. The boots were too small but the rest was not a bad fit. The girl made no effort to leave and Anwar thought perhaps he would have to kill her. He climbed into the driver's seat and saw the girl putting the seatbelt on in the passenger seat.

He put off the idea of killing her for the moment anyway. She was quite a pretty thing, and she seemed to be sensible to some extent anyway, at least she kept her mouth shut.

He drove off not really knowing where he was going, just getting away from the Hospital and the area.

***

In Adama, Colonel Hartog called into the hospital to see the man who had been brought in with concussion. It had taken this long to link the injuries to the man with the explosions at the millionaire's estate.

The empty bed made it urgent to find out what happened to the man. A search of the grounds disclosed the body of the policeman, killed with the strike to the throat. His car and uniform made a starting point for a search.

***

Anwar Parvis stopped the car and studied the map wondering where would be best to go. The girl took the map and indicated a route. With a shrug he put the car in gear and set off as she directed, following a route that she obviously knew by heart.

When they stopped finally they were at a farmhouse out of sight any neighbour. The place was empty and the girl was at home. She demonstrated her local knowledge by going straight to the pantry and retrieving food and cooking it and cheerfully feeding them both.

Anwar Parvis was mystified. The girl had not spoken a word since they met. He addressed her directly after they had eaten. When she did not answer him, he asked her why. She looked sad and opened her mouth. She had no tongue. She fetched pencil and paper and wrote quickly in Arabic.

'The policeman who died, kidnapped me, he had my tongue removed as punishment and to make me his slave, to prove that he was my master. For you I willingly serve for you have released me. My life is yours.'

She put her hands together and bowed to him. Parvis did the only thing he could do at that moment, He took her hands between his and leaned forward and kissed her forehead.

For the general this was an unprecedented situation. He was not accustomed to feeling gratitude to anyone. He needed to think about this.

As the evening darkened into night the girl took his hand and led him up stairs to a bed room. She opened another door and showed him a room with running water and a toilet. Then she left him. He felt disappointed that she had left him alone.

He would think about it tomorrow, he was tired tonight. He thought perhaps he should secure the girl, but then he realised he had trusted her so far. She could have betrayed him at any time.

He lay back on the bed and was asleep as soon as his head hit the pillow.

He woke in the night, suddenly aware that he was no longer alone. The smooth flesh beneath his hand was warm and willing under his touch, the subtle movements of her body invited and accepted his caresses and invited his intrusion when the moment was upon them. The whole episode was dreamlike and when he sank back into sleep it was with the comfort of her body beside him.

***

The enquiry into the death of the policeman turned up the news of the small, dumb girl who normally worked as a trainee in the hospital. The fact that she was missing was regarded as significant. The police sergeant from the local station knew where the girl lived. It was known that her parents had been found dead by the policeman who was killed at the hospital.

The sergeant decided to call and see if the girl was still at the house and if she was if she knew her former protector was dead. If a new protector was wanted he was willing to offer himself in the role. He took his own car and told no one of his intention or destination.

When the car drew up outside the house there was no sign of the missing police car. It had been put into the barn behind the house. The sergeant banged on the door and when the girl appeared he crashed the door open and grabbed her by the arm. He was surprised when she hit him round the ear with the heavy pan in her other hand. For a moment he stood still, then he swayed, and collapsed to the floor. His fingers had left a bruise on her arm where they had gripped her. The general appeared, having heard the noise. He took in the scene immediately. He noticed the girl's arm, he examined where the man had gripped her.

Then he went and checked the pulse of the man on the floor. It fluttered, a most unhealthy sign. He took the cushion from the nearest chair and placed it over the face of the sergeant. Leaning forward with both hands on the cushion he kept his weight firmly in place. After a few minutes he removed the cushion and checked the pulse again.

This time there was no response. He nodded thoughtfully and then stood, the girl helped him drag the man through the back door out into the back yard. Though there were no animals left on the farm since the death of her parents, there was still a heap of manure in the yard. They rolled the body over to the heap and stripped off the gunbelt and emptied the pockets, then Parvis took a shovel and dug a hole in the manure heap. They rolled the body in, then covered it and that was that. The girl drove the car round to the barn and it joined the other car out of sight.

Parvis examined the gear in the trunk of both cars retrieving two automatic shotguns and four loaded magazines. There were spare magazines for the two side-arms, both being cheap Star automatics of Spanish origin.

It was obvious they could not stay here. Parvis was certain of that. He had plenty clothing. The wardrobe was still full of the girl's parents' clothes, and there were more modern things left by the absent brother who was now in Jordan. He was concerned. Because of the failure of his mission, he could no longer return to Iran. Also there was the girl, he found that he was thinking about her fate at least as much as his own. For the first time in his life he was concerned about someone else. It was an odd feeling but it brought a warmth to his life absent up to now. He wondered if it was love that he felt.

***

For Col. Hartog gathering information about the dead police officer took time and it was not until later in the day that the suggestion was made that the girl might be at home. In the absence of the sergeant, officers were sent to the girl's home to question her about the dead policeman. She was not found the place was deserted except for the body in the manure heap.

***

Taking the sergeant's private car, Parvis and the girl had already set off for Antakya, on the border between Turkey and the Syrian province of Latakya. It was the opposite direction to the search; after all nobody in their right mind would go into Syria while the troubles were at their height.

The runaways guessed that it should be possible to pass through to Jordan and possibly lose themselves in that troubled country. Because of his position in the Iranian hierarchy, Parvis had access to considerable funds throughout the middle east. At Antakya he collected enough dollars to keep the two fugitives in comfort for the foreseeable future.

For the girl, it was as good as it gets. For the first time in her life she felt needed, and confident. The future was uncertain but this odd man cared for her.

Parvis was confused, uncertain but happy. It was a strange place for him to be, but whatever happened from now on, his past was behind him. The girl—he did not even know her name—cared for him, and he cared for her. It was enough.

***

They found the police car but nobody looked for the sergeant there. There was no sign of the girl and the eventual result was the case was closed unsolved. The unidentified man remained unidentified. Then a casual inspection of the fingerprints taken by the coroner showed a crescent scar on the left thumb. This explained the mystery of the sergeant, though not how he had stripped his clothes off and crawled into a manure heap to die. Or how he had received a blow on the head that should not have killed him.

Faced with all these questions and no answers, Col. Hartog decided to wait and see what developed, if anything; hoping that it would all go away by itself.

The routine of the regular business of the deployment carried on in the day to day succession of exercises and war games played between the allies within range including the force commanded by General Volkov.

For Summers the visit by three-star General Wallace was scheduled to be a problem. In fact it worked out a little differently than either anticipated.

The day started with the usual pomp and ceremony attendant on the visit by an inspecting officer.

The Lear jet landed and taxied to the parade where the General de-planed and stood to receive the general salute, and march past. Mike Summers was there to receive him and all protocol was strictly observed.

The base inspection followed and a formal lunch was attended in the special dining room with the senior officers and local dignitaries present.

Protocol demanded a private meeting between commander and the inspecting officer and it was here that the face-off occurred.

General Wallace opened the discussion "The turnout was up to standard," He admitted grudgingly.

"The turnout was immaculate." Brigadier Summers replied.

"I believe I will be the judge of that." General Wallace answered with some asperity.

"After the performance you have given over our last deployment I do not consider you fit to make any judgement of these men and women."

"How dare you speak to me like that, I will have you before a Court Martial for insubordination."

"I really do not think so. If you did, the whole story might come out. How you colluded in condemning my entire command to death, in addition to Colonel Volkov's command, in the name of security. And I can tell you that I have documentary proof of your part in the conspiracy, along with the instructions given for the collateral removal of Colonel Volkov's command."

General Wallace coloured and held back the anger at being spoken to in this way by the man in front of him. It was not all over yet.

"My promotion to Brigadier General was inspired. if I had actually been killed you could have pointed out that I have been the maverick who had been promoted under pressure from others against your better judgement. All my actions were suspect; thus the attack on Iran was obviously my idea, and I have reaped the reward for my sins. I ask what about the rest of my command? What would you call that collateral damage?

"You are the bastard who has dogged my career ever since I took part in that operation in the Gulf War. Tell me, what was it I did that upset you so much?"

"You actually disobeyed station orders, by flying non-American troops in a Blackhawk without specific authority, and you were under orders not to leave Kuwait with the helicopter. Neither charge was brought because the officers concerned refused to testify. It was my duty to try and en-sure that you were punished appropriately, so I made it my business to see that your career suffered."

"So why the promotion to Brigadier, back dated even?"

"That was to make sure that the regular commander of the Selfridge Unit would not be sent on that particular de-ployment."

"I was expendable and he wasn't?"

"I believe that was possibly the reason!"

"And the rest of the unit? Were they regarded as ex-pendable, too? Is that the reason some of the officers were transferred during the lead-up to the deployment? General Wallace, I am tempted to have you up on a Court Martial for the betrayal of your command and abuse of office. What we are now discussing is your resignation from the service for the good of the service."

The face of General Wallace grew angrier as Brigadier Summers spoke. Finally, he replied. "You fool, did you really believe that I was the authority behind the Iran raid?

That I ordered the destruction of your unit? I was a two-star when those orders were given. They came from the top, all I did was pass them on. Oh, I did suggest you to command, but only because I considered you would be better qualified for this job than your predecessor, who as you well know is serving out his time a long way from any action. You may believe this or not. I did not agree with the orders to the Russian unit. That was arranged by the CIA against my protests. Right or wrong, one of the main reasons you were chosen was because I thought you might do what you did do. I have never really liked you, Summers, but that did not interfere with my assessment of you as a leader. The other reason you were promoted with seniority was that it should have happened five years ago. And, finally, I will not be resigning my commission whatever you think. I worked hard to get where I am and for me the service always came first.

"The person who coordinated the CIA operations in the Iran area has just been promoted to the rank of Assistant Director Mediterranean Region. I suggest you watch your back while you are here because he has a long arm."

General Wallace, calm once more drew himself up and said "My congratulations for the safe extraction of your people after the Iran affair, and well done with this inspection. I may have overreacted in the Gulf, it does not seem to have harmed your efficiency as a Unit Commander."

After the General left in his Lear Jet, Mike sat back to consider what had passed between them. He had to learn to accept that the nemesis that had dogged his service life was not General Wallace. It had occurred to him that the escape from the Georgian Border was an embarrassment to the administration. What he had not realised was that the whole event had been stage managed by the CIA and that the loss of face had been unacceptable to the organisation that had suffered perhaps one embarrassing incident too many at that time.

It seemed that the incident had become a personal thing.

***

Ali Baranka came to see Colonel Chuck Hartog, looking very upset. The two men had formed an unforeseen friendship since their first encounter and the Turkish officer was concerned by rumours that the CIA was actively supporting elements of the FSB in actions against the forces of Georgia, and indirectly against the current NATO force in the Incirlik base. The serious problem was the gathering of forces, ostensibly terrorist, that were being aligned against the Georgian base occupied by General Volkov.

"The forces being gathered are actually Russian army troops and they appear to be spearheading a takeover of Georgia, returning it to Russian rule. The government opposition have been negotiating with people that they should not be listening to. They are under the impression that the incoming effort is directed as placing a sympathetic government to the current Russian regime." Ali was convinced that his information was correct.

Chuck Hartog listened attentively, "Ali, we've got to speak to the boss about this, I know he suspects the CIA and is aware of the threat to our people as well as that to Volkov and the Georgians.

Brigadier General Mike Summers sat back in his chair and looked at the two men in front of him, "How convinced are you that this is a Russian takeover with CIA assistance?"

Ali answered, "My Kurdish friends came across a surveying party, running lines along the southern border of the country. Since they were including a substantial part of what the Kurds think of as their land, they intervened. They found charts and field drawings that included the current areas of Georgia, both occupied and unoccupied. All the drawings indicate the inclusion of Georgia within the boundaries of Russia. When questioned, the surveyors all confirmed that their brief had been to include the areas they were covering in the greater Russian boundaries." He sat back, much happier now he had passed the problem on to someone who would listen, and perhaps act.

"Can we get hold of these drawings and charts?" Mike asked.

"I have some in my car outside." Ali said and rose to his feet.

"Let's take a look at them. Please bring them in and I will have a word with General Volkov."

The conversation was short and to the point. Within minutes Volkov was in the air, within the hour he was landing at the UN base.

He was preceded by a Typhoon flown in from Batman Airbase. The pilot was Group Captain David Sheldon, RAF. He was in the Brigadier's office when General Volkov arrived.

"So what is all this about Russia taking Georgia over once mo..."he spotted David Sheldon and stopped abruptly causing Katerina to bump into him.

Mike rose to his feet. "Gregor, I would like to introduce my friend Group Captain David Sheldon RAF, currently on attachment to Batman Airbase. David came to our assistance when your people paid their first call on us last year."

"Ah, the Typhoon, I should have realised. I am pleased to meet any friend of General Summers." He turned and Katerina stepped forward, "This is Colonel Katerina Shukov, my 2i/c.

Katerina stepped forward and shook David's hand and kissed him on both cheeks. "Hullo, David, it is good to see you again."

David smiled, "You are looking more beautiful than ever, Katt."

Mike noticed that she blushed at this, and he wondered. "Please sit down, everyone. I believe you know all the others here, so I'll ask Major Baranka to lead off."

Ali began, "The Russian government is invading Georgia, the initial plan is to first strike at the base commanded by General Volkov. The excuse will be that the general is Russian and he had, in effect, deserted from the Russian army. The protection given him by the Georgian government will be the excuse to continue the campaign against the Georgian government itself.

"They have been infiltrating people into the country for some time so that a nationwide upsurge of pro-Russian support can be demonstrated. This will be the excuse for the final envelopment of Georgia."

Ali stopped for a moment to look at a paper he had in front of him. Nobody spoke or moved they all waited for him to continue.

"Their plan will only work if the strike against General Volkov is successful, with some exceptions. The majority of the infiltrators will not rise unless that happens. If they are not convinced that Russia will win, they will not rise. I will go as far as to say they will become Georgians officially, and get on with their lives here. That is my assessment. As far as the position of General Volkov is concerned – without help they will succeed. The force they are building up in the territory they hold already is already, big enough to overwhelm the Batumi base, and it is still grow-ing."

"Where are they assembling?" Mike asked.

"Pskhu, which is in the north of the country, just 210 kilometres by air to Batumi." Ali answered, "There is an airbase there where they can bring materials and troops in without attracting too much attention, and of course launch an assault by the same means."

"Is the assault an official Russian operation or are they disguising it as a popular uprising?" General Volkov asked.

"It is to be an unannounced attack, and the success will be followed by assistance from Russia to sort things out from which the takeover will result."

"Colonel Hartog, will you look after our guests, I have some administrative things to do with Colonels Hamilton, Browning and Summers. This will not take long and we will , if you agree, get together at dinner in one hour."

When the others had left Mike turned to the three peo-ple closest to him probably in the world. "I will not see our friends wasted for the benefit of the CIA or the Russian government."

Sarah said "If the troops agree. You realise that your career will be over?"

He looked at her sharply.

"I am not opposed, I just want to know that you under-stand where this might go."

Peter spoke, "I'm with you. If we leave this for the Pentagon we'll be too late to pick up the pieces."

"I'm in!" Jessica said. "And I am sure that the troops will be. After all we were all in the same boat, and we know now that the CIA will be gunning for us as soon as the dust settles."

"Right, I want full assembly in the drill hangar at 20.00 tonight, I will be speaking to Chuck in a few minutes so that he can confirm with his duty men who cannot come to the hangar. Right. I will see you all at dinner."

Peter and Jessica left the office. Sarah stayed. "I'm proud of you. You know that, don't you? Even General Wallace recognised that he had misjudged you."

Mike stood up and took her in his arms, "Maybe I'll have more time to spend with you from now on, what d'you think?" He kissed her then and sent her out to join the others.

By the time he met the group at the dinner table he had his speech to his troops written. It was not long but it said what he felt should be said.

The dinner passed in friendly conversation; the pairing of David and Katerina was duly noted and generally approved. Volkov had once had hopes in that direction, but had settled for the Georgian liaison officer Colonel Carol Timoshenko, a vivacious lady from the Black sea coast, who had fallen for him within three days of her arrival at the base.

The hangar was full, the PA system echoed a little so Mike spoke slowly and clearly.

"Most of you were here in Turkey during out last deployment. The things that happened then have, up until now, been kept between ourselves. We survived that deployment for two reasons, one being our alliance with the people tasked to remove us to prevent any future embarrassment to our government, and the Russians. I will add at this point our government as represented by the CIA. Our survival on that occasion was helped immensely by the unstinting help of Major Ali Baranka, at the time a master sergeant in the Turkish army, and at considerable risk to himself."

He paused and studied the faces in front of him, satisfied he had their attention he carried on. "It has now come to our attention that our friends across the border in Georgia are threatened once more. I say, without being too pessimistic, that means our turn is next. The CIA have never forgiven us for surviving and, having survived not given the game away. Having survived and kept our secret, we have demonstrated that they were wrong.

"The threat facing Batumi base will be the first move to take Georgia back into the Russian State. The forces undertaking this task are gathering secretly at Pskhu in the north of Georgia, which is still under Russian control despite the orders by the Russian Parliament to leave. It seems that the real power still remains with the President."

Here he stopped again briefly to collect his thoughts.

Chapter eight

...The conflict

"So the reason for this get together is that judging from past performance, the UN will not interfere. The final negotiations for Georgia's entry into NATO have not been completed.

"We have our own survival to consider, but I am putting it to you that we should add our resources to those of our friends at Batumi, and stop this so-called rescue of Georgia by the popular uprising of the people, who will immediately turn to Russia for her backing against any interference by international bodies.

"If you agree, I will issue orders to all sections involved so that there will be no question in future that blame for the actions taken is passed on to you.

"Anyone who decides not to take part is of course free to withdraw at this point. Thank you for your attention and I am proud to have served with you over the past years."

Mike stepped back from the dais and left the hangar.

Chuck Hartog took his place. "For those interested, I will be with the Brigadier, not because he is my friend alone but I think this is the right thing to do. I will dismiss you just now but return here in one hour ready to commit, one way or the other. Thank you."

The hangar emptied with the buzz of conversation rising as the crowd split into their units, and returned to their quarters.

"So, what do you think?" Mike asked Sarah.

"I think I will start packing my gear and making out a stress list for the Squadron. Peter and Jessica are already collecting their bits and pieces together as is Chuck, I have no doubt. When the people return I expect the majority will be ready to volunteer, you should realise that the people look up to you especially so since that last deployment."

There was a knock at the door.

When Sarah opened it David was standing there, "I will be returning to Batman immediately, I will not say anything to the powers about what might happen today. I will be in touch. I am proud to know you."

He turned and left, walking outside into the short evening twilight. A figure approached him as he started toward the parked Typhoon aircraft.

The voice of General Volkov came softly calling him to stop for a moment.

"David, I may call you David? "

At David's nod, he continued. "About Katerina."

David stiffened and it was noticed by the general. "I wanted to say that I am happy to see that she and you seem to be good friends together. I also would be happy if you find happiness together. However I would just like to add that I would be unhappy if you hurt her in any way. I am fond of her and she has suffered in her life. Her husband and son were murdered by terrorists. Her parents were removed to a gulag where both died, because they lived in the same area as some Chechen rebels. You now know this so I will say no more."

"Thank you for telling me these things, I was not aware. You may be reassured to know that I am no longer married, and my feelings for Katerina are known to her, as are her feelings for me. We will sort our lives out when this exercise is over. Goodnight sir. I will be in touch." He turned and continued walking to his aircraft.

Katerina was there waiting. "I knew you would have to go," she said. "Will I see you again?"

"Sooner than you think, I will be back with a little help if it is possible. If not, I will still be back. Depend on it."

He took her in his arms, "Now we have found each other again I am not letting you go."

He kissed her, feeling her respond. Then she broke away, "I will be waiting." She promised.

He climbed into his waiting aircraft and waved, then in a roar of power he was gone.

Katerina stood for a few minutes letting her nerves settle and calming herself before returning to the others and the bustle of preparation.

***

The hangar was full once more. Chuck and Mike walked in as the NCO's called the men and women to attention. At the dais Mike paused looking out over the sea of faces before him. Then he said "All those who wish to abstain please leave the hangar now."

Nobody moved. "Do I take it that the Rebel spirit is alive and well in the USA, or at least here?"

The roar that greeted this was answer enough. In the front row a sergeant stepped forward, "I think I speak for us all, sir; we became the allies of our friends over the border when things looked rough for us all. We wish to stand by them now come what may!"

Mike stood for a moment getting control of himself, then he said "Thank you, orders will be posted – are being posted now. Movements start tomorrow."

The men cheered as he left the hanger, Chuck stood up in his place.

"For the record, all airfield protection personnel will be replaced by clerical staff as soon as the orders are cut. Aircrew and their ground staff prepare for campaign conditions. Special Forces Commanders, report to me now. Dismiss!"

The hanger emptied swiftly, the officers of the Delta and the SAS units stationed at the base joined Chuck as he left the building. As they walked across the tarmac he said. "The orders issued earlier are now open, you may act accordingly." One by one the men disappeared and by the time Chuck reached his office he was alone.

***

Jerry Peters had been in the SAS for three years now, his lieutenant pips were well and truly dull. The team he commanded worked together like a smoothly and professionally unit. He watched them all seated round the back of the flatbed truck, cleaning weapons and chatting quietly, well below the level of noise that the truck produced. All were in dark gear with cammo colour on their faces and hands, all were kitted out with body armour lifted from the Americans. It was better at its job that the British issue.

Jake Rider called from the front of the truck, "Obstruction ahead. They all lay flat below the level of the side panels of the truck. Jake continued to watch as they neared the barrier.

Jake shouted in Russian to the soldier standing there. The man replied also in Russian and the barrier rose to let them through.

"That should do." Jake commented "There should be no more barriers until we reach the airfield itself."

"What did you say to him then?" Charlie was one of the sort of people who always had to ask the question.

Well used to Charlie, who responded to any and every answer with, "Oh like that is it." Jake said "I told him that we were the brothel wagon taking the girls back home, they were all knackered having been worked over by the Mongolian company."

"Mongolian Company? What Mongolian Company? How did you know there was a Mongolian Company?"

"I didn't, you dummy, I just guessed that he wouldn't know either."

"Oh like that is it." And the discussion finished.

Jerry Peters smiled, wondering what Charlie was really thinking, then he gave it up; it was probably something he wouldn't want to know anyway.

Their progress was interrupted just five miles from the enemy base.

The Delta man who flashed the UV light had been placed there to give them a heads-up to park the truck.

Jerry knocked on the cab roof to let their driver know to stop.

They offloaded and ran the truck into a previously selected place behind a row of trees. The Delta team were already set up. Jerry and Peter Browning, the Delta boss, confirmed the arrangement s they had already made on the base.

The two teams deployed in a long, loose line and started for the enemy base.

The debacle of the attempted Clean-Sweep operation was now behind him and Elmore Heard was firmly establish in the re-supply of weapons from the former USSR to anyone who would and could afford to buy them. The inspired and long-planned takeover of Georgia was now left to get on with it. The plan already formulated by Heard and Zorin. The actual implementation of the operation was now in the hands of the Russian officers involved. The two agents had a far more lucrative business to arrange.

For Heard it was significant that in the cynical world of International Espionage there seemed to be no conflict of interest to interfere with his employment by Russia and/or Iran in an enterprise. Though initially scheduled to target the base of the newly promoted Georgian General Volkov at Batumi; the Turkish base of General Summers of NATO had now been added. This despite the fact that the main thrust of the operation was at a selected group of the Iranian people, and the city of New York.

The entire operation was based on the safe placement of six suitcase-sized nuclear bombs, already located and earmarked by Heard's partner, Zorin. Their involvement in this operation meant that they were not present at the latest developments of the Balkan Power struggle. With the profit anticipated from the current deal, the importance of a Russian takeover in Georgia paled into insignificance.

The bells started ringing in the wrong places in Langley. Official reports of the secret assembly of Russian forces in northern Georgia were coming in from Batman Base and Incirlik base in Turkey. The intercepted reports had been made to the Pentagon and to the other members of NATO including Great Britain.

The Deputy Director of the CIA Dennis Garrard sent an 'immediate response' message to the recently appointed area director demanding the reason that no information had been produced on the subject. The fact was that the reported detail was explicit, with facts and figures, equipment lists and a deduced raison d'être. This had been interpreted, because of the secret accumulation of men and materials, as an apparently spontaneous uprising of the Georgian people. The lack of communication on the subject was not only irritating it was criminal neglect of duty, and the Deputy Director was after blood.

In his office he awaited with trepidation for the summons from the Director, while still hoping for a reply from Elmore Heard, the area director based in the South West Asia office. As yet he was unaware of the de-facto desertion of Heard.

The email arrived two minutes before the summons to the White House. The email was useless, Elmore was away from his office and no information was forthcoming.

The CIA Director had called in sick and would not be available for today at least. The ball was definitely in his court.

The President looked at Garrard in astonishment. "Are you telling me that you are not aware of matters in Georgia at a time when they are being seriously considered as members of NATO?"

Travelling back from the White House after the most uncomfortable meeting of his career, Dennis Garrard swore that he would have the absent Elmore Heard filleted by the time he finished. To sit in front of the President listening to an Army General detail the build-up of forces that he had been told nothing about, was galling. The fact that his Director had probably been kept informed of the build-up, hence his diplomatic illness, was equally galling and it decided him to start the operation to remove the two-timing son-of-a-bitch sooner rather than later.

Back in Langley the bustle of busy people deeply immersed in their work, was suspicious to say the least.

Once back in his office he sent for the desk officer dealing with the Georgian area. When the man stood in front of his desk, he looked up at him. "Tell me!" He said.

The man looked puzzled "What do you want to know sir?"

Garrard looked at the man as if he had just crawled out from under a stone. "Tell me about the attack on Batumi."

The man suddenly looked haunted, "Batumi. sir?"

"That is what I said. Tell me about the attack that is about to take place on the Georgian base at Batumi using Russian special forces."

"I...but I can...." The man struggled to find some explanation.

"Are you saying you cannot tell me and if so why?"

"Sir I have strict orders not to reveal anything to anyone."

"Orders from whom?"

"The Director's orders sir."

"Tell me, what is your name?"

"Mason, sir, Roger Mason."

"Who am I, Mason?"

"The Deputy Director, sir."

"Is the director here?"

"No sir."

"In his absence I am in charge, am I not?"

"Yes sir."

"Speak, short succinct sentences, explaining all as if I know nothing about it. Do you understand?"

"Yes sir."

"Speak!"

"Mr Heard was tasked to eliminate elements of the forces involved in a clandestine operation."

"You are referring to a black operation?"

"Yes sir."

"Then say so!"

"The operation was a joint venture with Russian assets involved. Unfortunately the operation was successful but the elimination failed. The US elements were not removed by the Russians contracted to perform the task. They did in fact join forces, and eliminate the clean-up force.

"The US general concerned blackmailed our director into allowing the US force back into the States.

"The Russian force defected to Georgia. They now form a serious part of the Georgian army."

He stopped but Garrard just waited for him to continue, so reluctantly he continued.

"That occurred 18months ago, in the meantime the same National Guard unit was posted for deployment back to NATO in Turkey

Mr Heard had taken over the directorship of the area. The Russians were ready to get rid of the embarrassment of having the defectors laughing at them from Georgia. They have made no secret that they want Georgia back within Russian control. Talks of joining NATO are making the whole thing urgent. The plan to eliminate the Batumi force became the initial move in a takeover coup organised by the Russians. There is a secondary plan to eliminate the US force led by General Summers and his senior officers with a pre-emptive strike when the Batumi base has been reduced. It will look as if a missile has been fired by mistake and misdirected. It is a low yield nuke."

"You have got to be joking! Jas Heard lost his mind?" With a sinking feeling Garrard realised that the plan could just work. He might get away with it, but only if Batumi falls.

"Can you contact Heard?"

"No sir, he is off the grid until Batumi has fallen."

Get me in touch with General Summers, person to person, secure line .Now!"

Mason reached forward and picked up Garrard's telephone, he punched in several numbers, then he spoke. "Connect me with General Summers at Incirlik." There was a pause, then he put the telephone down. "General Summers is not available, sir."

"Get the base at Batman." Mason lifted the telephone again, and the same routine was performed. "Connect me to the base commander."

"The commander is not present, this is the base security."

"Where the hell is everyone?" Garrard demanded. "Code 7ZX." He quoted secure line ID and, general officer ID.

"Combined exercises with the Georgian forces, sir, according to the routine orders sir."

"Where are the exercises taking place?"

"Batumi, sir."

Garrard slammed down the phone, his frustration clearly beginning to show. Turning to Mason once more he said. "Right. Tell me what is going on/" Garrard was now sounding seriously pissed off.

"I don't know, sir, but if I may suggest. Both General Summers and General Volkov have shown extremely well developed talents for survival. May I suggest this is a time to wait and see?"

"From what you have just told me I have little option. Get the latest satellite pictures of the area. Let's see if there is any sign of what may be going on!"

Twenty minutes later the latest pictures were produced for the Deputy Director to examine.

"These pictures are for today. Let's have the previous set for comparison." Garrard ordered.

The previous set arrived timed two hours earlier than the current set.

"Who authorised the satellite coverage on this scale?" Garrard knew the answer before he finished the question. The only person who could arrange that level of cover was the Director. So what the hell was the Director up to?

"Talk to me, Mason!" Garrard was in no mood to be denied, "Tell me about the reasons for all this. I can live with the lack of facts so far. Now I want everything you know and what you think?"

***

In Turkey preparations were nearly complete. Reports were coming in on a regular basis from the Special Forces units surveilling the Russian encampment. They were all dug in at key points, tasked to start the ball rolling when the signal was given.

Before any action began as far as General Summers was concerned the enemy base would be given an ultimation.

As far as Volkov was concerned they shouldn't bother but he accepted that General Summers had a point in terms of international political diplomacy.

The two men were in the advanced control unit, a truck-trailer unit with communication links with all units. The air elements from Batumi were on the ground, showing normal activity, whilst ready for instant take-off when the signal came. The US squadrons were in the air over Turkey in mock battle games with RAF units from Batman Air Base.

The final reports came in.

Mike Summers turned to Gregor Volkov with a tight grin. "Time I retired anyway."

He thrust out his hand to his friend and ally. Volkov shook the extended hand, picked up the microphone and nodded to the woman radio operator. She raised her hand fingers extended, folding them one at a time: five, four, three, two, one. The thumbs-up was the signal.

"This is General Gregor Volkov of the Georgian Army. The unauthorised assembly of foreign troops gathered at Pskhu are ordered to disperse and return to Russia immediately under the supervision of my forces. You are currently surrounded and any attempt to resort to arms will be met with instant force. You have five minutes to respond and commence disarming your forces for safe conduct to the border."

The two men waited, coffee was produced and they drank without noticing the taste. The minutes passed without response until just before the final seconds passed a voice came over the loudspeaker with the reply.

"Fuck off."

Volkov pressed a button, and all hell broke loose.

Jerry Peters hit the flare release and set off the string of claymore mines set out around the enemy truck park. Despite their age the mines appeared to perform right up to specification. Jerry grinned; the box of claymores had been a present from one of Ali Baraka's Kurdish friends. Obviously it had remained in store since the Second World War, or possibly a little later. The marks on the metal cases which had remained in fair condition did not include date of manufacture, or perhaps they had been removed before being sold to whatever rebel band accepted delivery.

The damage inflicted by the swathe of ball bearings through the vehicle park was apparent. The men working there had, in many cases, been cut in two. Vehicles had pock marks where the steel balls had penetrated, smashing engine blocks on the outer ring of vehicles. The vehicles protected by the ruined outer ring, still worked, but the numbers were being reduced by the grenades being shot into them by the advancing SAS and Delta teams.

Aircraft were taking off from the airstrip as the flare burst over the main airfield buildings.

The huge Antonov aircraft parked with the tailgate opening to unload, shivered then with a subdued thump, it dissolved appearing to implode and explode at almost the same time. The area where it once stood was now a blast area with nothing of any size to be seen. On the outskirts were the scattered debris of men and materials plus two of the taxiing aircraft that were within range of the blast at the time.

Elsewhere the angry crackle of small arms mixed with the swish of missiles and the crump of grenades.

Jerry made for the noise since that was where he expected his men to be.

He was right of course Charlie was loading grenade rounds into his weapon, Jake Rider was sniping at the heads of the enemy troops with devastating accuracy.

The roar of engines announced the arrival of the main attack force comprising both US airfield defence units and Volkov's Georgian Guard regiment. There was a fierce fire-fight going on around the control tower and the attackers were not having it all their own way.

Overhead the F18s from Incirlik were mixing it with Mig 25s and 23s Volkov's Mig 23s were coming into the frame now and the fighting aloft was becoming more general, the aircraft scattering over a wider area. Then low level aircraft swept in with a scream of engines and the control tower disappeared behind a cloud of dust from the shattered concrete. The second wave dropped cluster bombs with pin-point accuracy. Targets, laser-designated by the ground forces, were removed instantly in the storm of ordinance. The Typhoons with bomb loads dropped, rose to take part in the dogfights in the air above them.

The battle was definitely going to the attack force, when reinforcements started to arrive from the Russian forces still encamped in Georgia. The first warning came from the Special Forces on the north side of the Airbase.

It had been pure inspiration that had caused Colonel Hartog to place men on watch that side, and arm them with mines and two salvaged 88mm anti-tank guns with 70 rounds of ammunition of questionable origin and efficiency, all dredged from the armoury of the Kurdish people at the time of the first deployment. The guns had been restored and reproved but never returned. The Kurds who donated them at the time pointed out that their tactics of shoot and move were not really compatible with artillery that required a tow truck of some sort. So there they were, on the faint chance that reinforcements might be sent from the Russian interlopers already in Georgia and dragging their feet over leaving. The report came in to the command trailer and Mike Summers thought fast. The rotating air group under Peter Hamilton were refuelling now. He picked up the microphone and called the base at Batumi.

He got through. "Peter, Chuck was right, the Russians are coming to reinforce the Pskhu base. Can you upload tank smashers and vehicle killers, more carpet bombs perhaps. We are holding them off at the moment with the two 88s."

"Will do, I'll get this lot started." The call cut off.

Twenty minutes later the call came in from the first flight of rearmed F18s. "Coming loaded for bear, can you give us a heads up, Delta?"

"Delta here, working on it. First mark now!" The lead aircraft was suddenly aware that the laser spot was now on his screen. "Got you, Delta, incoming."

The aircraft screamed into a dive and levelled off at 200 feet and released the carpet bomb. He was already at 3000 feet when the series of explosions occurred. A swathe of ground 30feet wide disappeared under a series of explosions that carpeted the first 60 foot of road in front of the Delta positions. His wingman followed going for the next stretch of road and revealed that she was actually a wing woman when she yelled bombs away in a distinctly feminine voice.

In succession the entire flight carpeted the road for a quarter-mile, wreaking havoc with the reinforcements.

Russian aircraft were rapidly appearing and the radio warning was now on continuous transmit. *"All Russian national aircraft are warned that an insurgent force is attacking national units. By entering this airspace there is risk of casualties from friendly fire. Leave this airspace immediately."*

***

In Langley the Deputy Director was watching the developing situation through satellite and AWACs broadcasts. Seeing the approach of the Russian forces from the occupied section of Georgia, his eyes narrowed. "Get me the President!"

Mason looked shocked. "But, sir, you have a red phone."

"Damn!" Garrard swore, having never used the red phone before, he had forgotten it existed. Dragging out his keys he opened the lower drawer of his desk and withdrew the red handset from its depths.

There was only one button on the instrument, he hesitated looked at the screens again, and pressed the button.

There was a short wait that seemed endless, Garrard tapped his fingers waiting, then a voice answered.

"Mr President, I am advising you that an exercise in the Georgian Republic conducted by NATO and Georgian forces has been interrupted by insurgent troops backed and funded by rogue elements of the Russian government. NATO and Georgian forces have contained the insurgents but Russian elements from the forces still occupying part of Georgia have mobilised and are attacking out people. NATO force has elements from Incirlik and Batman involved. If this is not stopped quickly I am worried it will escalate into international conflict."

He listened for a few minutes, interjecting the odd yes and no. Then "Thank you, sir. I will implement your orders immediately."

To Mason he said "Get me Batman on the phone now, and Afion-Kara-Hissar Base."

Mason grabbed the phone and started punching codes. "Afion on the line now sir!"

Garrard picked his second handset from its place and said "Order of the President. Get the Officer in Charge on the line now."

He waited, then a voice came on the line. "General Massy here. Who is this?"

"Garrard, Deputy Director CIA. By order of the President. There is an exercise between NATO and Georgian forces at Batumi Base in Georgia. It has been attacked by Russian-backed insurgent forces. The other occupying Russian forces have moved in to support the insurgents. Since they are illegally there anyway, the President had instructed you to open code B7 and mobilise air elements immediately to support the Georgian national army, led by General Volkov, currently supported by Brigadier General Summers from Incirlik, and Group Captain Sheldon and his Euro-fighters from Batman. Order your elements to report to General Summers for orders. Is that understood?"

The thoroughly irritated General Massy, answered "That is understood, Code B7." The phone slammed down in Turkey. Garrard smiled thinly, he was well aware that the general hated being instructed by the CIA, there was nothing new about it. He returned to the screens in front of him, noting that the Russian units were taking reverses.

The call to Batman came on the line. "Batman Air Base NATO, how can I help you?"

"This is Deputy Director Garrard CIA here. Put me through to the Officer in Charge!"

"Colonel Walker here 2i/c Batman."

"Colonel Walker, what resources have you on the base at present?"

"I cannot talk over an open line, sir."

"This is a dedicated line Colonel, and I know that Group Captain Sheldon is engaged with other NATO units in Batumi Georgia. Now what other resources have you at Batman? I do not have time to play the 'look up the records' game."

"I have two squadrons of Apache ground attack helicopters and a transit regiment of air cavalry, in C130s refuelling at present, for deployment to Izmir."

"Good , Contact General Massy at Afion-Kara-Hussar
base and hold the air cavalry until you have spoken to him,
is that understood?"

"Understood sir, contact General Massy immediately,
and hold the cavalry meantime." The call ended and
Garrard sat back. He had done all he could, possibly got the
Russians out of Georgia. He thought General Summers
must have seriously pissed off Elmore Heard for him to try
a stunt like this. And what about the Director? He hit the
keys of his computer and called up Heard's file.

***

In Georgia things were definitely looking up. Mike re-
ceived an eyes only message from General Massy. *'One
Squadron F18s en route in support of your force from here.
Batman sending 7th Air Cavalry in C130s plus 1 Squadron
Apache ground attack helicopters. Advise if further re-
sources needed. Good luck. Massy. Major General'*

Mike smiled and turned to Volkov, "Take a look at
this. Remember you never saw it."

Volkov read the message and smiled in turn. "I think
we may be changing history. I am going outside to take a
look."

Mike rose with him. "I think I will, too." He said and
turning to Katerina and Sarah. "Ladies you have the lead,
we will return after a quick tour."

Sarah said, "They never really grow up, do they?"

Startled, Katerina looked at Sarah questioningly. Then
she smiled. "That is exactly right," she said, nodding. "Exactly." She turned and held up her hand. Sarah high-fived
it. Demonstrating that women don't really grow up either.

Chapter Nine

...Aftermath

Generals Summers and Volkov stood at the border watching the last of the Russian vehicles cross on their way to Sochi in Russia. As the barrier dropped they both sighed with relief. The occupation of Georgia had ceased.

Volkov said "Michael, I am a hero of the Republic of Georgia as are you, but what will await you when you return to America? After all you have broken many rules and politicians do not like that sort of thing."

"Gregor, in my experience politicians look first at the end result, then they decide whether any rules have been broken, or if perhaps, by use of initiative, a realignment of the existing outdated rules may be more expedient."

As the two men strolled away from the barrier there came a shout from the Guard sergeant. A man had appeared with a gun that he was raising toward the two generals. Both reached for their own pistols, but it was unnecessary. The Guard sergeant's AK was up and firing before the man could set himself.

They went over to the man as he lay on the ground, his weapon out of reach. He was dark-haired and well dressed, his shaved face was that of a white collar rather than blue collar worker. Volkov bent close spoke to him in Russian.

The man spat blood and spoke quietly in Russian, then he swore violently and died.

Volkov said as they walked away "He was upset, his words translated as 'Fucking CIA' he also mentioned he was commissioned by a man named Heard and his Russian friend Zorin."

***

The final act in the Georgian saga was not the passing of the Russian army over the border. Neither Summers nor Volkov were prepared for the aftermath.

For Brigadier General Summers, waiting for him on his return to Incirlik was a summons to appear before General Massy at Afion-Kara-Hissar.

In his full dress uniform he presented himself at the Headquarters expecting, actually anticipating a demand for his resignation for any one of a dozen reasons that he could think of offhand.

General Massy was not amused at the task he had been given. In his mind Brigadier General Summers should be before a court martial for the actions he had taken over the invasion of Georgia. The fact that the result was, in the end for the benefit of NATO and the United States, meant nothing as far as he was concerned.

The orders in front of him were explicit. Brigadier General Summers was to be commended and sent to the Pentagon for interview and debriefing.

The call came through that General Summers was here, so he decided to get it over with. "Send him in."

The man that came through the door surprised Massy. For some reason he was under the impression he would meet some cocky, smart-aleck, jumped-up whiz kid. The mature, well set up man in front of him with the campaign medals and the Bronze Star and the Air Medal, was a surprise.

"Sit down General, coffee?"

"Thank you, sir. No."

"So, it is my duty to commend you on the action you took in the Georgia conflict, I also have to send you to the Pentagon for debrief and interview. I really do not know what that is all about but personally I would suggest extreme caution in your dealing with Pentagon and, I understand, the CIA.

Massy noticed the bemused look on Summers's face, he smiled.

"I confess I would have expected to have you here explaining to me why the hell you should be given the opportunity to resign when a court martial would be the appropriate action. Now I've thought about it I realise that it would be political suicide for a politician to suggest such a thing. What you did was the right thing, not the political thing, or the expedient thing. The right thing, and I understand because I respond to that. As a regular officer it is second nature to obey orders and pass the decision up the line if I am in doubt. In your case you made the decision, and stuck your neck out because it was the right thing to do, and for that I salute you. If it gone wrong I would be pulling the rope they used to hang you."

Summers now was looking wary. Massy got to his feet, and held out his hand. "Mike, you are officially a hero. Live with it and enjoy it, and pray there is no next time."

Mike took and shook the hand extended to him. "Sir, I appreciate the candour, and I get the message, thank you for your time and the help you extended when I was knee deep in shit."

Outside the office Mike donned his cap and breathed evenly once more. Whatever he had anticipated it was not the reception he had received or the remarks that followed. His thoughts were interrupted by the orderly who appeared to escort him to the aircraft ordered to carry him to his fate in Washington.

The flight in the Air Force Citation executive jet was comfortable and to his surprise Mike was able to sleep most of the way. He had removed his uniform and slipped on slacks and a Tee shirt for the trip. When he was wakened he took advantage of the facilities offered and showered and shaved before donning his newly pressed uniform in time for his arrival in the United States.

The aircraft was met by a staff car and a lieutenant who wore the aiguillette meaning he was a General Officer's Aide. He saluted and said "Sir, I am Lieutenant Hervey, aide to General McMaster. I will be your escort for your visit to the Pentagon and the White House."

"White House? I had no idea…."

"Sir, the President has requested a chat before we go to the Pentagon."

Bewildered Mike shrugged. "So, let's go talk to the President," and climbed into the staff car.

***

Jordon Robinson was looking a little worn around the edges. Mike thought, but then nobody believed that being the most powerful leader in the world was an easy job.

The famous smile greeted him as he approached the desk of the Oval Office. Robinson came round the desk to greet him and having shaken his hand, and been photographed doing it, the cameras were dismissed and the two men sat down in the easy chairs alone.

"You chose to risk total war with Russia without a 'by your leave' or even an email. Why?" Gone was the smile, the affable friendly face had hardened, the eyes piercing.

"If I had asked, I would have been refused, or even worse delayed while everyone here weighed up the odds and discussed the political issues. Sides would have been chosen. While Georgia was being annexed against her will by Russia. Protests would be discussed in the UN, which Russia would have ignored, and puppets in Georgia would be proclaiming their joy at returning to the Russian fold. Thousands of true patriots in Georgia would be arrested and imprisoned. I did the right thing for the right reasons, thereby cutting the bullshit, and saving the lives and livelihood of many thousands of people."

Mike sat back and waited for the explosion at his blunt reply.

The President looked a little startled at the response but then relaxed, "Let's have some coffee." He rang a bell, and a maid entered and placed a tray with coffee-pot cups and cream and sugar and cookies, on the coffee table next to the seats.

She left the two men to serve themselves.

Alone once more the President poured coffee for them both.

"Okay, I get the message." He said "You acted, if it had gone wrong I would have had to pick up the pieces"

"With respect, Mr. President, that is one of the responsibilities of your office."

Startled for a moment Robinson realised that what this man said was absolutely true.

"Right, you are saying you made a battlefield decision fully anticipating the support of this office come what may."

"Honestly? I didn't know what support I would get, if any, nor did my people. If I may say, sir, there have been a good few examples in recent years when there would have been active opposition to what we did. It was because it was the right thing to do in the circumstances, especially following the attempted betrayal of my people on our last deployment."

There was a silence that stretched for what seemed like hours following this comment, in fact it was perhaps three minutes. "I am going to decorate your unit with a Unit Citation. In addition you have been promoted to Lieutenant General." Mike started to say something but was stopped by a raised hand. "You will also receive the Congressional Medal of Honour at a ceremony in the Pentagon this afternoon. Your wife is on her way and your daughter will be present. Now, before you get carried away with the idea that we in Washington approve of all that has happened I will sum up my feelings in the matter, which I am sure are shared by your senior officers.

"Taking risks with an international situation as explosive at the Georgian/Russian dispute was indefensible. You try that again and I will personally see you locked away for as many lives as I can arrange. The only possible excuse for that action, 'because it was the right thing to do,' has only been accepted because it succeeded. The risk was unacceptable and you are sitting here because I am aware of all the circumstances surrounding your case, including the attempted assassination and revelations to both you and General Volkov at the border post. Your Guard Unit has been handed over to Colonel Hamilton and you are reactivated into the regular service and posted to Washington on the General Staff. Do you have any comments?"

Mike took a breath and realised that the wind had been taken out of his sails. "No sir, no comments."

"Good, so what was the reaction in Georgia after the coup failed?"

"The word ecstatic comes to mind! The celebrations were immediate and spontaneous. The United States has altered from being a dirty word, to welcome friend. I had problems retrieving my command at the end of hostilities, and I believe that the negotiations for the entry of Georgia into NATO have advanced considerably."

The knock at the door was followed by the entry of the First Lady accompanied by Sarah. Both men rose to their feet and Sarah, in uniform, saluted.

The First Lady smiled at the two men and turning to her husband said, "Jordon may I introduce Colonel Sarah Summers."

***

Life in Washington was not what Mike Summers had anticipated. His visit to the White House and the subsequent honours had been an embarrassing period that he hoped would finish with his return to Michigan. The White House had made it clear that was not going to happen for the foreseeable future.

His interview with the Deputy Director of the CIA had been something else, interesting and revealing. The man Heard had defected somewhere apparently and nobody really wanted to know. He had the impression that Dennis Garrard was embarrassed by the disclosures that had been made over the Georgian affair, as he called it, and the absence of the director of the CIA was still causing a stir in Washington circles.

It was generally concluded that Garrard would take the chair in the interim, possibly even keep it. From Garrard he learned that the likely location of Heard was with the allies he had cultivated when arranging the black operation against the Iranian nuclear fuel plant. Mike was required to return to Incirlik to hand over officially to Peter who was now the ranking officer in the National Guard Unit. He would complete the deployment and bring the unit home.

While Sarah found a house, and arranged the move from their Dearborn home to Washington, General Summers went back to Turkey.

He was received with full military honours by the Unit plus an Honour guard from the Georgian army. Gregor Volkov was there to congratulate him and David Sheldon flew down to join the party, to wet his stars. Colonel Katerina Shukov was also present but though she took part in the celebrations, Peter suggested that the arrival of David Sheldon was the main reason for her presence.

At the end of the day of parade and celebrations Mike managed to get together with Gregor Volkov and Peter. The three sat round the table in the headquarters building discussing the present situation in the area. The arrival of Ali Baranka caused the atmosphere to alter completely.

He looked haggard and though neatly dressed and shaven was obviously close to complete exhaustion.

When he had been welcomed into the circle of friends he drank from his chilled glass and then said. "Gentlemen, we have a problem."

The words dropped into the light-hearted chat like a lead balloon. All conversation stopped and the eyes swung to Ali as he sat tiredly in the easy chair he had been given.

Seeing he had their attention, he sat up and began to speak.

"The people who were associated with the occasion when we all first met have separated themselves from their former masters. My information is that they are currently working on a plan to supply the radical faction in Iran with several suitcase nukes. It seems that there is no suggestion of politics involved, strictly a cash operation. The difficulty as far as this country is concerned is that they intend bringing them through Turkey in a convoy of supplies for the refugees from Syria and Iran itself.

"The major factor as I see will be that the shipment will contain extra units to be dropped off in Batumi and Incirlik.

"The American has insisted that the two extra weapons be set off first, followed by a New York weapon to ensure that the ensuing conflict will be blamed on the extreme Muslim elements of the middle-eastern nations."

There was silence following this opening comment from Ali Baranka. Gregor Volkov was the first to speak. "What does that mean as far as we are concerned? I realise obviously that a Nuke on both bases would be inconvenient, but surely this is something we will have to pass up the line. Actually, what do we know? Have we any idea how, or when, the bombs are being delivered? Do we have a timescale? After all, convoys of relief goods are passing through Turkey on a regular weekly basis from all over the European Union."

Ali shrugged "I have my people out alongside my Kurdish friends, keeping an eye open and a watch on what is coming and going, but they operate by guess and by god. Without detection equipment they have no real chance of finding these suitcase bombs.

Mike lifted the phone. "Ask Colonel Hartog to come in please."

Chuck Hartog listened to the story Ali had to tell, showing little reaction. When Ali finished he nodded thoughtfully. "I would suggest we move a contingent up to Ciranu; the base is still in operation as a satellite. I believe we have C130's here to take 'Immediate Action' crews. I suggest we transfer operations there until this task has be sorted out. Here in Incirlik we are too far away for swift response. Leave the detection bit with me for a while. I may have some suggestions later." With this cryptic remark he left.

Mike felt better hearing that. There was something re-assuring about Chuck's calm acceptance of the situation and the suggestion that he may have some answers. He thought for a few minutes then shrugged, picked up the telephone and started to give orders. The first C130 left for Ciranu 30 minutes later.

***

Colonel Zeibari in command at Ciranu, called his HQ in Ankara, reporting to his general that the Americans were returning to the advanced base.

The general gave scant sympathy, "They are paying the bills, what would you like me to do? If you are unhappy go on leave for a few weeks, let your deputy start earning his pay"

The phone slammed down and the colonel looked un-happy. If he went on leave his wife would have to come with him. Perhaps he would take what the Americans called a familiarisation tour of the Black Sea bases. He could take his aide, Captain Ariane Kaya, to take notes. She could perhaps bring her swimsuit while she was at it.

He smiled and picked up the telephone to call his wife and tell her the sad news.

***

For Chuck there was only one man to speak to and Doctor Alan Clarke was the man. They had attended university together. MIT had not been the easiest option for Chuck Hartog, but he wished to have the correct qualifications to become a pilot in the Air Force and that required the right sort of background educationally, and while Chuck could graduate easily on a basis of football and athletics, his maths and literature subjects were another matter. Alan Clarke was a nerd, in the vernacular of the time and liable to maltreatment even in an educationally-orientated establishment like MIT. Mere sharing a room with a jock would not have been enough to preserve him from the standard hazing received by his peers. In fact what started as a partnership based on tuition by the nerd and protection by the jock, developed into a friendship that had endured for the past 22 years.

Chuck's dreams of earning his wings dissolved with the medical results following his initial application to enlist. His eyesight, sufficient for all normal purposes, was just not good enough for pilot training.

A practical man, Chuck gave up the idea of a flying career and concentrated on ground defence. His single-minded approach to this new direction was rewarded by regular progress through the ranks, commencing with Warrant and rising to Brevet Brigadier General. Confrontation with higher authority during the Gulf war ensured his Brevet rank was withdrawn and early separation from his professional Air Force career had followed. His commission in the National Guard had been offered in the rank of Lt Colonel. In accepting this demotion Chuck had realised that whatever he did in civilian life, he would not give up his Air Force connection willingly.

He thought, *Thank you lord for General Mike Summers.* This association had really kept him in the most intense action since the Gulf war, without the politics.

"Alan, it's Chuck!"

"Where the hell are you calling from? Did you realise I was just starting to make out with the most gorgeous blond in Texas? It is also, by the way, three in the morning here."

"Gee I'm sorry, so I'll just take my little problem to NASA, shall I?" Chuck grinned as he said this, Alan and NASA did not agree, and that had cost the government a fortune despite several warnings by Alan, who had predicted the whole debacle."

"I suppose you better tell me about it, since you must be costing Uncle Sam a fortune in telephone charges."

"The secure fax is on its way. Call me from the office when you have read and inwardly digested the content." Chuck smiled as he used the deliberately formal words, reminiscent of their college days.

"Piss off!" Alan's reply to this was anticipated. "I'll speak when I have something to say. Meanwhile, how the hell are you?"

"I'm enjoying life here in the blue yonder, and from the sound of it so are you."

"I'm getting along, doing a little research here and there. Hang on a moment!" The phone was put down, then it was picked up and Alan's voice came on once more. "Wow, you play dirty, don't you? I do believe you will have to arrange a flight to wherever you are on this one. I think the gadget I have will do the trick but I need to set it up under local conditions. You won't need anything too commodious, one of those Air Force Lear jets will do, with a pretty attendant of course."

"Are you serious?"

"Oh yes, preferably with medium-sized tits, I don't like those enhanced ones that are so popular with the young set these days."

"How soon can you get to your old haunt at Houston?"

"Couple of hours!"

"Plane will be waiting." Chuck rang off. He shrugged. The sort of problem that they were facing merited a little string pulling. He picked up the phone once more and called Houston.

***

Alan Clarke was seated in the comfort of an armchair in the cabin of the Lear-Jet two hours after the phone was put down. The neatly dressed, trim-figured flight attendant smiled in a friendly way at the comments issuing from their single passenger, who was probing the inner works of a small box with a complex-looking miniature mother-board.

***

When the Lear arrived Jessica was waiting at the foot of the air stair. Alan came out with a big cheesy grin on his face. Looking at Jessica, the trim blonde in her nicely filled uniform. he could not resist the comment, "Hell, Chuck, you've outdone yourself this time."

Chuck appeared at that moment in a jeep.

Glancing from the bemused looking Jessica to the ebullient Alan who was going to disgrace himself with some other comment, he called out, "Alan Clarke, meet Colonel Jessica Browning, USAF. Have you brought the goods?"

Distracted, Alan vaguely waved his briefcase at Chuck and then looked disappointedly at Jessica. "Hi, Colonel, do you have a sister maybe?"

"If I had I would be inclined to worry if I knew you were chasing her." The smile took the sting from her words.

Alan smiled back at her "I was only kidding, but if you did have an evening free I am a good dinner partner!" He said it wistfully, and hopefully.

Jessica shrugged "When would I get an evening free, I'm a working woman, you know."

Chuck broke up the conversation by calling Alan to get his ass in the jeep.

As they drove off in a cloud of dust Jessica ordered the Lear to taxi into the big hanger while the crew took a break, and the Lear got reallocated.

***

The first team left the base to link up with the Kurdish team allocated to them. The backup platoon of Airfield defence and Special Forces embussed and set out after them to link up with the Georgian troops detailed by General Volkov.

In the briefing room, Group Captain David Sheldon RAF was seated, talking to Katerina Shukov. The Georgian colonel was liaison between the Georgian forces and the NATO forces in Turkey. She was also wearing a three diamond engagement ring provided by the RAF officer who had arranged to marry her before she could escape once more. At least that was the way he put it.

Chuck and Alan came in followed by General Summers, who joined them at the long table. "We'll wait for Jessica, I think." Mike Summers was still not accustomed to his current exalted rank. He had hardly got used to Brigadier General, and now as Lieutenant General with three stars on his shoulders he found they weighed heavily.

Jessica came in like a breath of fresh air and the meeting started with the introduction of Alan Clarke, who gave them a quick review of the capabilities of the plutonium detector.

When Alan finished his dissertation, the drawing board was covered with chalk marks and the message had been understood. The device had limitations but was the best available at the moment, and better than none at all. It did mean that the spotting teams would need to be closer to the convoys than originally anticipated which would put them fairly into the danger zone.

The teams were informed and the six sniffer units were despatched to the teams with instructions for their use. Chuck decided to go out with one of the teams to get some idea of the problems they might meet. In his uniform greens, he called into Mike's office before he left. "I'll be away for several days. Meanwhile, I have asked Peter to keep an eye on Major Cameron; he is more experienced at the admin work than the practical soldiering."

Chapter ten

...Bomb disposal

The jeep containing Col. Chuck Hartog, also took M/Sgt Patsy McCoy, Captain Richard Samuels and as driver, Trooper David Bowman, SAS.

Samuels was new to the unit, a recent graduate of the new Special Forces School at Fort Bragg. A trained chef, his unusual selection for alternative training was based on the abilities coiled up in his slender 5'9" body. The qualities of endurance, combined with an ability to better all the unarmed combat instructors in Fort Bragg, gave him a shoo-in as a Special Forces operative. The fact that he was licensed to fly multi-engine aircraft and helicopters had brought him to this remote attachment. He was personally still wondering if he had made the right choice of posting. He had been on the base for three weeks already and his most exciting job had been to prepare the dinner for the visiting General Volkov from Georgia who was being entertained by General Summers. He grinned wryly; the reason he was here was that Gen Summers was in command. The guy had a reputation for being where the trouble started, and he had the added reputation of finishing it before it became a problem for anyone else.

He shifted in his seat. It seemed things were now looking up.

"You okay with our brief Captain?" the gravelly voice of the colonel came from the back seat behind him.

"Yes sir, I'm happy. Are we expecting trouble?" He nodded at the trailer bouncing along behind the four-wheel-drive vehicle. The trailer was loaded with a mini-gun, ammunition and hand-held rocket launchers. Spare weapons and explosives plus a sniper rifle were also included, and all the jeep passengers had their personal weapons, and ammo.

Colonel Hartog smiled grimly. "Captain, this is bandit country. Although the Kurds in general are our allies in this, not all support us, we are therefore, in danger at all times. Anything we don't need will come in useful for the units we visit."

M/Sgt Patsy McCoy, seated behind the Captain in the jump seat, readjusted her petite derriere to a more comfortable position. Despite her Irish name, there was little about her to associate her with Ireland. Dark hair, dark tan, skin that was Italianate or Spanish rather than anything else. The pretty face with the startling blue eyes, plus a trim, slender, toned figure might deceive a stranger into thinking she was a pushover. But she had earned her tapes and carried the bullet scar from an episode in Afghanistan to prove it. She smiled to herself. Captain Samuels was still an unknown quantity, but he was shaping up well.

She swept the area she could see ahead, noting the movement in the sage bushes about two hundred yards off the road. "Stop!" She called out sharply. David Bowman rammed the brake on and the vehicle skidded to a halt. All four bailed out of the nearest door and hit the ditches on both sides of the track. All were wearing earpieces. Patsy said "Two men, 200 yards, half left ahead of the truck. I think it might be an IED activated by wire link. Bowman, with me!" She waited while Bowman keeping the jeep between himself and the ambushers, snaked across the road to join her, then they set off through the scrub carefully avoiding creating movement among the bushes.

Watching through his binoculars Richard Samuels saw the slender figure of the sergeant rise to her feet as another figure came into view with a weapon raised. Then the second figure melted to the ground, the sergeant turned toward them and waved. Chuck and Richard rose to their feet and walked over and joined the M/Sergeant.

She swung round and indicated the small accumulator detonation device. The wires had been detached. There was a low tent and sleeping bags, the ambushers had been there for some time, perhaps waiting for a special target. "I found this." Patsy handed Chuck a Blackberry handset.

Chuck opened the memory. There was a message in the folder. It was in Turkish, it said the target was on the way and it was dated today. The sender had not left his name. He turned to Captain Samuels. "It seems we have a mole in the base."

Samuels looked at his face with a wry smile. "I would be surprised if there had not been a mole or two or three for that matter."

"What I should have said is that there is a mole among the senior staff at the Base. Apart from we four, the general, David Hamilton and Jessica Browning are the only people that knew where we were going.

:I guess there is a bug or so planted around the place. There can be no other explanation, meanwhile let's get going, I have the feeling that this little set up was because there is something in the wind, perhaps this convoy is a carrier."

He called the others back to the jeep and they carried on to their first rendezvous.

***

The team were located within a half mile of the road. So far, they had only seen the normal passing traffic. A call from the spotter at the border came just as they arrived, reporting that a convoy was on the way.

Richard Samuels was dressed as were the others in battle gear complete with Kevlar vest and comms. His chosen weapon was a Colt bullpup rifle with under-slung rail feed for grenades. His Fairburn knife was sheathed on his left forearm and the Glock automatic was in a tanker's underarm holster, rather than the hip-rig used by many of his compatriots. Out of the jeep, he took position on a grassy mound where he could see without being seen. He scanned the area between the ambushers and the road. He caught the flicker of movement out of the corner of his eye as he panned the glasses from left to right. Without deviating from the sweep he waited until the glasses covered the area again to search the location of the movement had had spotted. He recognised that what he had seen could have been any number of things, certainly not necessarily an enemy, but taking chances could be fatal in these circumstances and, since this was the first time he had been in battle conditions against a real enemy, it was better to safe than sorry.

On the third sweep he caught the movement again, this time it was possible to make out a small puff of smoke rising from the location. The person or persons hiding at that location was smoking a cigarette.

To Richard this was unforgivable. He called M/Sgt McCoy over and pointed the smoker out. "Tell me that is not one of ours!" he said.

"It is not one of ours," she said. "That means he is probably one of theirs."

"Why do you say he? It could be a woman. After all, there are many women in the ranks of most armies these days."

"A woman would not be stupid enough to smoke on observation or ambush duties." The M/Sgt was matter-of-fact on the subject and her comment discouraged any answer."

Richard realised that he might be treading on dangerous ground if he made the flip reply that trembled on his lips, so he buttoned it. Instead he said, "I think I would like to take a closer look, would you mind?"

She turned and looked at him calculatingly, then. "Okay, I've got your back." She turned to the others below them on the lower ground. "Trooper Bowman, take over here, the captain and I are going for a closer look at the watchers." She hesitated, then pointed out to Bowman where the watchers were located. "There may be others we have missed so keep a close eye on the whole area."

"Gotcha, Boss!" Bowman was a man of few words, but obviously was tried and tested because McCoy accepted the reply without comment and turned immediately to Richard. "Ready when you are, Captain."

As Richard moved forward and Patsy prepared to follow, she could not help noticing the easy way he moved snaking forward through the dusty scrub on his stomach with little apparent effort. He had a neat ass, too.

She shrugged and moved out after him but could not help wondering if there was any significant other waiting for the captain at home.

The pair worked their way to a point where the small outpost was visible. There were eight in the group, the smoker was apart from the main body, downwind and though the smell of the burning tobacco was obvious to the two watchers, the others were upwind and unaware of the sentry's lapse. There were three women, all in army fatigues.

Richard turned to Patsy who had come up beside him. "They are Russian."

"No badges on their uniforms." Patsy pointed out.

"They are speaking Russian, the tall one is from Gorky, he is bitching about the local food and the lack of women." There was laughter from the others in the group as one of the women clutched her groin and did a couple bumps in his direction.

There was another comment from the complainer and the woman replied.

"What was that she said?" Patsy asked.

"Freely translated, 'In your dreams, dickhead' or words to that effect." Richard chuckled quietly. "I think they are not the happiest bunch you would find in this delightful corner of the Earth"

"Do we take them out?" Patsy spoke calmly as if she were buying cereal for the breakfast table.

Richard considered the matter, then he said "Remove the sentry. He should control his smoking habit. It will worry the others as well."

Patsy unhooked her automatic shotgun and laid it beside Richard. "Do not lose this."

Richard nodded, bringing the Bullpup round from its place on his back, and unlocking the safety.

Patsy slithered off through the scrub. She returned within very few minutes and picked up her shotgun. "We may have a problem, there is someone approaching along the path, they will see the body, we do not have time to get clear."

She looked at Richard. He looked back with a small smile on his face, shrugged and said, "Shall we?"

As one they rose from concealment and opened fire.

Richard was on semi-automatic, holding his finger down, Patsy's shotgun reloaded fast. Between them they accounted for the entire group of eight within seconds. None of the Russians had time to more than grab for their weapons. None of them managed to lift them and get a shot off.

The newcomer coming along the path ran straight into the barrel of the shotgun. He collapsed unconscious to the ground.

Richard changed magazines and looked over at Patsy, The surviving Russian was beginning to stir. Richard frisked him and retrieved a despatch case from within the prisoner's blouse. Then each took an arm and they got him to his feet and dragged him back to where the others of their party were located.

Richard spoke to the prisoner in Russian. "Where did you think you were going?" He said mildly.

The man replied with suggestions about Richard's parentage and interesting things he should do to his mother.

Patsy casually smacked him round the mouth and said in Russian, "Your mother, if she is still working in the whorehouse, would be ashamed of you. Making suggestions like that reflects on the way you were brought up. Speak nicely to the gentleman and I won't remove your fingers one by one." The cold calm way she spoke caused the Russian to consider for a moment. Then he shrugged. His friends would be along shortly and dispose of these intruders.

"I was going to the officer stationed at the next security point."

The pouch he had been carrying was open now and the contents laid out for Richard to read.

"Aha, I see we are expected to try and ambush the decoy convoy! It seems our mole friend has been busy with his crystal set, letting the opposition know what our plans are."

He turned to Chuck. In English he said "I think we should kill this man and get on our way. He obviously knows nothing of value for us and he will only hold us up if we take him with us."

Chuck looked thoughtfully at the prisoner who was beginning to look uncomfortable, certainly less cocky than he had been earlier. "Perhaps you're right. Yes, I think you are. Take it easy, though. From behind, I think, with a silenced pistol while he does not expect it. It's not his fault that he is inconvenient at the moment." He shrugged. "C'est la guerre," and he turned away.

The increasing agitation of the prisoner made it quite clear that he understood what they were saying and he started speaking quickly, before these men could carry out their plan.

"Please!" He said in English, "I can show you where the ambush points are!"

"Why should we believe you?" Richard asked.

"I understand that my life depends on it." The prisoner said bluntly.

"Ah, you do speak English, then?" Robert said. "Do you have any idea of the contents of your despatch pouch?"

"Yes I do. I was involved in the preparation of the messages."

"So where is the local area command post?"

"If I have your assurance that you will not kill me then I will show you. Otherwise?" he shrugged.

"I will see you are treated in accordance with the Geneva Convention. However if you are bluffing!" He drew his hand across his throat in the universal sign for sudden death.

Chuck gathered the team together and with the prisoner in the lead they set off along the faint path to the local Unit HQ.

***

At base the careful search for bugs was under way General Volkov had provided the ultimate Russian bug detector to be used in conjunction with its US equivalent. So far three bugs had been detected.

***

M/Sgt Patsy McCoy breathed quietly through her mouth as she observed the unit site in front of the party. There had been a lot of water under the bridge since she had first begun infantry training seven years ago. In her mind at that time there had been a lot of anger, and her early career had been marred by disciplinary hearings. The intervention of her Top Sergeant had made the difference. At a time when it seemed she would be thrown out as unsuitable, her case had been taken on by 'Bull' Lynch. Senior Instructor at training school. The conversation between the two had been secret, and there was no way she could ever have expected to leave that office still a member of the Armed Forces.

Whatever her instructors imagined they did not anticipate the change in the attitude of their most difficult recruit.

It had been a hard slog, and she had been forced to control her temper, with the threat of exclusion if she lost it again. She found that the subsequent courses were easier. Her self-control had improved to the extent that her early record had been forgotten.

Having a natural aptitude for army life and really feeling at home in the service, she had concentrated on getting ahead. It had been at the expense of her private life which had been sparse in terms of romance. It was therefore disturbing to find that the presence of Captain Richard Samuels had created a frisson of interest in that direction, unexpected and not entirely welcome at this time.

There had been nudges about her becoming an officer. Up to now she had always been against the idea, some form of reverse snobbishness that would not recognise that fact that she was a born leader and deserving of the rank. The fact she was not college-educated did not help. Only now after serving under officers who were, in her terms inept, and realising that there were others who were worth working for and with, was she beginning to realise that an officers rank was the natural progression of her chosen career.

Her musing was interrupted by Captain Robert Samuels. "Over there, I can see the radio aerials." The whispered words were almost in her ear, she could actually feel the warmth of his breath, gently brushing her skin. She turned sharply toward him and found her lips brushing his cheek.

"Well I appreciate the sentiment but if you warned me I would have been ready to respond." The whispered words were for her ears alone and the blush that warmed her cheek embarrassed her.

"If I had known you were interested I would have made sure you were ready." The words were out before she realised what she was saying.

He touched her cheek and pointed to the enemy camp. His words were only just audible "I look forward to next time." Then louder he said "Can you see how many people are there?"

McCoy studied the encampment for a few seconds. "I'd guess at six. Three in view, three operating equipment." There was no sign of the incident now just strict professionalism.

Richard Samuels nodded approvingly, as it should be.

Lt Col. Chuck Hartog sighed and put his binoculars back in their case. "We are going to have to clear the ground here. There are other sites I know, but this seems to be the most important; Richard, any ideas?"

Richard turned to M/Sgt McCoy. "What do you think? Slink up close and personal and drop a few grenades, or the quiet approach?"

Patsy looked at Browning. "Can we get close enough?"

The SAS man looked at the approaches, "We three only." He indicated Richard, Patsy and himself. Colonel. you should wait with the prisoner, keep him quiet. We'll call you in when we are done."

Patsy looked at the Colonel wondering how he would take it.

Chuck looked at them. He then nodded and grinned tightly. "I get it, I'm too tall, and I've not had the training. I have heard it all before, and while I object to you guys having all the fun I guess you're right. I'll look after the gear while you subdue the opposition. Try not to wreck their equipment."

Patsy and the others stripped off their webbing, retaining only the holstered automatic and Fairburn knives, Bowman carries two stun grenades, just in case. All three set out across the intervening ground on their knees below the level of the scrub covering the landscape.

Chuck lost sight of them within seconds, so he kept the enemy camp in view through his binoculars. The raiders had nearly half a mile to go crawling, despite the enemy being only a quarter mile away. There was an open area that had to be avoided.

For a nerve stretching half hour there was nothing, then over the personal radio system came a brief word. "Go." followed by silence once more.

Patsy's voice came over the system only a few minutes later, though it had seemed to Chuck like hours. "Care to come and join us boss, the party is just about to start."

***

Group Captain David Sheldon RAF lay stretched out on his bed watching Colonel Katerina Shukov, of the National Army of the Republic of Georgia. On attachment from Batman Base with his wing of Typhoon multi-role aircraft, he was enjoying the opportunity to spend time with his fiancé pending their approaching wedding day. Katerina was modelling the latest addition to the uniform of the Russian army. Dressed in her own scant briefs she had a fitted Kevlar moulded bustier clipped on. Lined throughout with foam filled linen it was reminiscent of a Madonna outfit of an earlier year. Katerina put her hands on the twin projections protecting her breasts and giggled, as she strutted back and forth in front of her man, aping the mincing steps of the catwalk and swinging her hips in a manner David thought was more like Gipsy Rose Lee than Kate Moss.

The phone at the bedside bleeped. David reached for it "Sheldon here."

"David we have a problem!" The voice of Mike Summers was restrained but there was tension there.

"I'm on my way. Katerina is here, shall I bring her?"

"Please do!" Mike put the phone down and turned to Ali Baranka, the Turkish Security Chief who was sitting beside the desk. "So what is actually happening, Ali?"

The Turkish officer was looking serious. "The Kurds are very restless and the insurrection that is growing stronger all the time is affecting the entire area along the border of Iran. The problem is that despite the softening situation here and in Georgia, the Iranian Kurds want to return to their own lands. The increasing level of arms supply has encouraged them to believe that they can take on the Iranian army and force them out of their homelands. Despite the devastation that the Iranians have wrought there they believe that once they get home they can put things right."

"You believe that even if they succeed in driving the Iranians back, there will be nothing there for them except devastation and poisoned ground?"

"Exactly. My spies tell me that the spoiled earth will not be useable again for at least 30 years." He paused, his sad eyes lowered, then, "Our problem is that the conflict will spill over into Turkey and the Iranians will not be playing with conventional weapons. Not only the possibility of the suitcase atom bombs we are chasing at present, but chemical weapons that will destroy our people and soil as well as that of Georgia."

David and Katerina came in as Ali was making his last remarks.

"Iran again?" David asked.

"The Kurds, I'm afraid. They are reaching the point of returning to Iran and taking on the army there, in an effort to recover their homelands."

Katerina looked grim. "But they will not have a chance. The Iranian forces will saturate the area as they did before, and the earth is poisoned anyway."

Ali answered her, "There are fanatics in their ranks who are stirring people up. I am now led to believe that there is more to this than it seems."

?Two of my people think there is a group of Kurds who have been infiltrated into the refugee contingents, who are in the pay of Iran."

"Do you mean that the Iranians are provoking this re-surgence?" Peter asked.

"That is exactly what I believe, I was not sure up until now, but when we got the news about the suitcase bombs it all started coming together."

The three friends sat looking at Ali, concerned at this information.

"Does that mean the use of the suitcase bombs here and at the Georgian base will be coordinated with the upris-ing to offer a cause and effect to the rest of the world? Probably allowing them to shrug and blame the Kurds for the whole thing?" The general looked at Ali, eyebrows raised.

Peter came in and heard the latest updates. "It makes sense from their point of view, the world knows nothing of the theft of the bombs, but they are aware that there are bombs available on the black market. It would all make sense, even the accidental collateral damage to the two bases."

Mike Summers said mildly "There is something else."

Both the others looked up at this.

He carried on "Ali, perhaps you would like to explain."

Ali walked over to the large map of the area on the wall of the office. He pointed at a region which was close to the border on the Iranian side. "Here there are abandoned iron mines, they date back to Biblical times and they have been taken over by this group as a forward base. My belief is that one of the bombs will be placed here and probably exploded with the garrison still in place. The location allows them to control the uprising from the place where the action should be centred."

"So what do we do? Drop in and clear up the hideout?" Katerina asked.

"We can do little from the ground I'm afraid, there is no way we can get near the place without premature discovery. The only possible way is by air and even that is difficult because of the terrain. It is very broken hummocky rock. The road winds between small hills that obscure the target for fast movers. This will be very difficult to target for any aircraft. The final approach to the mine entrance is over a cleared area that is guarded by integrated heavy machine guns."

"How about helicopters?" Peter was already thinking the problem through. "Obviously we need to seal off the place after the arrival of the villains."

"We would need more firepower." Mike put in.

"How about an Osprey? The Marines use them and they can carry the ordinance, plus they have vertical ascent and descent capabilities. Either drop an assault group or perhaps a land mine of some description"

"That sounds do-able if we can get hold of an aircraft in time." Katerina said "I have an air assault group who have been training to drop from low and high levels. In fact a Ha-lo drop could be one answer to get a pre-emptive bomb in place. But what about alternate exits to the mines? Do they have escape tunnels?"

Ali said "My information is that they have deliberately sealed all located escape routes. These people are fanatics. There is no leeway as far as they are concerned. The possibility of failure is not to be considered. Of course it means that there may be a way out but only if one has been overlooked either deliberately or by accident. Deliberate would indicate the presence of someone a little more pragmatic than the main body. It would also indicate a person of influence."

"I presume we are searching for this possible entrance?" Peter said.

"We certainly are and we think we may have found it. My agents have been using thermal imaging to watch over the area and they found a zone where intermittent hot spots have been seen. Definitely not wild animals. They are working on locating the actual spot at present. I am sure that we will be successful and have the place covered shortly. Whoever tries to escape, we believe, will be someone of importance."

General Summers turned to his telephone "Right. This meeting is over, we will reconvene at 1800 for an update on progress. I'll see what we can do with getting an Osprey from the Green team."

Chapter eleven

...Just one thing after another

The team of Special Forces troops arrived at the base that evening, the men were already acquainted with the base garrison from the earlier alliance against the dissident Russian forces.

The Osprey came in after dark, settling down on the apron in front of the main hanger. The Georgian team were already accommodated within the hanger awaiting their start time.

***

At the ambush camp Chuck studied the approaching convoy through his binoculars. Captain Richard Samuels directed the seeker at the convoy vehicles in turn. The fourth truck produced a response. Bowman sighted the shoulder-mounted missile at the vehicle and fired.

Chuck watched the smoke trail following the missile to its destination, braced for the last glimpse in this life if the missile set the fission in progress.

The truck exploded and the sympathetic explosion of the explosive in the suitcase bomb caused a secondary blast, but there was no all-embracing blast to flatten the entire countryside for miles around. Chuck let his breath out slowly, realising that he had been holding it ever since the truck had been identified.

"Call it in," he said to Samuels. "Strike one!"

***

In the convoy Hazel Cantrell was in the lead vehicle when the explosion occurred. It came as a complete surprise. When the shock wore off she went back to find that the truck in question was completely obliterated. The truck ahead was scorched up the back but the side curtains were still in place and the cargo undamaged. The truck behind was completely free of damage, it had dropped back a little and was around a bend the trees in line with the blast were blasted and singed. Of the crew, the driver and his mate, there was no sign at all. Whatever had caused the explosion had been powerful enough to clear the scene more or less completely.

The convoy continued on its was minus one truck. Hazel spoke to her driver, he had been with her on several trips by now. "Tell me, Stefan, do we carry arms and ammunition in out trucks?"

"Madam, how would I know? I do not load them I only drive." His shrug however was expressive, and his cynicism showed."

"What are you not telling me, Stefan? You can tell me. We could have been driving that truck."

"All I know is that the food we carry is provided by the Mafia in Russia, I do not believe they ever do anything for nothing."

"But this company belongs to my guardian and his partners. Are you saying they are Mafia?"

"What can I say, Madam? What I have said already is too much; if they find out, I am dead already."

"This is between you and me only, no one else will know, no one else must know. I had no idea that Mr. Rankin was Mafia."

For the rest of the journey Hazel was deep in thought. At Jolfa she considered speaking to Mahid but decided to keep it to herself for the moment.

***

At the base, General Mike Summers was embarrassed. His being here when further incidents were occurring was almost a provocation. Though it was nothing to do with him officially, he was on the spot. Reluctantly he concluded that he should report the situation to the Pentagon. He spoke to Peter who was in command of the base and told him what he was doing and why.

"Between us, General, that is the wise thing to do, and if there is anyone with the sense they were born with, they will order you to stay and take command of the situation. After all, who else is there with the background knowledge to react correctly in this situation?"

"Peter, I should point out to you that you are here, and that you have the knowledge."

"But, sir, you have the rank!"

Mike conceded the point and picked up the phone and asked for a dedicated line to the Chief-of-Staff in the Pentagon.

The Chief-of-Staff had been a Lt Colonel in the Iraq war, serving under Storming Norman Schwarzkopf. His career had been a succession of action postings before being caught up in the Pentagon trap. It had been a lucky break for him, as the serious action had just begun in Afghanistan. Because of his recent field experience his input was important and already a Lieutenant General, his fourth star had followed. A tour in Afghanistan proved his tactical abilities. The emergency medical situation that caused the retirement of the Chief-of-Staff General Abernethy coincided with the return of General John T Manners from a successful tour in Afghanistan. The rest is history.

Mike Summers call was put through immediately. "Manners here, Mike, what can I do for you?"

"Sir, I am in Turkey at this time, handing over to my former second in command Colonel Peter Hamilton. Unfortunately a situation has arisen involving the rogue CIA man Heard. It seems he is involved in the sale of suitcase size WMD's to Iran. They are, we understand, being shipped to Iran via mercy convoys supposedly directed to the Kurdish refugees. I'm told there is one dedicated to this base, another to the Georgian base where the defecting Russian forces are now based, and a third to New York. The intention is to attribute all bombs to Muslim fundamentalists.

"The base defence team here has already destroyed one of the bombs, carried as suggested in a food convoy.

"My orders are, come what may, to return to the Pentagon as soon as the handover is completed. However, in the circumstances as ranking officer in place here, I feel it is my duty to stay until the present situation is resolved."

"You are asking me to extend your orders to cover this?"

"Sir, with respect, that is bullshit, I am informing you of a tactical situation in a location where on two previous occasions I have had to make decisions that have not been approved by higher authority."

"What is your opinion of the gravity of this situation?"

"I would rate it as maximum risk sir. The destroyed bomb was exploded without fission occurring. A similar bomb in this base exploded as intended would wipe out not only the entire base but also the local town and housing within a 10-15 mile perimeter."

"I will cut you new orders to remain in place for sixty days. I am sticking my neck out on this, but I actually approved the actions you took on both occasions in the past and in Iraq, if that means anything to you. I will run interference for you with the President if it is needed but whatever I say your butt will be in the wringer if it ends in tears, you understand?"

"Thank you, sir, I understand and I'll try not to let you down."

Mike put the phone down and realised he was sweating. He called Peter in.

"You are officially stuck with me for 60 days; the orders will come through on fax. It means I will be here to advise you and help in sorting out the current problems." Watching Peter, Mike looked for any signs of resentment.

Peter grinned openly. "Well, that's a load off my mind. I was beginning to think you were going to bug out and leave me to save the world on my own. Boss, you are welcome."

He reached out his hand and gripped Mike's. "Welcome to Hell once more, General."

"Glad to be here, Peter. So, shall we get on with it?"

***

Mike's first effort was to call Sarah and let her know the new situation. Not surprisingly Sarah, still ranking as Colonel pending her retirement, immediately set about arranging to fly out to Turkey to join him.

"Sarah is on her way," he said to Peter.

"Quite right, too!" Was Peter's immediate response "The more the merrier!"

***

The Osprey was scheduled to fly in two days' time. The troops tasked to drop and locate the bomb at the site were briefed. The carry handles were fitted to allow them to locate the piece where it would do the most good. Meanwhile, at Batumi, the halo-platoon was being briefed on its task – to suppress the defences at the cave mouth. The special operatives that formed the group would be under the official command of Major Sergei Adamov, a former Spetsnaz captain, who had been part of General Volkov's defecting group. Not the biggest member of the squad, the major was 5'9", but broad shoulders and a trim waist demonstrated his fitness for his job. A recent convert to the Halo drop system he had trained his platoon to a very high standard, and as far as his troops were concerned, they would follow him anywhere.

His 2/ic was Captain Sasha Sikorsky, no relation to Igor of helicopter fame. She was quick to point out.

Adamov thought differently, possibly because Sasha Sikorsky was one of the best helicopter pilots he had ever encountered.

"The men are ready, sir." Captain Sikorsky saluted as she made her report.

"Good, let's get them loaded up." He answered her salute and watched as she trotted over to the waiting transport, thinking to himself that even in her bulky coverall there was no hiding her elegant figure. He smiled to himself, she was far too young to have any interest in an old man like him. Her generation considered forty-five ancient, after all. He stirred and picked up his gear. As he walked over to the aircraft he was joined by Colonel Shukov.

"This is a difficult one, Sergei, these insurgents are Kurds and they know their way about."

"After Afghanistan, boss, I trust no one I haven't personally trained on a job like this. I have a good bunch here and Sasha's the sort of back-up you wait a lifetime for."

Katerina gave him a sidelong glance at that remark. Her thoughts regarding the suitability of Sasha as back-up were fully in agreement with the major's, but unlike the major her opinion of the private preferences of Captain Sikorsky ran rather on the lines that the attractive captain would gladly drop her knickers for the major given the slightest encouragement. Being fond of them both she thought if they did not get themselves sorted out soon she would need to give the situation a nudge. It was about time.

At the aircraft, a modified Boeing 737, she boarded with the platoon and strode down the aircraft exchanging the odd quip with the seated paratroopers. Satisfied that all had been done as she had arranged, she took a seat at the front of the cabin where Captain Sasha Sikorsky was already strapped in. The door was closed by the crew chief, and the operation began.

***

At Incirlik NATO base Lieutenant General Mike Summers met his wife Colonel Sarah Summers as she stepped off the Air Force tanker that had brought her from Andrews Airbase.

"Another fine mess you've got us into!" she said with a smile.

"Just can't seem to get out of the habit." he answered, grinning. "And incidentally, I am very happy to see you, Colonel Summers."

He took her arm and slipped it through his and they walked off the tarmac into the Headquarters building. As they walked he briefly brought her up to date on the situation at present.

"Do you mean to say you have deliberately brought me into a deadly dangerous area on a whim." Said with a straight face, she almost had him going.

Equally straight-faced he said, "Damn right I did. Now you are my wife I feel it's my duty to give you the opportunity to share the dangers of my life, as well as the pleasures."

"So where are the pleasures?" Having reached his quarters by this time he proceeded to demonstrate said pleasures in no uncertain terms.

***

They lay side by side, content to be sharing the moment for a while, then Sarah said, "So, tell me about it, what have you got set up so far?"

Over the next half-hour Mike laid out chapter and verse of the current situation and the measures he had taken so far.

Later, back at the office they were in time to receive the initial reports of the raiding parties.

***

The Halo team took to the air from the modified 737, dropping through the floor hatch in pairs. They had all been paired off throughout their training. Dropping from 30.000 feet was a lonely business. All the team members were fitted with a small light on the back of their coveralls just for the long drop. When they deploy their chutes the lights disappear, and the team is down to buddies only until they land at the target.

Major Sergei Adamov soared through the thin air, his buddy Sgt Karol Roman off to his right about 20 feet away. Below the skein of lights of the platoon stretched forward into the distance. The Major checked his GPS, they were still on course for the target, he checked the altimeter. They were dropping close to the predicted rate. Captain Sasha Sikorsky, leading the drop several thousand feet below her Commander, reported that the drop was going well and they should soon be in the zone for the controlled glide to the drop point on the hills above the cave mouth.

Sergei acknowledged the report, "Good luck." He added and switched off.

Sasha glided down to the point indicated on her GPS, touching down gently. She gathered her parachute and stuffed it in the bag brought for the purpose. There were figures dropping all around her now, as the platoon arrived in their pairs. The parachute bags were all gathered together and stacked, weighed down with rocks, to disguise as well as keep them from being scattered by the wind.

Major Adamov arrived with his buddy. He allowed his buddy to deal with the parachute while he got together with Sasha and the map to get the men moved into position as soon as possible.

Two hours later the platoon was poised above the mouth of the cave. The gun sites had been identified and squads allocated to deal with them. The teams detailed to abseil down the rock face were waiting for the go ahead, under the orders and direction of Captain Sikorsky.

She was standing in her harness ready to clip on and descend. Sergei walked over to her and tugged the harness verifying that it was securely attached. He faced her, she was inches away from him. He looked her directly in the eyes. Without thinking, he said, "Look after yourself, we have things to discuss when we get back."

Sasha looked at him directly. "It's about time."

For a moment they stood, then swiftly she kissed him on the lips and turned "Time to go, boys and girls." She called out in a low voice. The murmur of the engines of the Osprey could be heard in the background.

Adamov watched as they lined up on the cliff top. With a lift of her hand, Sasha dropped over the edge along with the rest of the team.

The major walked along the cliff edge waiting for the Osprey to get a little closer. Below the signs of movement in the gun emplacements warned that the Osprey was noticed.

"Hold it, lads," he whispered in his mouth-mike. "Not too soon."

"We're in position." Sasha reported from the foot of the cliff.

"All together now. Open fire!" The major spoke sharply, and all hell let loose as the sited gun positions scattered across the broken land below lit up with the explosions of the missiles from the raider's weapons. 30 seconds of noise. Then nothing but the flicker of flame from burning clothing then the occasional crack of overheated ammunition.

Captain Sikorsky heard the shouts and the alarm bells within the cave and murmured quietly to her group. "Here they come, choose your targets and put them down."

Her crew of 18 were placed across the entrance where they could see the doors set into the wall built to shut the cave off from the outside world. It was a substantial wall built of blocks of stone cemented together with big steel doors, open at the moment but liable to be closed in the event of attack and as she watched Sasha saw the near door start to quiver against the large rock leaning against the foot of the door to keep it propped open. She grinned, it was typical here in the Middle East. Sophisticated electronic door controls, combined with a doorstop. She waved for her people to advance to the doorway. Rolling rocks for cover, they crept forward as a loudly complaining officer wearing a colonel's insignia came walking through the cave, followed by a group of soldiers and civilians. At the doorway the colonel stopped and looked up towards the nearest gun position.

There was nothing to be seen from the ground. He lifted a hand communicator to his mouth and spoke rapidly. Then he shook it and Sasha clearly heard him say, "Russian shit!" The Colonel banged the handset against his hip and tried again. Then he threw the instrument at the cliff face where it shattered with a satisfying crunch. He turned to the men behind him and detailed two men to walk up to the gun sites and conform that all was well. He was speaking in Farsi, and Sasha who had learned the language before being posted to Batumi, could understand exactly what he was saying.

The Osprey had made a wide circle round the area and was hovering well behind the major's location at the cliff top, waiting for the signal to make the drop of the land mine.

Sasha called the major. "Time for us to get together, I am just about to open the party."

The two messengers had not returned, it was not surprising since both had met a silent unanticipated end on the point of the fighting knives favoured by the raiders. At the cliff top, Adamov ordered his men over the edge to join the Captain below. He then called the Osprey into hover at his location until the ground below had been cleared. The suppressed beat of the big dual purpose propellers closed on him and hovered close enough to the ground for the major to step onto the cargo pallet containing the trolley-mounted bomb, suspended under the aircraft.

The burst of suppressed gunfire from below went unheard on the cliff top. The voice of Sasha through his earphone reassured Sergei that all was well and to come and join the party.

The Osprey crept over the cliff edge and positioned itself to lower its cargo to the ground. As he reached the ground Major Adamov looked to see the situation.

Apart from the bodies beside a now closing door it seemed all was in order. The other door was still straining against its retaining rock.

The group unloaded the trolley bomb and pushed it through the door. Adamov set the timer for fifteen minutes, and stepped out of the door signalling for the removal of the rock. The first group mounted the pallet and were raised up to the cliff top. By the time the final group were lifted there was only five minutes on the clock.

***

The column of trucks with reinforcement troops approached the base as the attackers were still being lifted. The pilot of the Osprey coolly rotated the nose to point at the approaching vehicles and then he pressed the uncapped red button and a blizzard of depleted uranium bullets shredded the first three trucks and their human contents. The remaining trucks stopped suddenly and disgorged their men. There was no risk involved for the raiders. The men had seen what had happened to the leading vehicles, it was enough for them, half of them did not even take their weapons with them.

The pilot raised the final group without pausing to check the effect of his gunfire. The marine pilot knew exactly what he was doing, just as he knew there would be no serious response to his fire.

***

Sasha had moved the first and second contingents from the cliff top to a rendezvous point where they boarded the Blackhawk helicopter in Georgian Air Force livery. The other members of the party boarded the Osprey, which ditched the pallet and waited to see the effects of the land mine. Sasha persuaded the Blackhawk pilot to join the Osprey in time to see the mountain collapse. The steel doors blew out to smash against the lava hillocks opposite, and a huge cloud of dust rose from the site. When it started to clear, the wind blowing it to the East it was clear that there would be no survivors. In the place of the small mountain there was a crater. The cave system that had existed, honeycombing the area within the mountain had been filled with rubble from the blasted rock. The sharp edged ridge surrounding the crater was broken at the point where the cave entrance had been.

Chapter Twelve

...Where angels fear to tread.

Lt Col. Chuck Hartog was passed the news about the destruction of the enemy site, but though it was good news, in his present situation he had problems of his own. M/Sgt Patsy McCoy was leading the way through the scrub covered landscape with Trooper Bowman bringing up the rear. The pack carried by Captain Samuels was stuffed with the paperwork and vital bits of the monitoring camp that they had briefly occupied. They were now being pursued by a party of soldiers, thinly disguised as peasants, armed with Kalashnikovs and grenade launchers and wearing bullet-proof vests.

So far the party had managed to stay out of reach, but they had lost their transport and were currently paralleling the road looking for alternatives.

They stopped at the signal given by Patsy. Chuck pushed the button on the GPS indicating their position to the listeners and watchers at base.

Over his headset Chuck was suddenly aware of a voice he recognised.

"Keep your heads down, guys, I'm passing through." Mike Summers passed the crouching group, the Merlin engine of the Mustang announcing its presence accompanied by the chatter of machine guns as he made a pass over the pursuing troops. The swoosh of the impact of the single carpet bomb relieved the immediate pressure, as the eighteen soldiers kept their appointments in paradise in the holocaust of the hail of bomblets that left no survivors.

"Thanks for the help." Chuck called.

"Anytime." Mike Summers answered cheerfully carefully avoiding the area he had just devastated. He climbed to survey the area around the escaping party. "There's a truck heading your way. It looks like you'll be able to thumb a lift. Good luck guys."

The radio squawked. "Mustang!" Mike answered.

"There is a light aircraft approaching from the east, not answering radio, flying erratically, can you intercept, our CAP is too quick."

"Mustang, on my way."

He spotted the civilian aircraft, flying low and bouncing around in the thermals rising from the hot ground. He throttled back and coarsened the pitch on his propeller to keep station beside the small Cessna. The pilot looked over at the Mustang and spotted the US insignia that had been replaced on the sides of the fuselage after the completion of the black operation.

It obviously reassured the pilot who nodded when Mike indicated that he follow him down to the airfield that was now in sight.

The pilot of the civilian aircraft was a small man who spoke good English but he looked and was ill. When he left his aircraft he warned everyone to stay away from it without protective clothing. "It has been irradiated," he shouted. "It needs to be hosed down by people in protective clothing, please." His final words were almost a wail. Major Cameron, in charge of the security in Chuck's absence, swiftly organised a team to hose the aircraft down, and two protectively-dressed nurses to take the pilot to the isolation room in the sickbay, where he was taken through the entire process of decontamination.

He was escorted to the briefing room where he declared he was Professor Razi of the Iranian Nuclear Unit. He had been seconded to SAVAK the Secret Service and brought to the border base, and from there to the advanced base in Armenia to accept and service six suitcase bombs.

"I am a scientist, I do not worry about politics but I also have a brain and a conscience. I discovered that the bombs were not for use by my government but had been put in the hands of mercenaries to perform tasks that my government wished to distance itself from. The conditions for the service were appalling, little attention had been given to the safety of the people involved. There were two people running things, an American and a Russian. They both kept well away from contamination." He stopped exhausted and an orderly came over and took his blood pressure and temperature, then injected him with a small morphine dose.

They attempted to take him away to rest but he refused.

"I must finish," he said, "This is important. The leaders were not saying what the bombs were for, but when I was working on the one I have with me, I heard one of the Russians laugh and say that Wall Street would never be the same after this case was delivered." He paused again and drank some water.

"It was then I realised that these bombs were not going to Tehran for research. I was horrified. They are dirty bombs and would cause horrific damage, and if the wind was right the damage could be extended over a huge area." He rose to his feet unsteadily. "I am dead already. I have absorbed more than one lethal dose of radiation. I will unload and clean the bomb I have on board. Your people can examine it and assess the damage it can do better than I, but I do not wish to die from this radiation, it is a disgusting way to go. Perhaps you could shoot me?"

The stunned listeners heard the words but could not believe them. The man was asking them to kill him.

Mike looked sympathetically at the man in front of him. "I hear what you say but rather than shoot you, do you know how to get back to the base where you were working?"

"I do, what are you suggesting?"

"If we loaded your aircraft with say, Napalm or perhaps an airburst bomb, it would be a clean way to die and you could take some very nasty people with you."

Professor Razi looked at him steadily, his bloodshot eyes keen despite his sickness. "Apart from the single bomb already despatched, there are still four there and maybe the men running the operation. Why not? I will go now and take the bomb out of the plane and then you can load it up and tell me what I should do."

He staggered slightly then recovered, "First things first." Before he left to work on the bomb he said "If I may I will write a letter to my wife and children, they are unaware of what I am doing and I would like them to know that I stayed true to my principles."

The professor wrote his letter and the doctor prepared a booster shot to keep him going as long as possible. The Cessna was cleared inside and out until the residual radiation was at a minimal level. The professor worked on the bomb outside at the edge of the airfield, he finally declared it secure and leak free. The outer case was cleaned and the bomb shipped off to Washington for investigation and evaluation.

Professor Razi rested for a few hours before taking to the skies once more in the Cessna. Now with a cargo of Napalm the small aircraft was escorted from the area by the Mustang, now flown by Colonel Browning. The flight did not take very long. The professor found his way back to the concealed lab where he had been working. As he flew he found he was raging inside at the unfairness of it all. He had been a lecturer at University, happily married with two children, when the Ayatollah took over the rule of the country. At first there had been flattery and fine accommodation for the research team, his family had been allowed to live with him on site. But as the power and influence of the extreme brand of religion took hold of the country, the austere set of rules had come in.

The professor's wife had been a modern forward-looking person who had not enjoyed the strict regime and had actually said so in front of the wrong people. For this reason she had lost her place at the research establishment and been banished to a settlement where she was forced to wear the chador and, for the sake of the children, keep her mouth shut.

He missed both his wife and the children terribly. There was no chance of ever re-joining them now. Even without the fatal level of radiation poisoning they were never going to allow them to get together again. He adjusted the autopilot, setting the controls to descend gradually. The entrance to the facility was an innocent looking service station set beside the road. It sold no fuel and it would not provide service for any vehicles. As he covered the intervening ground descending gently he prayed to his god for forgiveness and for the souls of the innocent in the laboratory below. He knew they were all hopelessly irradiated whether they realised it or not so he prayed for them anyway.

There was a smile on the face of the doomed man when the plane touched down on the main road, a touch of the near rudder pedal swung the nose directly at the entrance below the canopy.

The spinning propeller shattered against the door frame and the aircraft decelerated from 45knots to zero in a flash. The professor died there and then, flying through the windscreen headfirst into the doorpost. The cargo of Napalm was discharged through the opened doors and down the stairs to the floor below. The two containers exploded when they hit the floor below, the sheet of flame spreading throughout the area melting metal and crisping flesh. Nobody escaped. Unfortunately the American was not there and though two bombs became blobs of metal, the other two had been taken away by the American that morning.

***

The satellite picked up the picture in its pass over the area; the plume of petrol-fuelled fire and smoke created a finger in the sky that could be seen fifty miles away.

Nobody bothered to advise the professor's wife. The letter was sent but the circumstances of her exile did not permit communications with outside sources. Iran intelligence who intercepted the letter read it, noted the Turkish postmark, and filed it with the other items of little interest to their masters at the time.

***

Elmore Heard stopped the Humvee on the rise above the research lab. Established in this remote valley of

Trchkan, Armenia, the concealed base was well sited and unlikely to be found. He heard the aircraft as he turned to set off once more. He stepped out of the vehicle, automatically checked the two aluminium suitcases wedged between the back seats before lifting his binoculars to search for the approaching aircraft.

He located the Cessna, idly wondering if it was the one used by the lab staff. As it approached closer he recognised the letters on the side and relaxed when he became aware that it was the aircraft from the lab.

He watched as it lost altitude and touched down on the road. With horror he saw it turn sharply into the canopy over false front of the petrol station.

The crump of the explosion followed and he started to turn and run. Realising that if it happened it was a waste of time, there would be no escape, and if it didn't there was nothing to worry about, he watched as the column of smoke and flame rose in the air. A fingerpost marking the grave of the 30 men and women working there.

He shrugged, he was still alive, and of the people within the lab only six were in any state to survive. The others were hopelessly irradiated whether they realised it or not.

He climbed back into the Humvee and put it in gear heading for the Georgian border and Zorin's new base of operations in the hills above the Black Sea.

***

Mahid Vahidi was a patriot, his love for his country was only matched by the love he had felt for his wife of two weeks who had been shot and crippled by the fanatic followers of the new rulers of Iran. Despite his rank as a major in the army at that time there was no apology, and the medical services would waste no time on the expensive treatment that was required to return his wife's mobility. Her badly patched body was now condemned to a wheelchair for life, and his colonel had merely said, "So take another wife, there are plenty to choose from."

Mahid thought of his beloved partner, with her degree in English and Law, his hatred for the colonel started at that point.

When his wife committed suicide, her message written to explain this act mentioned the Colonel's suggestion and that she would make it easier for him, and also end the daily torment of her existence.

His reaction to her suicide was not to rage against the people who had created the situation. His life just stopped, he carried on with his work, but inside he was watching and planning. It was not just revenge, though he was human and that came into it. What really motivated him was the complete lack of human feeling in the government that rode in on a wave of religious fervour. Since then the leaders seemed to be carried away by power and their reaction to the rest of the world, supporting insurgence, encouraging people to commit suicide by strapping bombs to their bodies. Worse were those forced to protect their families by giving up their lives as human bombs. The merciless imposition of the strict rule of Islam, with no concession to modern life was the final straw that turned Mahid from passive to active.

He used his military rank to find out ways to fight back. It was not surprising that he was contacted by opposition groups, most of which he ignored. There was one incident that made a major difference to his life. His unit was part of the perimeter defence of the so-called innocent research of nuclear powered electricity. The raid on the facility destroyed the underground factory and set the whole program back by years.

He applauded the initiative that had led to the raid and over time became aware of their identity and the fact that they were back in Turkey. When the base at Ciranu was reopened recently he managed to make contact with one of the network of informants controlled by Ali Baranka. The border post that Mahid commanded had been used for the passage of goods and people both into and out of Iran. The aid convoys sent for distribution among the Kurdish refugees passed unharmed or touched through his post, and it was because of this that the contact was first made.

***

He met Ali and Peter Hamilton-Davies at a secret rendezvous, over the border in Turkey.

The two NATO officers waited as the headlights of the jeep swung round and were switched off. The ticking of the cooling metal of the vehicle was clearly heard on that still night.

"Major Mahid Vahidi?"

"Colonel Davies and Colonel Baranka?"

Introductions over the three men sat down in three picnic chairs round a small table and shared a selection of drinks from the cooler brought by the Ali.

"We are aware of the work you have been doing on behalf of the people of Iran. Because it is obvious that you really have the interests of the people, rather than the government at heart, I felt it was important that you were aware of the reasons why we have reopened the base at Ciranu."

Mahid smiled "You underestimate me, Colonel. I believe that the reason you have placed yourselves here is to stop the renegade CIA man from importing suitcase bombs from the former USSR atomic arsenal. I understand you have managed to destroy one and that my former friend Professor Razi has managed to destroy the transit lab itself. However I have been told that the CIA Man Heard is still at large with an unknown number of the weapons."

Peter said "I'm impressed. Tell me, Major, why are you offering your services like this? I presume you do not support the present regime in Iran?"

"I understand that I am suspected of attempting to infiltrate the insurgent forces, but I would like to draw your attention to the fact that I am still a major, though I should be a colonel by now. Of that I say nothing for it means nothing, I have no interest in furthering my career in the Iranian army. I have never approved of the religious take-over of my country. For many years religious tolerance allowed all races and religions to work and live together with no real problems, now we have degenerated to the sort of regime that the Nazi's in the twentieth century perpetrated. Children are being taught to accuse their parents of transgressions unheard of, prior to the change of government.

"But the main reason was that my wife was shot and seriously injured during a fire-fight between police and Muslim fanatics. There was no suggestion of regret because of her innocence at that time. The suggestion that expensive surgery was needed to give her back the use of her legs, was rejected on the basis that she was only a woman, thus not worth the expenditure." He stopped at that point and collected himself, obviously upset at passing on the story of his wife.

He continued. "I was told to find another wife if this one was no longer fully functional. They told me in front of my wife who was wheelchair-bound because of her injuries.

"Two weeks later my wife killed herself. Gentlemen, make no mistake, I love my country, but I recognise that as long as these self-obsessed bigots are in power there will be little chance of my country becoming once again a land worth living in."

The force of passion that accompanied these words made a powerful impact of both the NATO officers.

"Let's get down to planning how we can co-operate in this matter." Peter said and all three put their heads together to formulate a plan.

***

As Mahid returned to his border post in the early morning, he considered the meeting he had just attended. The two men, despite being Infidels, had been professional and he realised he had liked their open attitude to him and the situation. Having been brought up to distrust the British and American military, he wondered not for the first time how many other things he had been led to believe were untrue. Certainly the performance of the Iranian governments since the deposing of Pahlavi family had shown no improvements as far as the people were concerned. In fact from his own experience most of the ordinary people were considerably worse off. There was no doubt that the rule of the Ayatollahs had worsened the lot of the ordinary people by the imposition of such strictly administered laws that social life had deteriorated dramatically.

There was a rightness about the agreement to cooperate with the Westerners Mahid decided. The sooner the country developed a democratic form of government the better. And anyone and anything that could help in that purpose would receive his support.

His return was greeted with relief by his deputy. Despite the agreement they had about the injustice within the country he was inclined to be nervous when left on his own.

***

They came for him in the evening of the following the day. They arrived in a people carrier and a truck. The command of the border post was given over to the deputy who had reported him and the arrested man was placed in the rear of the truck and driven off. The snatch party had no intention of taking the arrested man to Tehran, there it would be possible that he might have friends in high places who would not only have him released but could also bring retribution down on the heads of the kidnappers.

The SAVAK team that had taken him wanted to interrogate him on suspicion that he was communicating with the insurgent Kurds. Based entirely on the word of the 2i/c of the border post, whose brother was a member of SAVAK.

The one thing the snatch squad had not taken into account was that the border post was under constant observation by the Kurdish insurgents.

The arrival and departure of the team was noted and Ali Baranka was informed. The movements of the snatch team were recorded and the location of their base of operations duly recorded.

Ali reacted fast and produced a team of men to surround the house being used. Having established that the prisoner was actually being held in the cellar, his men moved in. They took the entire building over, killing only one man and taking all the other SAVAK men captive with deceptive ease.

Mahid Vahidi, released, discussed the situation with the newly-promoted Colonel Baranka. "I do not believe that this was a sanctioned arrest. See, here we have the brother of my so-called deputy; I think this was personal. I can guess how it would be. Kurdish rebels kidnapped me and murdered me. Captain Korda came to my rescue; alas, too late. Something like that anyway. I think I can work better from the border post so just stick the dead man in the people carrier and I will return to the post and resume command." He hesitated. "I would appreciate it if you would stay close until I am proved right, just in case."

The colonel looked at him silently, then he nodded. "Sounds like a good plan. Right. I will keep close until you signal me that everything is alright."

The return to the border post was enlightening for Mahid. Captain Korda had already moved into his quarters. Mahid's possessions were piled up on the veranda outside the door. Captain Korda was sitting in the C.O.s office with his feet on the desk drinking Mahid's whisky.

The people carrier drew up outside the door in a cloud of dust and Mahid stepped out and brushed dust off his sleeve. He walked into the office without knocking. The Captain had his back partly turned. He swung round angrily. "What the devil do you mean coming into my office without knock...."

His voice trailed off as he realised who it was. The angry face was replaced by a look of horror, half-risen and off balance, Mahid kicked the chair and the captain tumbled to the floor.

"I am sure you are delighted to see that I have been released from that silly attempt to kidnap me. Now tell me why you decided to arrange such a thing. I presume the dead man in the car outside is your brother, or maybe it is just his friend. Whatever the story he tells me is that you arranged the entire affair so you are actually responsible for the deaths of six SAVAK agents."

The Captain was still crouched on the floor but now he was past the fear and shock and his hand went to his holster and he drew his sidearm. He shot at the Major but the Major was no longer there. As he lifted his gun looking for his target the Major clouted him with the base of the desk lamp. The soggy thunk as the lamp connected made it apparent that the Captain had a thin scull.

***

Igor Zorin was pleased with himself having established that there was an easy way of delivering the bombs for Batumi and the Turkish base. Already in possession of the case for the Batumi job he was waiting for his partner to appear with the other two scheduled for their personal use.

The deserted farm that he had taken over was at least still watertight and with the equipment that had been brought in quite comfortable. He was reclining on a heap of cushions strewn across the carpeted area of floor when the phone rang. His companion was pushed to one side as he reached for the instrument, half buried beneath one of the cushions.

"Yes?" he said.

The voice at the other end was cultured and the language English, accent free. Zorin had the impression that the English had been learned from a teacher rather than at a mother's knee. "I understand you have in your possession something that belongs to me."

"And what might that be?" Zorin could be formal himself when necessary.

"The suitcase currently lying in your barn is mine, bought and paid for. I want it!"

"Who are you then and what gives you the idea that I care what you imagine is yours or not?"

"If you do not arrange to pass that case over in the next half hour when I call back, then I will have to take it back with prejudice. Do you understand?" The voice asked.

"What makes you think I give a shit for your threats or your so-called ownership? You are welcome to try taking it, but I would advise you to save yourself grief and leave things alone." He laughed as her put the phone down thinking, "Stupid man, who did he think he was kidding?"

At the other end of the line the caller replaced the telephone carefully. He relaxed back in his chair looking thoughtful. A knock at the door stirred him out of his reverie. "Yes! Come in." He said briskly now fully alert. The door opened and the woman came in bearing two mugs of steaming coffee. He looked at her approvingly, as she placed the two cups on opposite sides of the desk and fetched a chair to sit on. Five foot six inches of slender but shapely womanhood was how he described her to his associates. Beautiful green eyes a tanned complexion and short blonde hair. With a brain as sharp as any he had encountered, Hazel Cantrell PhD, graduate of Harvard, visiting consultant at MIT, by the age of 19. She was his ward, and she was now 25, having spent the past two years in Africa working on the Mercy Run to Ethiopia and Somalia. She had joined her guardian when her tour in Africa finished.

Her appearance and presence had not gone unnoticed when she joined him in his charity work. The initial remarks being of the: "Have you banged her yet, what is she like in bed?" variety.

She having worked with him now for over a week and the associates firmly put in their place, the office had returned to a normal sort of simmer enjoyed by most of the other offices in the building.

The charity work carried out by the organisation collected food and goods for the relief of the Kurdish peoples of Iran and Turkey, currently subsisting in the Refugee camps in Armenia and in Northern Iran.

For Hazel Cantrell the work was worthwhile and effective. The convoys she had collected on site had gone through with little trouble largely through the cooperation and assistance of the commander of the Iranian border post at Jolfa. She had been running the convoys herself until two weeks ago. When one of the wagons had blown up, her guardian had insisted that she come and work in the office to protect her from the possibility of injury.

Up until that time she had been happy travelling through the length of Armenia into northern Iran delivering the goods and helping out while they were there, waiting for their return papers to fetch the next convoy through. Since this sometimes took a week, she had got to know the people at the border and at the camp.

Captain Mahid Vahidi had escorted her to dinner in the City on three occasions and as she got to know him better she realised that she missed the regular contact that they had. Though he had made no advances she herself was aware that there was a growing empathy between them that excited her. She had not much experience with relationships as her college days had been mostly study and research, the only hasty fumbling excursion into sexual relations had been painful and off-putting. She had later realised that this was down to the callow fumbling of her selected partner at the time. When the thought of getting close to Mahid occurred to her, she realised that any physical contact would be rather more practiced, and she found the idea increasingly more attractive as their acquaintance grew. Being trapped in the offices under the leering eyes of her guardian's associates was wearing and frustrating.

"Avo, we need to talk!" She was as always direct, a trait he encouraged, though it was on occasion disconcerting.

"Yes, my dear, what do we need to talk about?"

"I need to go to Jolfa, we have come up short on the last convoy because of the accident." She was referring to the explosion that had destroyed the bomb carrying vehicle, in the last convoy. "We need to coordinate the provision supply to take up the dietary balance created by the shortfall created in the rice supply."

"Can it not be done by telephone?" Avo Rankin said reasonably.

"On this occasion, I think not!" Hazel looked into his eyes and smiled. "I know you do not want me to travel with the convoy, so I intend taking the Sky-van. It can carry an interim load of rice at the same time. I can fly it myself so I don't need a crew as such. I will take Albert with me, he can help with the loading."

Avo thought for a few moments. "All right you can take the Sky-van, Albert can bring it back. You can wait at Jolfa for a couple of days so that you can bring the Lear jet back. It should be returned from its refit. I'll have them deliver to you there, it will save having the delivery pilots snooping around our facilities here in Kars. I will have letters for my agents in Jolfa so please call in before you go to collect them."

Hazel finished her coffee and rose to her feet. "I'll be back!" She said with a smile, and with a wave of her hand, left the office with just a trace of scent to remind him she was there.

Her cell phone was at her ear as she passed the other offices along the corridor on the way out. "Abdul, get the Sky-van ready to go to Jolfa, I'll need a full load of rice, please." As she reached the exit door she found her way blocked by a big man, he was grinning and sweating, and she did not like him. "Out of the way, Fedor!"

He continued to grin and said, "Make me, give me a kiss." He reached for her.

Hazel shrugged. "You asked for it!" she stepped into him and lifted her knee into his groin. He was completely unprepared and collapsed clutching himself, his face twisted in agony.

She stepped round him and left the building.

In his office Avo Rankin considered what he was going to do about Zorin. He pressed a button on his desk.

Fedor came in, grimacing still from the blow to his pride and his person.

Avo looked at him and shook his head "When will you learn that my ward does not want you in any way shape or form? You are stubborn and stupid, I think."

"Boss I just have this thing about her."

"You are aware that if you force her in any way I will personally relieve you of the embarrassment caused by your sexual urges permanently, at least for the period it takes for you to be skinned alive." There was a cold certainty about the suggestion that left Fedor in no doubt that the threat was genuine.

"Now I need you to go and fetch the suitcase from Zorin. I have no objection to his being hurt in the process, he is trying to cheat me out of my purchase and I have a client waiting in Tehran who has paid in advance. Take whoever you need and fetch the bomb here. Do you understand?"

"Yes, boss. Is Zorin still at the farm?"

"He is at the moment, do not hang about."

Hazel was returning to get the keys for the runabout when she heard the conversation between Fedor and Avo Rankin. *Bomb?* He was telling Fedor to fetch a bomb. The thought that her guardian knew about the carriage of weapons and explosives in the food convoys had occurred as a possibility, but she had discarded the notion. After all the man had been a friend of her parents, they would never had become involved with a criminal to the extent they would invite him to become her godfather. Would they? She really knew nothing about her parents, they had died when she was pretty young and her memories were of the order of sunny day picnics and parties where Avo had been a regular visitor, or had he? She really was beginning to wonder how much she remembered and how much she had been told she remembered. She picked up the keys and left before Fedor came out and drove to the airstrip.

The Sky-van had been wheeled out and the mechanic was working on the engines. The covers were off and he was half buried in the depths, his feet firmly planted on the gantry as he worked.

"Valery, what's the problem?" she called.

"No problem, I'm just replacing the oil filters, she'll be ready to fly by lunchtime. Will you take me with you this time?"

"You trust me?"

"Of course."

"Then I'll take you."

The head appeared from the engine, red hair and a creased smiling face. "I love you, Hazel, marry me?"

"I'm busy this week, ask me next week." She laughed and turned watching Fedor and several others pass the gate on his way to collect the bomb, she presumed.

Suddenly the day was not so sunny and the implication of Rankin's words struck home. Perhaps the bomb was scheduled to go on the next convoy. But why send a bomb to Iran? They surely had enough weapons there. Then she recalled the stories she had heard about the destruction of the nuclear plant. Surely it could not be an atom bomb they were talking about?

The rice was being loaded at noon when Fedor returned. He turned into the airport and drove to the secure end of the hangar where the valuable stores were kept. At the door he stepped out of the vehicle and using his key he opened the sliding door.

Hazel walked over. "So what is my wounded soldier doing now?" Fedor turned and she saw he had a bloody graze on his other cheek. "Why, you are wounded indeed. Did she object to you advances?" she said lightly.

Fedor's shoulders slumped, "We had to collect a suitcase for the boss, the idiot decided to keep it, so we took it anyway." The simple statement seemed to cover everything. "Gregory got wounded." He added, "He'll need the hospital, I guess."

Hazel looked into the people carrier. Gregor was laid out on the floor holding a bloody towel to his abdomen. He looked terrible.

"Get him to the hospital quickly, that looks serious. Why have you come here?"

"I have to leave the suitcase. It is to be loaded on the Lear when it comes back."

He swung the aluminium case out of the vehicle and slid it inside the warehouse door. Then he slid the door shut and locked it.

"Go, go quickly, Gregor needs urgent attention." Hazel pushed Fedor back to the driver's seat, "Hospital now!"

She watched the vehicle depart with the squeal of its tyres. Then she turned to the warehouse door and unlocked it with her own key.

She hauled out the aluminium suitcase and studied it. It looked innocent enough, just a couple of false notes that made it something other than a standard suitcase. There was what seemed to be a flap about 8x6 inches, she reached down and flipped it open. It revealed a keypad and a small LED screen. She closed the flap and looked about to see if she was observed. There was no one in sight. From the warehouse she brought a trolley and hauled the case onto it, covering it with a piece of canvas. She locked the doors once more and dragged the trolley round to the Sky-van hauled the trolley up the open ramp and lodged the case against the bulkhead still wrapped in its canvas shroud. The remainder of the rice cargo was loaded with some few things to replace other losses from the last convoy. Then, with an impatient sigh, Hazel raised the ramp and settled into the cockpit to run through the start-up routine. Valery appeared and climbed into the cabin, settling himself into the co-pilot's seat and strapping in.

"Did you bring your passport?" Hazel asked.

"Of course, we are going to Iran. are we not?"

"We are but it would not be the first time you've forgotten!"

Hazel started the port engine and, once it was running, started the starboard. When she checked the magnetos on both engines she opened the throttles and started to taxi to the strip. The take-off was smooth and once they were in the air Valery undid his seat belt and went to the little galley area to put the kettle on.

"How long today?" He asked.

"About two hours." She answered.

***

At the airstrip Fedor arrived and went to the warehouse section of the hangar. As soon as he realised that the bomb had gone he thumbed his cell phone to the speed-dial of Avo Rankin. When Rankin replied he said tersely "The bomb has gone, it has been taken away."

"What do you mean taken away? Who could take it? Nobody knew it was there." Rankin sounded dangerously calm.

"Hazel knew, she was there when I left it, and she has a key."

"Shit! Has she taken off yet?"

"Yes I saw her leaving as I came back to the airfield. But she would not know it was a bomb, so why would she take it?"

"How do I know, perhaps she does not want it sent on one if the convoys like the last one." There was a pause then Rankin said, "Send Karloff after her in that fighter of his, what is it?"

"Focke Wulf 190."

"That's it, it is armed I believe?"

"Yes sir, machine guns and cannon."

Get him airborne and I want that Sky-van back her pronto or a blazing wreck. Do I make myself clear?"

"But it is Hazel flying, boss!"

"Shit happens." The phone cut off.

Fedor looked at his phone stunned, then he shrugged and pressed another number.

"Karloff, boss's orders. Get that German junk in the air and chase after the Sky-van. Boss wants in back here pronto; if they won't come a burning wreck will do."

"You mean it?" Karloff sounded happy.

"Do it!" Fedor put the phone away and walked into the hanger. He switched on the RT and called the Sky-van. When Hazel answered he sighed with relief.

"Hazel, Fedor; the boss has ordered you back here, he's sent Karloff with his German toy to come and persuade you. He has ordered Karloff to shoot you down if you don't come."

"Thanks for the heads-up Fedor, Hazel over and out."

Hazel thought for a few moments, then "Sky-van XZ 230 calling Ciranu base over."

"Ciranu base, what can I do for you Sky-van?"

"I am carrying mercy stores to Iran from Kars to Jolfa. I have been informed that I am pursued by a FokkeWulf One niner zero armed for bear, sent to force me back to Kars. Do you mind if I drop in? Over/"

"Wait one, Sky-van."

The operator pressed the panic button that was direct to the colonel's desk.

Peter Hamilton answered immediately. "What?"

The operator answered with the recording of the Sky-van call.

Peter said "Affirmative, and roll out the Mustang."

The call came back to the Sky-van, "The welcome carpet is out for a direct emergency landing on E-W runway. You may notice a Mustang taking off. He will greet your follower if he appears. Over."

"Thank you, Ciranu I am approaching from the East at 3000 ft 10 miles.

***"

Jessica Browning settled herself in the seat of the Mustang and opened the throttle. As the wheels came up she saw the Sky-van on its final approach to the runway. To the East she saw the shadow of a fast moving aircraft, and turned towards it. She tested the guns and, reassured that all was in order, opened the throttle wider and zoomed up into the path of the German fighter aircraft.

"FW 190 are you lost? Over."

"Mustang, P51. Are you joking? Get out of my way woman this is serious."

The two aircraft were approaching at high speed, Jessica slammed on the air brakes and full flap, The Mustang seemed to stop and rise above the approaching 190. The burst of fire across the nose of the 190 caused Karloff to jerk the control column back and the 190 went into a steep climb.

Noting he was still aiming toward the Sky-van now close to touch down, Jessica closed the airbrakes and raised the flaps and with throttle wide open she dived to regain speed and lifted the nose of the Mustang opening fire with the cannon. The punch of the kickback caused by the cannon firing slowed the aircraft down and she had to drop the nose or stall.

The Sky-van was on the ground now and the 190 diverted by two cannon hits in the fuselage behind the cockpit turned to meet the Mustang now picking up speed once more.

Roskoff soon discovered the difference between the inspired amateur and the professional.

The Mustang started scoring hits on the 190, while Roskoff blazed away with no apparent result. Jessica fired short bursts at close range within the cone of fire created by the range setting of the guns.

The Sky-van disappeared into the hanger and there was no target that Roskoff could see. Short of firing at the hanger in the vain hope of hitting the escaped transport, an act which would bring rapid response from ground based missiles and possibly jet fighters. There was nothing else he could do, so he turned to run.

The cannon in the Mustang had a limited magazine. In turning away Roskoff placed the belly of his pride and joy in the direct path of the final ten shells in the Mustang's magazine for the cannon. The second shell passed through the seat, parachute and body of Rudy Roskoff exiting through his shattered collarbone and the canopy of the cockpit. The other shells severed the cables and controls to the tail causing the aircraft to fall out of the sky carrying the dead pilot in a final plunge into the mountains, where the wreckage would probably not be found for years.

When Jessica returned to base there was no sign of activity to the naked eye, but in the main hanger a certain amount of turmoil was present.

Chapter fourteen

...Needles, Haystacks, what the hell!

The MP captain was pointing out that it was his duty to ensure that no forbidden substances or equipment entered the base.

"I wish to speak to the commanding officer and no one is opening my aircraft without my say so. Do you understand, buddy!" Hazel Cantrell stood in the way, determined not to move.

The captain was considering having his men move her by force when Jessica arrived and said "Stand down, Captain, I'll deal with this."

He turned and, seeing who it was, saluted. "Thank you, Ma'am. Shall I leave guards here?"

"Yes, please, Captain. Make sure no one touches the aircraft without my permission."

She acknowledged his salute and turned to the young woman. "Who is your friend?" She indicated the worried looking figure of Valery who was standing beside the cockpit door.

"Valery Adamski, the mechanic who maintains our aircraft. I am Hazel Cantrell and I run charity convoys to Jolfa from Kars for my guardian's company. I need to speak to someone who knows about bombs."

"Bring your friend and come with me. No one will touch your aircraft, these men will make sure of that." She indicated the guards who had taken up positions around the Sky-van.

Jessica unzipped her flight suit and shrugged out of it, tossing it to one of the maintenance crew in the hanger, revealing her uniform, the badges of rank gleaming at her collar. Her hat had been tucked into her belt and she donned it as they walked out of the hanger and across to the Administration buildings.

In the office she introduced Hazel to Colonel Henderson and General Summers. She left Valery in the care of the Adjutant and called for coffee while the four people seated themselves in the general's office.

"So, what is this all about, Miss Cantrell? Colonel Browning tells me that you were under attack from that FW190. Would you like to tell me why?"

Hazel had lost a little of her defiance now she was here in the presence of these officers. She started her story, stopping when the coffee came in, having explained the operation of the convoy system and reached the point where the explosion had occurred.

"So you see when I arranged to take the extra provisions in the Sky-van to make up the losses from the convoy explosion I had already suspected that our trucks had been loaded with explosives in addition to the food we carried. Then the bomb arrived. I heard my guardian tell his subordinate to collect the bomb, whatever it took, from a man called Zorin."

At the mention of the name the general looked sharply at the other two officers.

Hazel said, "Does that name mean something to you?"

Mike Summers said "We know it, but please carry on."

After a moment Hazel continued. "Fedor returned while I was at the airfield, he had a wounded man with him. He placed a suitcase in the secure store and took the man to hospital.

"After hearing about the bomb I took a look at the suitcase, and to cut a long story short I decided to take it to the border guard at Jolfa whom I know quite well and trust."

"Major Mahid Vahidi?"

"You know him?"

"We have met and he is working with us in some matters." Peter Henderson said, "And why here?"

"Fedor called and told me that my guardian had ordered that I be turned back or shot down if I refused. I knew you were here and I hoped you would protect me if I called for help. It was as simple as that."

"So this suitcase is in the Sky-van then, can we see it?" Jessica made the suggestion.

"In the circumstances I can hardly refuse, and I confess I am curious myself."

General Summers suggested that they adjourned to the hanger and took a look at the case.

As soon as the case was produced Mike raised his eyebrows. "Do you think the professor was right?"

"He said that there were four left in the Lab. He brought one to us and another was blown up in the convoy. If Heard got away he would have taken at least one, probably two. It is possible therefore that there may have been seven altogether, not six as reported."

Hazel broke in at that point, "Are you saying that the explosion in the convoy was an atom bomb?"

"It was, but the bomb was only blown up with the conventional explosive, no fission took place otherwise the entire convoy, the area up to fifteen miles radius would also have been devastated."

"While you all are discussing what to do about the bombs, if you don't mind I will take the cargo in to Jolfa. I'll contact Major Mahid and deliver the rice. I was supposed to return with the Lear jet, but I guess that would not be a good idea in the circumstances. So if you don't mind I'll return here with the Sky-van, it does belong to the charity that I operate."

"Before you think of moving I would like to speak with Mahid about it." The General sounded quite serious about it. "If Avo Rankin is deprived of his regular convoy route he will have to find an alternative. Also if Hazel flies in to Jolfa there may be an attempt to snatch her. She knows too much now."

"Surely if he's her guardian he won't harm her?" Jessica sounded uncertain.

Peter said "We are talking Mafia here, there is blood and there are the others, even as her guardian Avo will be required to deal with her, and people who interfere with Mafia business don't get second chances."

"You are saying that Avo would hurt me?" Hazel sounded shocked.

"I do not think he will have a choice."

Jessica went off with Hazel to have the Sky-van checked out before it departed for Jolfa, if it was allowed to.

Mike got onto the phone to Mahid.

Mahid was in the office when the phone rang. He picked it up and hearing Mike on the other end he said quickly. "I'll call back on my cell."

In Ciranu Mike put the phone down and picked up when Mahid called him.

"I am not sure but I think my office is bugged. In the circumstances I will not risk using the office phone. I am outside away from people, so what is up?"

"Hazel Cantrell discovered a suitcase bomb in the hands of her guardian. She smuggled it aboard the Sky-van, which had been loaded with rice to replace that lost on the last convoy. Avo Rankin sent a man after her in a fighter aircraft to either turn her round or shoot her down. She was warned and turned to us for help, the Mustang removed the problem. Now Hazel wants to bring the Sky-van over to you to deliver the rice. She can turn round once its delivered and come back here.

We can guard her in the air both ways but we can do nothing on the ground."

"I can alert the charity here and guard her while she is on the ground, but I will have to come out with her. I have already been advised to watch out for her and to arrest her on sight by my people, they will not forgive me helping her escape."

"I will make sure that there are a couple of friends aboard to help unload if that is alright. Anything else I can do?" Mike was concerned what they were planning was not protocol, but what the hell? "Right, Mahid, I'll get the show on the road to arrive after dark, and I look forward to seeing you in person later tonight. Good luck, I'll make sure you are contacted from the plane on the way in." Mike put the phone down, but there was something worrying him, it did not feel right.

Chuck and his party had returned to base yesterday evening and they had all been off duty up to now, but Mike Summers could not get rid of the unease he felt after the phone call with Mahid.

He picked up the phone again and asked the operator for Colonel Hartog. He might have guessed, Chuck was in his office already, putting together his report with assistance of Captain Samuels and M/Sgt Patsy McCoy. He answered the phone and listened to what Mike had to say. "I've got Captain Samuels and M/Sgt McCoy here with me, sir. I would like to bring them in with me, if I may."

"Come ahead, Chuck, and bring your team."

When the group had all settled down Chuck passed on his verbal report on the activities of the patrol over the past week. First the removal of the threat of the bomb, then the getaway and the subsequent pursuit, finally when the enemy picked up their trail again, the intervention by the Mustang. This he acknowledged with a nod to the General who had flown the Mustang. Last, the acquisition of the truck and return to base.

"Now we have another problem. We are pretty sure that Heard is loose with possibly two bombs. The guy is a seriously skilful operator. He has contacts throughout the Western world and also pretty much the Eastern.

"Apart from that he seems to have gone completely rogue. We are an obvious target, mainly for having the temerity to survive when he had decided to eliminate us. For that reason alone I am of the opinion that there is a bomb with our name on it. The other was designated for New York. I realise that the New York bomb was for the benefit of the Muslim extremists, but I have the idea that since he lost his connection with CIA and is currently on the 'Most Wanted' list, he still thinks of New York as a target, although now for personal reasons. If he manages the New York strike he will undoubtedly receive the reward promised for that action.

"I think so far he will perhaps dump one of the bombs in our vicinity. Taking regard of our high level of security, I do not consider he will push the button on us until he can be sure that he will get us all. That means he will probably wait until we are more relaxed on the subject after a little time has passed, and our security not quite so hair trig-gered. Comments anyone?"

Patsy raised her hand "Sir, I think you are suggesting that Heard will be going to New York with one of the bombs now as we speak?"

"I am, Master Sergeant."

"If he has left the other bomb in the vicinity of the base, we have the chance and at least some time to locate it. I presume Heard does not know about our bomb-seeker gizmo?"

"I think that is correct, he was not informed because, as far as I am aware, Doctor Clarke produced a prototype for our use, untested and prior to any field trials. He has promised to keep his discoveries to himself until we have this matter sorted out. Do you have something in mind er....Patsy is it? Can I call you that?"

"By all means, General, most people do. Yes, I do have an idea that I'm sure others have thought of. If Colo-nel Hartog sweeps the area with the gizmo, a second team concentrates on finding the second bomb and Heard. To get to the States he needs to use some sort of underground method. After all he can't just hail a cab, of hop a flight. However well that thing is shielded it cannot be success-fully X rayed. So it had to be a back door entry. It cannot be delivered by light plane, they don't allow over-flights these days and landing at one of the airfields in the vicinity still requires clearance. My guess would be sea passage to the vicinity with offshore transfer into a power boat that can be taken straight up the Hudson River to Manhattan Island for the detonation. Slap-bang in the centre of the pride of the USA." Patsy sat back embarrassed now that she had spoken out so boldly in the presence of so much brass.

Chuck said "I think Patsy has pretty much summed up what we should be concentrating on. I would like to add that in no circumstances should this matter be publicised in any way."

The silence following Chuck's words lengthened, as the significance of his words sank in.

They were interrupted by a knock on the door.

"Come in." Mike called. Sarah entered and, with a smile on her face, presented Mike with a message and a small package.

"Stay with us. Colonel," he said as Sarah turned to leave. She turned and closed the door with her back to it, while Mike read the message form.

***

The general smiled and broke the silence. "Before we go any further I have something to say on a different subject. Since we are all here together I'm happy to announce that in confirmation to my recommendation, the promotion in the field of Master Sergeant Patricia McCoy USAF to the substantive rank of Captain effective this day at 12.00 hours.

He stood and opened the package his wife had given him with the message form." Step forward, Master Sergeant McCoy."

Patsy was shaken and the prod from the smiling Captain Samuels brought her to her feet at attention in front of the general. "I do not need to read all the recommendations that have led to this moment. Most of them came from the people in this room already. He reached out and tore off the Velcro secured stripes from the arms of her tunic and pinned on the silver bars of her captain's rank. "Stand at ease, Captain. Congratulations, you've earned it."

The others in the room all stood and added their support. As she turned to resume her seat she caught the eye of Captain Richard Samuels. He was smiling along with everyone else.

***

Chuck got together with Ali Baranka on the subject of the possible location of Heard, basically to try and trace his movements, and Ali was able to contribute the information that a car driven by a foreigner had crossed from Georgia into Turkey two days ago. The car had been spotted at several places and was apparently en route to Istanbul. Though he had not requested particular surveillance on Heard he had set up a system to cover all strangers travelling through the area on general principles, if only to ensure that he could have some cover on anything that was happening in such an explosive political climate.

He promised to pick it up and follow the trail on the chance that it had been the man they were after.

Captains Samuels and McCoy were detailed with Private David Bowman, all now in plain clothes, to fly to Istanbul and keep in touch with Ali Baranka through the local security office. They would comb the waterfront for information of any Europeans hiring or purchasing a sea going boat suitable for transiting the Mediterranean. It was a slim chance but if Heard were the traveller Ali had turned up then there was the chance that he would try to leave the country that way.

Despite the close security maintained by the Turkish authorities there were still people who regularly passed unseen, unnoticed in the throng of fishing and pleasure craft that cluttered the waters of the Bosporus.

Chapter fifteen

...Join the Air Force and sail?

Two Americans and their British friend blended in pretty well. They settled into their hotel, and from there one of the first things they did was to hire a boat. Captain Richard Samuels was the proud owner of a forty-foot ketch back home. Kept in Chesapeake Bay, he sailed it whenever he got the chance. Among group two he immediately became Captain Pugwash, a name selected unhesitatingly by David Bowman. The hired boat officially named Ceyda immediately became the Black Pig. This apparently was a product of David's childhood TV education that completely mystified both of his American colleagues. As these things happen the names stuck, though it was just between the three of them. The relationship between the three was bound to be relaxed because of circumstances and mutual respect. The two men shared a room in the hotel. Once they moved onto the boat they had a cabin each and shared the cooking and cleaning equally. It was not long after their arrival in Istanbul a foreigner who had beaten them to it, was spotted negotiating for a boat to hire. Ali had set up a contact with the boatyards in Istanbul through the local security office, to report any foreigner trying to hire a sea-going boat.

It was essential that they got a picture of this man so that he could be identified as their target. It was Richard who managed to get a CCTV picture of the man from the charter company. Based on the Special Investigator ID provided by Ali Baranka, he was able to pry the surveillance tape from the Manager for sufficient time to copy the picture of the foreigner. Though slightly pixelated, the likeness was there and they were confident that their man was in the city. They split up the boat charter companies between them, to visit personally. Just to ensure that the rental agencies were aware of the importance of the request. Richard found the yard that had leased a thirty-six foot sloop named Alicia to Charles Nightingale, from Birmingham Alabama, using a valid credit card in that name. Leased for three months the boat was provisioned for a cruise of three weeks initially and had been boarded by Mr Nightingale and a female friend one hour ago. They were expecting to leave just about now. The boat was moored at the main Marina which was apparently the base for the Bosporus cruises.

As soon as he realised that they had found Heard, Richard called the others on his cell phone and arranged to meet at the boat.

The Black Pig was moored in the Samatya sahil Marina, at the suburb Yedikule, further down the coast of the sea of Mamara, between the City and the Bosporus. By the time they sailed they were able to identify the Alicia as she sailed down the sea of Mamara en-route to the Mediterranean.

The sails on their ketch drew well. Though Richard had not been aware of it, David Bowman had been brought up in Christchurch on the south coast of England. He had been messing around in boats ever since he could remember. He had crewed for the wealthy sailors in Christchurch and for the club members in Poole Harbour, both the Royal Poole and Parkstone Yacht Clubs. On the other hand, Patsy was not a sailor, but she was willing to try. Being of a practical nature she picked up the mechanical things involved very quickly, changing sails and the reasons for the raising and lowering. Both her companions were happy to show her how to use the helm, and it was not too long before she started taking her turn at the wheel. She did most of the cooking, because she was best at it, and bluntly she preferred food properly prepared rather than thrown together, which seemed to be the limit of both men's capacities in that particular area. All in all it was a happy crew on the Black Pig and the crew accepted 'Captain Pugwash's' orders willingly, recognising his command abilities and skills in boat handling.

Elmore Heard, to the contrary, was beginning to regret inviting his lady friend along. She was irritatingly competent at boat handling and seamanship. His own skills in that direction were adequate but no more. In addition, despite her exceptional good looks, on the boat she decided that intimate relations were not really appropriate at sea when there were only two people aboard, thus he was feeling more and more frustrated, faced as he was with the scantily clad, gorgeous woman who seemed to present different aspects of her inviting body with every task she undertook. After three days at sea, he had grabbed her as she stumbled over his foot in the cockpit. It was too much, and he did not release her immediately, but kissed the breast that was thrust near his face as he held her.

The elbow descended on the crown of his head, the knee punched his face her other hand grabbed his groin with excruciating results.

As a CIA officer he had been taught to fight dirty, but this sort of conflict was way out in left field. He finished up curled up on the deck. And they said no more about it.

In pursuit the Black Pig was set to catch up in the Mediterranean, not before. Any action they decided to take had to be discrete, out of sight of the rest of the world.

***

Meanwhile at Ciranu Base, the Sky-van departed with its load of rice piloted by Jessica Browning. There were two men on board with her. Sergeant Jake Rider SAS, and Charley Smith, trooper SAS, neither looking the part of a soldier, both had long hair and both dressed in jeans and tee-shirt. Charley was obviously a follower of the Grateful Dead. Jake made do with Led Zeppelin.

The flight had taken off under protest from Hazel Cantrell who was convinced that the presence of Major Vahidi would ensure her safety at Jolfa. It was as well that she remained at the base because the Sky-van was surrounded as soon as it landed. They dropped the ramp and the captain and sergeant who entered without invitation were swiftly assured that their presence was an intrusion. Both had their drawn weapons removed and they were escorted to the tail of the ramp where they arranged for the major to be brought out to the aircraft. They then organised the charity crew to come and collect the rice consigned to them.

The major arrived in rather battered condition, and he was able to confirm that the so-called soldiers were not in fact of the Iranian army. A telephone call to his new deputy produced a cordon of official troops who gathered up the protesting pseudo soldiers and on the major's orders, threw them in cells. The secret police documents they produced were disregarded as forgeries.

Jessica spoke with the charity authorities and arranged for future supplies to be routed from Georgia, by-passing the base at Kars, in effect cutting it out of the loop.

They returned to Ciranu bringing Major Vahidi with them.

Hazel was able to arrange for Mr Vahidi to become the charity representative in the local village outside the base and warehouse facilities were arranged for locally sourced provisions.

Her mechanic Valery Adamski was a renegade Russian—well, Ukrainian, perhaps even a Chechen. He chose his origin to suit the moment, his passport said Russian and dated from the days when the entire USSR was Russian. He had no objection to working in Turkey, the women were friendly, his red hair was popular with them for some reason. He was officially appointed to look after the Sky-van, but it was not long before he took over the maintenance of Mike's beloved Mustang. Valery had a magic touch with piston engines, and the Rolls Royce Merlin was a challenge he could not resist.

For Mike the search for the local bomb was a nightmare he could have done without. None of the people who could be spared wanted to leave. Whenever he found spare personnel he received extra volunteers for the bomb search. Sarah would not leave, having wangled an attachment to the flying wing as Wing Adjutant.

Doctor Alan Clarke had been working flat out on enhancing his radioactivity detector or as the troops called it the 'bomb bug'. Since his return to USA he had sent three further versions each better than the last. The latest could now be used from a helicopter at a strict height of 150 feet. It gave a ground sweep 50 yards wide, at a range of 200 feet. Two further models were on the way.

As it happened they were not needed for this particular exercise as the local bomb turned up with tragic results for two burglars. The house where Elmore Heard had left the bomb was only four miles from Ciranu base, nobody had anticipated that it would be quite so close.

The house had been burgled over one week earlier. The thieves had made off with the shiny aluminium case. It was a sad mistake, by one of them to open the case and find out what was inside. Having found the LED screen he guessed that it was a sophisticated lock of some sort and forced it off with a pry-bar. The aluminium was no match for the steel and it collapsed in a satisfactory manner to allow the interior to be accessed. His disappointment at finding a bunch of electronic wiring and circuit boards was somewhat reduced when he noticed the globe of what he thought was lead, a valuable commodity in this day and age. So the burglary had not been a total failure then. He weighed the lead in his hands possibly two kilos he thought, he wondered idly why it was in two sections, he presumed it made it easier to carry. He admired the beautiful finish, a perfect globe shape. He then put it back in the case until he decided who should have it.

The call to the Medical Centre for help with a patient, gave the game away. The local doctor called for help from the Base Medical Centre. As soon as the base doctor saw the patient she knew what the problem was. She called Colonel Hartog immediately.

A team went out with suits and decontamination sprays to the house where the patient stayed. The bomb was picked up on the hand-held detector as the team approached and they were warned to arrive fully suited. A screened box was used to transport the bomb to the base and the house was isolated and sprayed down. The patient died. His associate was never found and it was presumed he had left the house before the bomb case had been breached.

For Hazel things were looking awkward. In the first instance she was a little troubled by Mahid. She had begun to suspect that there were matters that he was not being completely honest about. This led to a distancing between them that she found uncomfortable.

Ali Baranka came up with the answer, it was a happy one from her point of view. It seemed that there was a possibility that Mahid's wife and child would be returned to him through the good offices of the underground group controlled by Ali's Kurdish friends. Mahid had been advised of the possibility, this accounted for the mood swings he had been experiencing.

Hazel's rift with her godfather was unlikely to be repaired. Since she had her own income from her deceased parent's trust fund, living was not a problem. What was a problem was that there were reasons why Avo Rankin needed her back in touch. Several of his properties were registered in her name. This meant it was difficult for him to vary their use without her physical presence. The other reason was her physical person. Despite the hints and winks of his colleagues, he had maintained a strict protocol in his behaviour where she had been concerned. Nothing was allowed to happen between them that could ever be described as improper.

Now the situation had changed, being found out after all these years, allowing his guard to drop and letting her know just what he was.

He felt that despite all, after all he had done for her over the years, he had been betrayed. That unbidden idea brought thoughts of revenge, and what better vengeance on the woman whose virtue he had defended all these years than to take that virtue and degrade it, turn her into a whore. The though caused a smile to come to his lips though it did not reach his eyes.

"Fedor!" His call caused Fedor to waken with a jerk. "Fedor!" He jumped to his feet and ran through to the office. "Yes, boss?"

"Think of a way that we can get Hazel back here. I wish to arrange a few things to teach that young lady that she belongs to me."

Fedor walked slowly back to his chair. He had worked for Avo for twelve years now and he had been well paid for it. Hazel was something else. He had long craved for her attention and never thought that he had a chance, but now after warning her about Roskoff, perhaps?

He was rather worried about Avo Rankin's remark about Hazel belonging to him. He had always wondered about the fact that this Armenian was godfather to an English girl. He had heard all about the so-called friendship between Cantrell, the father, and Rankin. But something had happened on one of the few occasions that Avo had got drunk, Fedor had helped him to his bed and he had been rambling that it was 20 years since he had taken Cantrell out. He had turned to Fedor and said gripped his lapels speaking directly to him. "We had been partners for years, friends, and then he found out that I had been having an affair with his wife for most of those years. The fool had seen a doctor about his repro...reproductory functions. He was told that he had none. Barren, firing blanks. So who had fathered his daughter? Eh....Eh... I fathered his daughter. I shot him. Stupid bastard, kept shouting he would kill me so I killed him. Melanie came in and screamed at me so I shot her, too." He slumped and was sick, Fedor lifted him and dumped him on the bed. "When she is old enough I will have her......." He muttered and fell asleep.

Fedor sat deep in thought for a long time, could Rankin really be the father of the girl? Perhaps it was just bravado? If he was her father how could he speak of having her?

He shook his head, it was beyond him. He went out to have a talk with the men of his team about the possibilities of a kidnap from an American Airbase.

***

The Sky-van dropped into the circuit at Tbilisi, Hazel flew the circuit and landed, taxiing over to the storage hanger maintained by a group of charities. Her two bodyguards were with her, Jake stepped down and looked around before waving her down, Charley followed as they walked together over to the offices in the corner of the warehouse.

In the office Avo was waiting to see Hazel, Fedor stood behind his chair. Avo rose as they walked in.

"Hullo, my dear, it's good to see you, we have all missed you, especially Fedor here."

Hazel looked at him coldly, 'So I'm here, what did you want me to sign?"

"It was just the deeds for two properties that are held in your name."

"So bring them out and we'll be on our way."

"Oh come now there is no need to be in too much of a rush, I have arranged lunch in the restaurant."

"I hope you enjoy it, I have business to conduct, so bring out the deeds and I will gladly sign them and we can get this unpleasant business over with." Hazel's voice was firm at it was apparent that there was no way she would be conned into eating or drinking with her godfather.

"Very well then! Fedor!" As Fedor reached into his pocket, both Jake and Charley reacted.

"Slowly now," Jake said, "Just keep things open and above board."

Fedor drew out a folded file and passed it to Rankin, who opened it and produced two deeds. Hazel read them both. She signed one and lifted her eyes to Avo Rankin and said, "There is no way that I will sign away my parents' house in London, nor will I sign away their company registered in London. They were both willed to me, and they will stay mine."

Avo looked as if he might protest, then he closed the file. Hazel held out her hand. "I'll keep my documents, thank you!"

Avo passed over the deeds and once more closed the file and passed it to Fedor.

"I will say goodbye then." He spoke with dignity and followed by Fedor he left the office.

When the two men had gone Charley turned to Hazel. There is a team of his men here, Jake has found them and we could be in trouble."

Hazel looked at him quizzically. "Why am I not really worried?"

Charlie grinned, "Boss, Chuck sent a backup team, just in case."

"They wouldn't try anything, would they?" Hazel said hesitantly.

"What do you think those deeds are worth? Especially since your godfather took over control of your father's affairs." Charlie's comment echoed her own feeling in the matter. She decided to find out just what the business was worth as soon as she got back to base.

There were no further incidents, the Sky-van took off with no interference. Hazel never saw evidence of the back-up team, whose presence was part of another operation entirely.

In his Kars office Avo Rankin sat brooding. The business he had handed over plus the deeds to his former partner's house added up to no great sum financially. The two together totalled no more than two-three million at most. What rankled was the fact that he considered them his. Some might think he had stolen them, but in his own mind he had earned them. How to get them back was what was occupying his mind at present.

He rang for Fedor.

"Yes, boss, what would you like me to do?"

"Shut up and listen to start with!" snapped Rankin!

Fedor winced, so that was the way the wind blew. He stood silent, waiting.

"How far are you on with the attack plans for the American Base?"

"The boys are unhappy at the idea, boss, they say the Yanks are well armed and without real heavy ordinance they would have no chance."

"If you had not lost the bomb, we would not be having this conversation. Between you and my ward you have cost me time and money and I am not happy, so what do you intend to do about it?"

For a moment Fedor was at a loss for want of an answer he ventured "The Russians, perhaps?"

There was silence at this suggestion and Fedor wondered if it meant he was deeper in trouble.

Eventually Rankin looked up, "That could be an answer. Tell that cowardly bunch of ingrates sitting eating my food and drinking my booze that when I say jump, I expect them to ask how high, Understand!"

Thus dismissed Fedor left the office and went through to the restroom where his men gathered. As he entered he clouted the first man he saw, and laid him out with the force of his fist.

"Listen, you bunch of layabouts, you get fed and paid and have a roof over your heads. Either you remember that or you walk, and I mean walk. That is if you still can. If I ever hear that you are unwilling to do something because you might get hurt, you will get hurt, depend on it. If I tell you to walk naked into a furnace I expect you to ask how long should you stay. Do you understand me?"

He swung round and looked at the others in the room. "Do you get the message?"

The silence that followed this speech made it clear that they got it.

Meanwhile Rankin was using a satellite telephone to talk to somebody in Chechnya. The conversation was short and cryptic, both speakers on the same wavelength immediately.

A listener may have picked up the odd word perhaps a reference to money. But there were no other references to give the game away. Which was not so good. Ali Baranka ha after all taken the trouble to bug the office for the purpose of gaining information, and it was only because of the previous conversation it was possible to put two and two together and assume an assault was planned using Chechen mercenaries.

Chapter sixteen

...Executive decisions

Major General Michael Summers looked at Colonel Sarah Summers as she lay contentedly in bed watching him dress for work.

"Just between us, what do you think Peter is going to do about Jess?"

Sarah shrugged her shoulders, settling even more comfortably in the bed. "I think they will sort things out in the end, but not if they are pushed. Their problems are both of them have danced around the prospects of marriage several times in their careers. Always something has come up to allow them to excuse themselves and bow out. I think with each other they have reached the point where there are no more excuses they can use."

Mike tied the tie and set it in place neatly. "So it's crunch time, for them both, you think?"

"Yup! Put up or shut up. I hope it will be put up, but...." She shrugged "I just do not know."

***

The objects of this discussion were leaning side by side over the map table in the briefing room of the base. On the table there was a blown up photograph of the border region with Georgia/Chechnya. The Caucuses Mountain chain ran along it for virtually the entire distance. Though there were passes, it was not the easiest way to get to Turkey.

Peter turned to Jessica, there was a smile on his face. She turned to him at the same time and, with her face so close he could not resist the impulse to close the distance and kiss her lightly on the lips.

Startled, Jess drew back and looked at him. "What brought that on?"

Peter reddened, "Sorry Jess...I...I...it just seemed right at the time."

She looked at him seriously, "Well, well, fancy hearing Peter Hamilton apologise for kissing a woman?"

She turned and stood facing him, he just stood there for once at a complete loss.

She stepped forward pushing him back against the table. Reaching up she took his face between her hands and said, "If this is going to happen at last, do the job properly, and she drew his face down to hers and kissed him with a passion that drew his whole-hearted response.

When they returned to earth, she stepped back and looked at him, "Now we have cleared that up at last, let's postpone things until later and get back to work."

Peter smiled, "They have to come by sea." He said. "At least any heavy equipment will." He traced possibilities on the photograph. "It's useful having the CIA owing us, I cannot see us getting this sort of satellite photo service otherwise. Especially for the backside of a jerkwater republic at the end of nowhere."

"Why, Colonel, I am surprised to hear you, of all people, making comments like that." The honeyed Southern tones belied the seriousness of her comment. She knew just how much respect Peter had for the local people of this corner of Eurasia. And what it had cost in lives over the past centuries in the struggle for survival.

The moment passed, and both went back to the problem at hand. An assault on the base would be more likely taken on with hand weaponry plus adapted civilian vehicles. If the transport in is by air, then it would be possible to bring in a few armoured vehicles.

Depending of course what aircraft were at their disposal. Having decided that as far as the immediate defence was concerned it would be necessary to rely on what was in place until more intelligence was gathered, Peter returned to his chair behind his desk. "Why? That is what I would like to know. Why are they doing this? Is it just anti-American, anti-NATO, Muslim extremism or let's go and kick-ass for the hell of it."

Jessica, seated at the other side of the big desk, looked thoughtful. "I cannot help thinking that Heard is the initiator. The bomb was supposed to wipe the slate clean after the Iran raid clean-up failed. We reappeared at the scene of crime against all the odds. Heard started the ball by sending the bomb. By surviving we became unfinished business, and with that in mind the word went out, everyone who fancied a go at us and realised that, on their own they wouldn't have a chance, suddenly was offered the opportunity to join a group in an alliance based on a common enemy.

"The fact that it is based on a criminal organisation means little in the circumstances. The important thing is a chance to beat us up."

***

In the Mediterranean the Black Pig was closing up to the Alicia, There was a fair wind and the waves were no more than two metres. Though the two boats were moving in a lively manner they were able to place Captains Samuels and McCoy on board without any fuss. The autopilot was in operation and there was no one on deck. McCoy cautiously stepped down through the open cabin hatch. The cabin was not occupied and the door to the forward cabin was undone and moving in time with the boat, swaying to and fro.

Richard joined Patsy. With guns drawn and ready, they moved down to the forward end and eased the door open. The woman was lying on the double berth, her legs were spread and tied in position at the ankles her hands were tied extended to the bulkheads on each side of the berth. She was gagged and had obviously been raped, violently. Her head jerked as they came in, but she could not move to see who they were. Patsy ripped the tape from her mouth. The woman said "No more please!" The voice was small and pleading. Patsy said "You're alright, safe now," and she untied the lashings on her wrists while Richard cut the ties around her ankles.

He then left the two women and went through to the main cabin and put water on the stove. Over his radio he told Dave Bowman what they had found, "The trace from the bomb is still moving" Dave said.

"Obviously. Looks like he raped the crew, and left, I suppose she should be happy to have survived. Lie off for a bit and I'll get back to you, over!" Dave signed off, promising to report to Colonel Hartog on the satellite /phone.

The two boats continued on course toward Africa and Gitta Swensen, Elmore Heard's victim, told her story.

She had been crewing a yacht for a regatta series of races, and had agreed to crew for the return to Istanbul. It was there that she discovered her employer wanted a little more in services than he had contracted for. She had jumped ship at the quay. Apart from her passport and a little cash she was stranded.

The boatyard arranged charters and Heard appeared out of the blue, needing a crew to cross to Oran. He looked alright, and she felt confident that with him she could be secure for the voyage at least. When they got sailing she felt even more confident. He had tried it on once only and she ruthlessly put him down. He spoke several times on the satellite /phone he had with him. "After the last call on the phone he came up behind me and dropped a loop of rope round me, trapping my arms. I had no room to use my feet, so that was that. The bastard tied me up and got busy, he raped me then and there. He left me and collected his gear together. I could hear him moving about in the main cabin. He came back and raped me again before he left. I could hear the noise from a quiet engine through the hull, I guessed it was a rib of some sort from way it came alongside. I got the impression that he did not expect me to survive."

Richard had been searching the boat while Patsy was looking after Gitta. He called out that he had found a nasty surprise but nothing to worry about. There followed the noise of him stepping carefully across the cabin floor. At the hatch he stopped. There was a pause, and over-side there was a faint splash. A few moments later there was a whump, as something exploded under water.

The door to the forward cabin opened and Richard's face came into view. "He used a water-triggered fuse, so I dumped it into the briny without the C4 attached. I suppose he was expecting the bilges to set it off in time. Now how much of a lead does he have?"

Gitta looked up, "What time is it?"

"14.50 give or take?" Patsy peered at her watch.

"Then he has been gone three hours." Gitta said.

"He kept me without the blindfold in the cabin until he left the boat, The clock on the bulkhead keeps pretty good time and I noticed the time when he put the blindfold on." She still sounded bitter, but recovering all the time. "Go get the bastard, and shoot him in the groin for me."

Patsy nodded thoughtfully, "Sounds reasonable, I'll see what I can do."

On deck once more she called across to Dave Bowman. "Any signal?"

He called back, "Still moving toward Algiers, now slowly."

"Come alongside, Dave, we should be getting on after him again."

The Black Pig came alongside and Patsy and Richard boarded her. Richard had spoken to Patsy before returning to their own boat. He turned to Dave Bowman. "I think it might be a good idea if you sail with Gitta in the other boat. We need to get after Heard and I don't think Gitta is ready or able to sail on her own yet. We need to keep pressure on Heard and we can't if we are having to keep company with the other boat. If you make direct for Algiers you can put her on the plane for her home and we'll probably be able to pick you up there. If things go wrong for us, then you are going to be close enough to possibly provide back up."

***

Major General Mike Summers was on the telephone to the Chief-of-Staff. "There is a very critical operation on at present. I have a team chasing the last of the nukes and Elmore Heard across the Mediterranean now. They are hoping to connect with the people involved with Heard who funded the entire operation in the first place. I think my place is still here until the operation is completed one way or the other."

The other end of the phone was silent for several seconds, Mike began to think they had been cut off, then "I agree, you stay until this is all over. We will discuss your future when the emergency is over. In the meantime I'll extend your orders to cover this contingency. How are your relations with the Turkish?"

"So far, extremely good. The operation to neutralise the local bomb was handled carefully with the full knowledge and cooperation of the local authorities. I believe you are already aware that the head of the Turkish Intelligence in the region has been on our side from the beginning, and the Kurds have been providing intelligence through him on activities over the borders with Armenia and Iran. I think that the activities of Avo Rankin, already curtailed, are likely to be finalised with prejudice if you take my meaning. There is little I can do in that case. The local people are very upset by the casualties entailed in the bomb transportation, and the interruption of aid to their Iranian brothers." Mike waited and sure enough the Chief-of-Staff had been listening and had comment to make.

"There is no question of you interfering with people over the border, the fact that Rankin operates within Turkey could be embarrassing but if the local people take matters into their own hands there is little you can do except help pick up the pieces, if any. Carry on and keep me in the loop as much as possible. You could be finishing up the tour with your old outfit. Don't quote me but don't be too surprised. Keep up the good work. My best regards to your wife." The call ended and Mike replaced the receiver thoughtfully.

Sarah came into the office with the latest report from the chase. "How did it go?"

"It looks as if I will be finishing the deployment with the group, at least if the Chief has anything to do with it. He actually seems to have some sort of confidence in what we are doing here."

"Of course, and why shouldn't he? You have dug him out of what could have been a deep hole, him and his boy President. He is no fool, his own career is based on the performance of his generals and no matter what the politicians say, you are a good commander and you do work on doing the right thing, regardless of its effect on your career. That makes you special, but it also makes you a target if things go wrong.

Chapter seventeen

...The plotters

In Teheran there is a building that no-one enters without good reason. It is a featureless square lump of concrete complete with the average set of leaking pipes and peeling paintwork. All the windows are protected by iron grills. The innocent-looking door with peeling blue paintwork is actually backed with a steel plate. It has a sophisticated locking system worthy of the other security fittings that protect the headquarters of the SAVAK. (Sazeman-e Ette-la'at va Amniyat-e Keshvar) The Iranian secret police. There was much written and believed about the Iranian security system under the deposed Shah. That hated organisation's reputation pales by comparison to its present day successor.

SAVAK demonstrates ruthlessness to friend and foe alike. Its powers, used apparently wherever its controllers designate.

General Arin Corman, Deputy Director of SAVAK, sat in his office contemplating the report in front of him. Things had been deteriorating along the border with Turkey and Georgia for some time. Putting the situation right had been preoccupying him since the problem had been dumped on his desk.

He was not too worried about Georgia at this time, he had been assured by his Russian sources that the man Putin would soon have Georgia back under his control.

However Turkey was another matter. Ciranu Base that had been the origin of the airstrike that caused the destruction of the nuclear facility in Iran was occupied once more by the followers of Satan. The American general there had been in command at the time of the raid. Though the aircraft involved had not been marked, he knew they came from that base.

The general thought for a little longer before he pressed the button to summon his assistant to join him. The major that came through the door and saluted was every inch a soldier. His uniform was pressed and fitted perfectly to his tall athletic frame. The lean face had sharp intelligent eyes staring straight ahead, as he stood at attention in front of his general.

"At ease, man, I have told you before, when I ring for you, just come in and take a seat. I wish to discuss something with you."

The major, Reza Gilani, removed his hat and sat in the chair on the other side of the general's desk. The dapper handsome major was one of the protégées of the general, son of a second cousin. The general saw no harm in advancing the career of a family member, providing it was to his own advantage. Loyalties within the hierarchy of the Iranian government were transient at best, so family membership gave just a slight edge over gratitude alone, and every little helped.

As Reza sat and waited, he wondered what the old fool wanted this time. Some new wild scheme to depose his boss perhaps; or could it be that he was contemplating another shopping trip to Paris. That would be welcome indeed. It had been some time since he had last managed to get away from the restrictions imposed by the Ayatollah's regime.

Eventually his patience was rewarded, and the general lifted his gaze from the paper that lay on the desk in front of him.

With his penetrating gaze fixed on the Reza, the general slid the paper across the desk to him. "Read that!" He said quietly.

Reza lowered his gaze to the paper placed in front of him. It was headed, 'Most secret', and contained details of an aircraft that he did not recognize. The description was interesting and Reza found he was getting more and more excited as he studied the specifications listed.

"Where....How? Have we got any of these aircraft?.....Sir"

"Interested are we?" The general asked drily.

"Why yes, these are better than the Americans, possibly better than the Euro-fighters, and the newest Russian machines. Where do they come from?"

The general relented and stopped teasing the major. "They are Chinese, and we have three arriving at the end of the month. They will be shipped in by sea in containers partially assembled."

"Will we be able to assemble them here?" Reza was by no means confident that the Iranian Air Force had the technical expertise to maintain such aircraft, let alone assemble them.

"The Chinese are sending an assembly crew and a training team to prepare our own people for the subsequent maintenance of the aircraft."

Reza looked keenly at his general. "May I ask how and why?"

General Corman returned his gaze. "How is easy, if you have enough money or other resources, anything is possible, and we have the money, oil, both. Why is another matter. In the minds of our masters, insults and slights are seldom forgotten. They may appear to be resolved, but that is often protocol, nothing else. Within these walls I have only my own opinion to offer. Though I do not know officially my own thoughts would be that there will be a plan in being already perhaps, to strike a blow against the Americans that destroyed our nuclear processing plant."

Stunned Major Reza Gilani looked at the paper in front of him, then back at his commander. "It will mean war, reprisals, the Israelis will come in, as will the Georgians. It will be suicide!"

"Only if they know it was us." The general said.

"We would be the first people that they would suspect."

"Perhaps the Russians? Don't you think? In the circumstances they make a very tempting target. Already they have clashed with the Americans in Turkey. Putin is sick over the defection of the Russians to Georgia, and is even now plotting to get Georgia back into the Russian federation."

The major started nodding, seeing the way this could go. "If the Russians started things, nobody would even suspect that we would be involved, or have the capability to do a sneak raid on the Americans."

The general nodded, "Why don't you take a look at the possibilities? I have the suspicion that I will be tasked with the operation. The last time they attempted reprisals they entrusted it a political policeman. His rank of general was a joke. This time I think they will give it to the professionals." The general sat back with a self-satisfied smile on his face.

The major rose to his feet realising that the interview was over. As he saluted and turned to leave, the general said "Send my secretary in, and tell the orderly I must not be disturbed for the remainder of the afternoon, I have a lot of planning to do."

As Reza left the office, he bent close to the attractive secretary seated beside the door. "The general will need you for the rest of the afternoon. Tell the orderly he is not to be disturbed for the rest of the day." He noticed the grimace that flitted across the girl's beautiful face; there for an instant, then gone. He sympathised with the girl, but that was life in the Army today. Still smiling to himself, he left the building.

***

The Squadron of Euro-fighters, Typhoons to the RAF who were flying them, arrived at the Ciranu base with a roar of engines and the swish of wet tyres as they followed the leader to the parking area designated for their stay.

Group Captain David Sheldon climbed down from the accompanying jet courier aircraft and walked under the umbrella held by the flight attendant, over to the dispersal area. The Wing commander leading the squadron saluted him as he approached.

"Hullo, Sir; Richard Brooks, stationed at Batman, here on attachment."

"So I believe, Wing Commander; I understand you are looking after my lads properly."

The surprise showed. "Sorry, sir, I was not aware that you were that Group Captain Sheldon."

David laughed, "The rank of Air Commodore was never confirmed." He shrugged. "Cuts in the budget intervened. I still do the job but at the lower rank. The option was to leave, and I am not quite ready for that yet. Shall we stroll over and see who is keeping the coffee pot warm for us?"

The two RAF officers walked the rest of the way over to the offices of the base commander.

Colonel Chuck Hartog USAF greeted the two men as they entered the building. "Hey, David. I thought you were up with the general these days?"

"Hi, Chuck, what about you? Don't they reward virtue in the USAF anymore? This is Richard Brooks, Wing Commander in charge of my old unruly mob. Who is in the chair here now?"

As the three men turned and made their way to the commanding officer's suite, Chuck explained that though Peter Hamilton was the CO. In fact, General Mike Summers was in residence for the foreseeable future, owing to the strained conditions in the area at the present time.

The trio entered the CO's office and found Colonel Hamilton sitting with a large coffee cup in hand chatting to Lieutenant General Mike Summers. Then, Colonel Jessica Browning entered through the other door and introductions over, the group of friends were soon at ease scattered round the generous room, used for briefings in other circumstances.

***

"You have another crisis here with the Russians?" Sheldon asked.

"Not the Russians this time though it would never surprise me to hear that Putin had been undermining the leadership of the Ukrainian and Georgian Governments. His latest statements and the support he has been giving to the pro-Russian elements is definitely showing signs of success. No it's a little closer to home this time. We have in this country the usual assortments of villains, one in particular had got hold of some so-called suitcase bombs for use by Iran amongst others. We were put on to it by our old friend Ali Baranka.

"Chuck went out with a scouting group and bagged one of six, one of the scientists who had been working on the bombs managed to dispose of three others, another was found in the vicinity of this base, and defused. The last is en-route to New York to blow up and enrage the US to attack Iran and start the war to end wars. More or less."

"More or less? I would regard that as more rather than less. Anyway how do you know it's on its way to New York?"

"The team we have chasing it has told me so."

"I see, you have a team chasing it, so where is it now?"

"Approaching Algiers by sea, last I heard."

"And the chasing group?"

"Approaching Algiers by sea, last I heard."

The update given, Mike relaxed back in his chair and not having been advised of the day to day activities of the NATO force, it being the responsibility of Colonel Hamilton, he asked "What brings you here?"

"Would you believe joint NATO exercises?"

"But you were promoted to Air Commodore surely?"

"Britain is undergoing big cutbacks in service personnel, I was one Air Commodore too far. It being either revert to Group Captain or out of the RAF, so here I am. Onlooker on behalf of our leaders, poised to condemn the slightest mistake."

"Well I'm sure I speak for all present, you are welcome as you always will be where this National Guard Unit operates. So how is Katerina?"

"She has gone to visit her friends at Batumi. Gregor Volkov is considering standing for the Georgian Parliament, he is unhappy about the way too many Russian Russians are getting in on the act. Katerina is there to drum up local support, for a week or two anyway. She will be with us in two weeks' time for the final week of the exercise."

***

The Black Pig overhauled the fishing boat delivered to Heard when he left the Alicia and abandoned Gitta on the final leg to Algiers. The rib used by the delivery man had long gone.

The boat's radar was of the primitive variety. The former owner of the boat decided not to waste money unnecessarily, on an American fool whom he would never meet.

The proximity of the followers seemed completely disregarded until, with a bump, the Black Pig came alongside and the chasers boarded.

Patsy McCoy and Richard Saunders found Elmore Heard sitting beside the wheel of the fishing boat. He made no sign that he had heard them. The only sophisticated electronics on board the craft was the GPS linked autopilot, and this was adjusting the wheel periodically, maintaining a mean course that had been programmed in to its memory.

Elmore Heard was quite dead, and had been for several hours at least. When Richard ran the Geiger counter over the stiffening corpse it only registered background radiation. Whatever had killed him it was not exposure to any lethal rays given off by badly insulated radioactive material.

Richard sighed with relief. "No irradiation here."

He called out.

"Thank god for that." Patsy replied. "I have found the bomb. It looks as if it has been kept carefully. There has been no setting loaded, so I presume he was actually going to set it off in New York.

There was no way for them to know how Heard had died. Neither of them were doctors. Richard suggested a heart attack, or perhaps an aneurism, even a stroke?

Patsy took the bomb over into the Pig while Richard searched the body and the luggage that Heard had brought with him. There were papers, and several weapons, pictures and money. Lots of money.

Patsy returned to help transfer the things he had found to their boat. "Viking funeral perhaps, with a little C4 to help it along?" She suggested.

"I guess, yes it would be better than the alternatives. Let's do it."

Between them they ripped up the upholstery and tore out bits of the old wooden framework from the table and bunk. Then with the remaining luggage they constructed a pyre in the centre of the boat. The body went on top, still frozen in the seated position that they found him in.

Neither considered Heard had earned any consideration. The stepped across to their own boat and Patsy pointed the 'Very' signal pistol from the boat's safety kit, at the open cabin door and fired the flare into the stacked heap of material under the dead man. There was a violent splash of red light from the flare swiftly lost in the heap of paper and cloth and broken wood. Then the combustible content of the flare, asserted its power and flames rose and danced through the cabin of the fishing boat. They motored away from the burning boat, and from a safe distance watched, standing side by side as the flames reached hungrily through the timber framework of the boat. The explosion was not as loud as they thought it would be but the shower of fire was spectacular for at least 10 seconds. Then it was gone, just a drift of smoke across the water, shredding and ripping as the wind dispersed it.

Under full sail they made for Algiers to collect trooper David Bowman.

Richard reported back to General Summers on the satellite phone, merely that the chase was over and the team were all unharmed. "The task has been achieved, despite the terminal loss of carrier. With retrieved item, we will be returning to rendezvous with the aircraft where we left it, in ten days' time."

***

"Well done!" the relief in the voice of Mike Summers was easy to discern. "Take it easy and look after the luggage, report if there are any problems."

Robert closed the phone and put back in its case.

"Ten days? We will be back within a week." Patsy said.

Richard turned. Reaching out, he took her chin in his hand and kissed her gently, then as she responded with enthusiasm, he took her in his arms, broke off the kiss and whispered, "Three days to Algiers, maybe four?"

Chapter eighteen

...The lady said no

Hediyeh Kashani, Hedi to her friends, did not like the position that she had been allocated by her masters at SAVAK.

Her work for the Secret Police was forced by circumstance anyway, and the type of work had come about after her initial induction into the organisation.

The rape of her and her sisters occurred during the series of disturbances following the early imposition of strict Muslim rule. The sudden reversion to religious fervour had no effect on the cruel and lustful behaviour of the revolutionary followers of Islam. It made no difference that the family had committed no crime. Pretty girls had been targeted as soon as the street youth groups had been let loose.

Her subsequent recruitment had allowed the rest of her family to survive and live within the constraints of the times. In her own case, the assaults that she had suffered had resulted in the loss of any chance of having children. Damage caused to her at a time when the child she and her husband had conceived only three months before had been killed in her womb. Her husband had been made to watch her rape, and then she had been made to watch the abuse he suffered, before they finally killed him.

When she recovered, she had been told that the people involved had all been punished. She knew it was a lie, in her work she had come across two of the men involved. Both men, thanks to her training by her new masters, were now dead. They had been made well aware of the reason they were dying, and of why they were made to suffer in the process. It had not made anything better, it was just something that was necessary, in her own mind.

Here, in her present post, she was expected to submit to the attentions of her boss, to make sure that she was in-dispensable personally, as well as officially.

It was not a particularly pleasant way to spend the odd afternoon, but since the loss of her husband that area of her life had been of little interest to her. The regimes' attitude ensured that the people she was expected to service, were at least free from infections.

Discovery of such things led to instant dismissal if not worse.

The general was a poor lover, his idea of sexual grati-fication was basic. Hedi found that if she presented herself ready to perform, it was soon over. A minimum of groping followed by a rapid invasion. His self-obsessed satisfaction took little time. All that was needed thereafter was the compliments on his prowess and it was all over.

Hedi left work early that day, avoiding contact with Major Reza Gilani who always made the effort to get close to her at every opportunity. She had no illusions, all the ob-vious attempts to get into her pants were a cover for his real aim, to recruit her as one of his private network of moles, planted through the various ministries and headquarters here in Teheran.

She was walking extremely carefully around that particular problem. Eventually she may need to succumb to his demands, but as long as she could avoid it she would.

At home and locked in her own room she used the small shower room to scrub herself clean of the smell of her afternoon's activities.

Afterward dressed in her dressing gown she sat at her dressing table and drew out the tape she had retrieved from the recorder installed under the General's desk. Slipping it into her Walkman, she listened to the conversations recorded during the day.

Satisfied that she had learned all that was to be gleaned from the tape, she turned to her shower room and lifted a section of floor that appeared to be a section of tiles, integral to the backsplash. In the recess disclosed was a cased satellite phone.

Hedi plugged the phone into the electric socket and waited for it to warm up. As she waited she spent the time summarising the information she had acquired.

She checked the phone was charged and the connection was set. Then she pressed the connect switch and spoke. "This is Cassandra."

The reply was instant. "Mark Anthony here, report!"

Hedi read out her summarised version of the tape she had downloaded.

"Do you know what the aircraft are called?" Mark Anthony asked.

"I only know they are Chinese aircraft, modern, new even, they said they can compete with the latest Eurofighter and are better than most of the American aircraft in service at present. They are expected to arrive by sea, at the end of this month. I have seen elsewhere that there is a consignment of small arms expected to arrive at Bandar Abbas at the end of this month. There are no other sea arrivals at either Bandar e Shapur, or Bandar Abbas, for seven days on either side of this shipment. I suspect that the aircraft are part of the arms shipment."

"Well done Cassandra. Would you like us to extract you, now your family have moved to Oman?"

"Do you think I am at risk?" Hedi asked.

"Reza Gilani is taking a serious interest in you. He has been investigating your background and I think the time is right to bring you in."

"How can I get away?"

"There is a plan in place for just this situation. Don't wait, get into your car and drive to the Airport Air freight section. Call at the office of the Sagem Security Corporation. Mr Sawali will look after you, password Cassandra. Good luck, I look forward to meeting you when you arrive here."

Hedi did not waste time. She packed up the telephone and packed an overnight bag. The telephone was put into the base of the bag which had wheels at the corners. Then she dressed in travelling clothes and slipped on the veiled head-dress that was now expected of all women when outside their home.

***

The small Fiat started as always, immediately. She set off in the early evening through the traffic-filled city streets on her way to the airport. As she turned out of the side road on to the main street, she noticed a Land-rover turn down the neighbouring street which led to her family house. She trod on the accelerator and at the top legal speed made off down the road. Once on the Rajael Highway she was able to push her speed up to 120 kph and she managed to sit in the stream of traffic for most of the way. The 12 k drive passed swiftly and twenty minutes later she turned into the area beside the Khomeini Airport signposted Air Freight only.

The Sagem Security Corporation was accessed down a side street from the main artery through the freight area. Hedi parked in the visitor parking area among several other vehicles. She walked over to the office and peered through the window before ringing the bell.

Through the glass she could see two men facing the seated man in the office. The nearest man had a gun in his right hand. She recognised him as a member of SAVAK stationed in midtown Teheran. From her handbag she retrieved the Walther automatic, issue for all SAVAK agents. She worked the action and tried the door handle. It was unlocked. Opening the door she stepped through in one smooth movement. "Mr Sawali?" She said brightly, her gun concealed at her side. The man at the desk made to get up, but the gun in the SAVAK agent's hand, came into view and stopped his movement. The whole scene confirmed Hedi's opinion and she brought her gun up in turn.

"I am a SAVAK officer. Drop your gun now!"

The agent with the gun started to turn. "Stand still and drop your gun or I shoot."

Reluctantly the agent laid his gun on the desk saying, "I am an agent of SAVAK as well, and this man is under suspicion."

"Stand still!" Hedi repeated, then "Who is the man with you?"

"He is the man who reported this man Sawali. He is an informant employed by me."

"Is there anyone else with you, or are you acting alone?"

The agent started to say I am al…. part of a raid group."

Sawali shook his head.

"Mr Sawali, does the name Cassandra mean anything?"

Sawali, nodded without speaking.

Hedi fired twice, the gun making a loud noise in the confines of the office. The agent and his informant dropped both men shot through the upper body, Hedi did not hesitate she stepped forward and shot both fallen men again this time in the head.

Turning to Sawali, "Can you dispose of them and their vehicle?"

***

Sawali picked up his telephone and barked. "Clean-up crew here now. Cappa, bring the SAVAK car inside and collect the keys for the lady's car and bring that in, too.

Men appeared from within the warehouse behind the office. Hedi picked up the agent's gun and unloaded it, replacing her own magazine with the fully loaded one from the other gun. She snapped the remaining bullets from her own magazine and dropped them into her purse.

The two bodies were already gone by the time she followed Sawali into the warehouse. At the far end a twin Beechcraft stood with the cargo doors open, there was a group of people stacking boxes and a truck with a part-loaded container, waiting at the door.

Sawali took her arm and steered her to the part-loaded container, up close she was able to see the chair with foot and headrest sited in a crate within the stack of other goods inside the container.

He gave her a bag containing two bottles of water and a packet of sandwiches, paper towels and two miniatures of Brandy. "The chair is a commode if needed," he whispered. "but you should be out in twelve hours at the most, at best in three."

She turned to him. "Thanks."

"No, it is thanks to you, that bloody agent would have made me pay, on the basis of some trumped up charge. It would have made it necessary to either close down, or kill him. So, thank you, Cassandra and good luck."

Hedi was not happy when the case was closed around her. More crates and cases were loaded to fill the container and conceal her presence. It was dark and confined and though she did not suffer from claustrophobia, it was not the most comfortable or cheerful journey. The reaction from the shooting set in, and for several minutes she shivered and suffered. The picture of the two men falling, surprised at the sudden attack. It had been necessary to finish them off she knew, but it was still a traumatic experience and she thought she would never get used to the killing, however justified.

The container was shipped that night. It arrived in the warehouse in Bahrain eight hours later. In the security of the closed warehouse the goods were unpacked and the confining case opened. Hedi tottered out and made it to the restroom with a sigh of relief. Her case was placed inside the door of the room while she was still in the shower washing the dust and smell of Iran from her body.

Dressed in western clothes once more, summer blouse, chinos and slip on shoes, feeling comfortable finally she walked into the office trailing her case.

The man behind the desk produced an American passport, and a set of documents, credit cards, and a wad of dollar bills. He was American, clean-shaven, with brown hair and blue eyes. He was in a wheelchair.

"Take the next flight to Istanbul Airport, check into the Holiday Inn, You will be contacted by either Richard Samuels or Patsy McCoy. They will escort you on by private jet to meet," the man studied his written instructions. Then, "Mark Anthony?"

She nodded. "In my own name?"

The American looked impatiently at her, "Of course not, look at your passport, please!"

Hedi looked inside her passport, the photograph was her, but the name was Margaret Stewart, from Tallahassee, Florida."

She looked at the American, eyebrow raised?

"When you speak English, you have a slight French/American accent. So you come from Cajun country." That seemed all the explanation necessary as far as he was concerned. "Leave me your gun and ammunition, and empty out all your personal things onto the desk here."

With a fatalistic shrug, Hedi emptied her handbag onto the desk. The clutter of objects that fell out were swiftly sorted through. Two piles were rapidly made.

When he had finished, the American pushed one pile over to Hedi, the other was pushed into a bag containing the gun and ammunition. "This will be saved for you until after the assignment is over." There was no argument or explanation. "A car is outside to take you to the airport, get your ticket with the credit card. Sign it first," he added.

Having signed the new name on the back of the credit card, and the store cards, she swept the pile of bits and pieces into her handbag. Picking up her trolley bag she went out to the waiting car into an uncertain future.

***

The Black Pig made the final turn into the Marina, and came alongside the pontoon with a flourish. Richard and Patsy gathered their gear together while David Bowman went ashore to arrange the car to take them to the airport.

When they were satisfied, and had handed over the boat to the charter company, they drove off through the streets of Istanbul.

They were all silent as David found his way through the traffic, each occupied with their own thoughts.

For Richard there was still the shock of meeting someone who had, within such a short time, completely captivated him. The fact that it seemed to have happened in the same way to Patsy was amazing. The trip to Algiers had been a real voyage of discovery for both of them.

***

"Boss, boss there is a problem." David Bowman's voice brought him back to earth.

"What?"

"We are being followed by a grey Mercedes. It has four or maybe five people in it."

"Let's take them on a detour, turn right now!"

Their vehicle swung right suddenly, leaving the main road and darting down a side road that led to private houses away from the shops and bars. The grey car followed the tyres screeching with the stress of the sharp last minute turn.

Bowman swung left then right then left again losing the grey car that dropped further behind with each turn. Finally they lost it altogether.

"Get to the hotel pronto, I want to pick up our passenger as fast as possible and get out of here.

Patsy, call the Hotel, ask to speak to Miss Margaret Stewart."

Richard pulled his gun out and checked the action.

Patsy spoke to the Hotel and was connected to Hedi. "Is this Miss Stewart?"

Hedi said "Yes..s." Hesitantly.

"Cassandra?"

Hedi answered swiftly "Yes."

Patsy said " I am speaking for Mark Anthony, Get ready to leave immediately, there is opposition about. Richard is 6ft tall, dark hair, blue eyes, dressed in blue shirt and khaki chinos, I am 5ft 6 fair hair in white blouse, and jeans. We will be in the foyer in five minutes. Are you armed?"

"No, well, I have a blade."

"Keep it handy. See you in five." Patsy rang off.

The car made it in three minutes, and Richard and Patsy were out and into the hotel before the car was completely stopped.

As they entered the hotel they saw Hedi come out of the elevator with her trolley bag. As she stepped out two men closed in on her one from each side. Richard and Patsy split up and as the men steered Hedi toward the side entrance Richard bumped into the man at his side sending him sprawling across the floor, his gun flying loose and hitting the reception desk. Patsy slammed the other man under the ribs with her straight fingers, driving the breath from his body with an explosive whoosh.

Richard and Patsy took Hedi's arms and steered her back through the main door to the waiting car.

David let the clutch out as the doors were closing.

The tail car was still around the corner waiting for the pickup. By the time the first man had recovered his weapon and run to the front door, the car was gone.

He turned in disgust and hauled his companion to his feet and they left through the side door. "Airport!" He snapped at the driver. Then Major Reza Gilani sat back and contained his impatience, preparing a suitably story to explain why he had failed to arrest the runaway Hedi Kashani.

***

The Lear jet took off for the short flight to Ciranu Base. As it gained height, it was joined by two Tornados from Ankara Base. When the F18's from Ciranu approached, they waggled their wings and peeled off back to their own base.

Chapter nineteen

Reprisals?

Colonel Chuck Hartog was on the tarmac when the Lear jet arrived. The door dropped down. Captain Patsy McCoy and Trooper David Bowman exited, Bowman carrying the aluminium bomb case. Captain Samuels came next followed by Hedi Kashani.

Chuck acknowledged the salutes from the team and when Hedi appeared he stepped forward and too her hand. "Cassandra, I presume. I am Mark Anthony."

The others looked on astonished when Hedi flung her arms round the colonel's neck. He hesitated then his arms hugged her tight as her tears ran unheeded.

The release of tension after months of fear and disgust was at last allowed. She did not care who saw it, she was free at last and Mark Anthony, her handler had made it happen.

For Chuck, the feeling created by the close embrace of this beautiful woman was dramatic. His one-time wife had divorced him after the first year of his posting to Iraq. She had said she loved him but could not live alone for long periods. He believed that, had there been children, it would have made the difference. They had been sensible about the whole idea of family, they had decided to wait until they were in a position to afford the extra expense involved, of course it had never happened. He had distrusted women ever since. The few attempts at meeting other women had never really worked. The establishment of the contact with Cassandra had happened because Ali Baranka needed a secure 24/7 answer service for the agent who had inherited the satellite phone used by her former husband. He had been one of the richer contacts that Ali had set up during the turmoil of change brought about by the arrival of the Ayatollah. Her recruitment had followed her discovery of the satellite phone. She had found it during the time she was being trained by SAVAK. When it had come to light, she had realised immediately what it had meant. Her first call to the fixed frequency had found Ali. It had been a shock for him as he knew his agent had been killed.

Hedi had explained who she was and suggested that the career that had been laid out for her could produce information of use. Over the next two contacts they had arranged a routine and code words. Because of the nature of Ali's own work it had been necessary to set up a permanent contact. That had been where Chuck had come in, he had run agents in Iraq in both wars and so had been perfect to become the contact Mark Anthony for Cassandra. They had never, up to now, met, but the close contact through the phone calls had created a bond between them that neither had realised up to now.

He suddenly became aware that the others were looking at them curiously, so he gently disengaged Hedi's arms and staying close he steered her over to the office block and into his office.

"Hedi? May I call you that?"

She smiled and nodded, "Of course, but what do I call you?"

Confused for a moment, he realised their entire relationship had been conducted between them as Cassandra and Mark Anthony.

"My name is Charles Hartog, Chuck to my friends."

"Do I qualify?" Hedi said with a small smile.

"Do you need to ask?" He answered.

And that was that. Colonel Chuck Hartog USAF, rejoined the human race, and Hedi Kashani learned that her life was not over, in fact it was just restarting after an intermission.

The de-briefing of Hedi took place over the next week. Information that she had not realised she had, came to light.

Her program then was to visit her sisters and mother in Oman to ensure that they were safe and settled. But her return to Ciranu was assured, with a post on the base as liaison between Ali Baranka and the American allies.

To ensure that there would be no problems with her situation at the end of the Deployment a Green card was arranged, and a passport issued in her own name.

Having noticed Chuck Hartogs' reaction, Jessica Browning mischievously suggested; by marrying Hedi, Chuck could save the administration involved.

In fact between the two people in question there was now a clear understanding. If nothing changed meanwhile, they would discuss marriage after they returned to the United States.

It has to be said that Chuck Hartog still found it hard to believe that he had fallen so completely. He had never met the woman before the occasion on the tarmac, but from that point on there was no question in his mind, or apparently in Hedi's.

***

Revenge was taking longer than Avo anticipated. His contact in Chechnya was dragging his feet. It had been over two weeks since he had been promised there would be action and nothing had yet happened. He had discovered that the Americans on the base where Hazel had taken refuge, were scheduled to leave in two weeks. He called Fedor.

"What are the Chechens doing? I thought they were ready to act last week."

Fedor stood in front of the desk looking at his boss. He was worried. He had never seen Rankin in such a furious state.

"Speak to me, idiot! What are the Chechens up to? They promised action in return for a fortune in weapons, so where are they?"

"They started out three days ago, boss, they have heavy gear with them, it will just take time for them to make it from Russia to Turkey. I spoke to them yesterday, They will be in position to act by Friday, in five days."

Avo Rankin glared at Fedor for a moment, then he leapt to his feet and strode up and down the length of the office. Calmer now, he said "Well, I suppose that is better than nothing. His impatience was driving him relentlessly, "Isn't there something we could do to stir things up? I hate this sitting around waiting for other people to act. I want that bitch in my hands." His hands curled into fists slowly, and his face hardened into a grimace of sheer malevolence. That was when Fedor realised that finally, his boss had lost it. The frustration of the loss of the bomb, combined with discovering his ward's part in that loss, seemed to have snapped something in his mind. All he was really thinking about was revenge upon the Americans, and his desire to inflict pain and humiliation on Hazel before killing her.

To Fedor it was obvious there was not a lot of time left, especially if he wished to survive this latest madness. When he left the office that afternoon, he returned to his rooms, where he carefully selected what he regarded as essential things. These he packed ready to leave. Carefully concealing the bag among the empty suitcases stacked in his closet, he sat down to plan his departure.

***

The Chechen was actually approaching the position he had selected where he could view the enemy base. He was worried because he had only received promises, plus a few weapons from that Armenian bastard Rankin. There was as yet no money, and money was the real reason the Chechen had for undertaking this idiot scheme. The weapons he dismissed so casually were in fact sufficient to re-equip his entire company. They had not been issued of course because his men were already armed; they each had an AK47 and plenty of ammunition. What else would they need against an airbase in a neutral country. The whole business should be a walk-over. How did the Americans put it? 'A walk in the park'.

He settled down with his binoculars and studied the airfield and the defence perimeter. He noticed the odd guard, and the circulating APC weapon carrier that made periodic sweeps around the outer fence. He did not see the network of tripwires that could be armed at the flick of a switch, as suggested by their Kurdish allies.

He was making up his mind already where he would begin the assault. Satisfied that his men would be able to manage with their existing weapons, he was already working out where he could sell the weapons supplied by Rankin. They could actually increase his profit margin over one hundred percent, provided the bastard actually paid up.

Danek Abramov was not what anyone might call the fatherly type when it came to leading his men. His reaction to argument was usually to pull out his gold-plated Colt .45 automatic and shoot the offender. If the man was not killed he might get another chance, but only if ammo was short at the time. He always had such statistics at his fingertips, it had saved the lives of some, and more important saved Danek's life, simply because of this instinctive awareness that told him there was another round in the magazine, or not!

So here they were, and not even Rankin was aware of it. The problem was none of the heavy weapons had yet arrived. The other thing that Abramov admitted to himself was whether the Americans knew he was there. If they didn't he could attack, take them completely by surprise, and do the business without recourse to the heavy weapons, that were so expensive to fund.

He lay there for several more minutes contemplating his choices. Finally, making up his mind, he rose from his place on the reverse slope of the rise in the ground. He put the binoculars away with care. Though they were taken from a dead Russian, they would have been expensive to replace. Then he walked over to his command car. The Land-rover Freelander had been modified and now carried a clutch of aerials that allowed him to connect with what-ever mobile forces he had at his disposal. At the moment there was only one other mobile unit under his command on the spot. That was the companion Freelander on the other side of the base.

He ordered the driver to connect him with the other vehicle.

"Rocco, what does it look like over there?"

The voice from the other vehicle sounded raspy and hung-over., "Piece of cake, boss. They are all asleep and wide open."

"Are your men in place?"

"All ready, and raring to go." The man at the other end was not Chechen, he was a mercenary named Howard Rockingham-Evans, from Brentford, west of London, England. Despite Danek's reluctance to pay out unnecessary money, Rocco did well because he was good at what he did. A former British army soldier trained as a paratrooper then, at Hereford for the SAS, he was dropped from the course because of excess zeal in unarmed combat that resulted in the crippling of two of his fellow trainees. It also meant the end of his military career.

His present situation was earned during the campaign against the Russian army, when it had invaded Danek's country. Rocco had found a home in the forces of Chechnya, the brutality that was standard activity in the ranks suited him, mainly because his skills and genuine ability gave him an edge in the many conflicts that he survived. When Danek broke away from the Army and went private, Rocco came with him. No one knew his other name, to all he was just Rocco.

Danek said "Take it easy to start with, just slip in carefully and see if they have been prepared."

"Got it boss, I'll take it easy, over and out."

The trip wires were not live, but they were still trip wires, the claymores stayed unblown, but the warnings went out to the defence units. The reaction was instant. Bullets sprayed the area where the trip wire had been jerked. The man involved never knew what hit him. The other four of his squad also became casualties when in

258.........Hell is another place/O'Neil

haste to get back to their friends the squad hit another wire, that was now live, and the claymore for that section fired and the lethal spread of ball bearings caught them all. Three plus the man they were carrying died on the spot the other two made it back on their stomachs, leaving their dead behind.

The radio squawked. Danek picked up the handset.

"Yes?" He said.

Rocco said "Oopse! They have hidden depths. I have three dead one wounded one unhurt."

"What happened?"

"They have a net of tripwires. Inert they give warning; live they set off Claymore mines. They now know we are her, or at least that there is someone here."

"Has there been any activity?"

"I have seen none, it is almost as if they have electronic security only, but I don't trust them. There is something nagging at the back.....Fuck! They're here"

The radio went off in a hurry.

"What's happening?" Danek shouted.

The operator who was seriously scared of his boss said "Sir, they have cut us off, no one can hear you."

Danek looked at the man, who quailed under his gaze. Then he turned and walked off.

The operator sighed with relief and powered down the set, leaving the receiver open.

The radio squawked fifty minutes later. "It's Rocco, get the boss!"

The operator answered, "Wait one." He ran to the small encampment and knocked at the door of the HQ Tent which had a wood-frame entry section.

"Come!" The voice of the boss was still not happy.

The man entered, "Sir, I have Rocco on the radio."

Danek rose to his feet and followed the man to the Freelander. Picking up the handset he said "Yes."

"Rocco here boss, I managed to get out of Dodge with half of my men, 15 were captured before they realised there were troops around. Two sentries were killed, which saved me doing it. Boss, these guys are good, we'd better wait for the big guns before we tackle the base."

"Thank you for the advice, Rocco, I will consider it in due course. Meanwhile, get your men back here in a hurry. If what you say is true we need to go to ground for a while."

Danek put the handset down thoughtfully. Time was running out, two weeks left to perform, then the Americans would be gone. There must be a way, maybe he had not given it enough thought. Still deep in thought he returned to his tent and lay down on the cot.

***

Chuck Hartog smiled at the report he had just been given, sixteen prisoners, mostly Chechen. He picked up the phone and called David Sheldon. "Is Katerina there David?"

"Yes she is, is this to do with the skirmish today?"

"Possibly, put her on"

Katerina came to the phone "Yes, Chuck, what can I do?"

"I have sixteen Chechen prisoners and I cannot talk to them, can you help please?"

Katerina laughed, "Chechens, wow! Of course, I will be right over."

***

As it happened there was little they could tell. When Katerina asked them about what they were doing in Turkey, they did not realise they were actually in Turkey. All they could or would say they were promised payment and reward if they succeeded in their task.

In Chuck Hartog's office, after the interrogation, Katerina said that the men were part of the force brought by Danek Abramov. "One of them knows more, but he is not talking, for some reason he believes that he will be rescued."

"Let's see what the pictures show." Chuck Hartog said, his curiosity piqued; pressing the switch to the intercom he said "Re-run the CCTV for the west side of the base perimeter."

"Yes sir, coming up now." The screen of the wall mounted TV lit up showing the area on the west side of the perimeter fence. The screen showed a fixed view of the area, taken from several cameras mounted at intervals along the fence. The cameras were minute, and unless a watcher was aware they were merely part of the poles they were mounted on. The clarity of the pictures was breathtaking. The door of the office opened and the analyst came in with a laser pen. With the pen he high-lit the location of the intruders, then he pointed out the arrival of the base security team. The watchers saw the capture of the prisoners, they also saw the escape of the rest of the group. They followed the progress of the escapees along the fence to the south, where they joined one of the many tracks that crisscrossed the land in the vicinity of the base. The escaping group passed out of range of the cameras as the party started to turn eastward.

Chuck said "Best guess of their destination?"

The analyst, Sergeant Harry Talbot USAF, said, "Best guess, observation point on the east side of the base, probably on the reverse slope of this hill." He pressed a switch in his hand and the scene changed to the view on the eastern fence cameras. The hill was highlighted though there was nothing to be seen at present.

At Chuck's nod the Sergeant switched off the recording and selecting another channel on the TV, brought up the map of the area. The hill in question was painted and the details enlarged until the area filled the screen. "As you can see," Chuck said, "There is plenty of room to park any vehicles at the foot of the hill in that area of trees at the foot of the downslope.

"The hill is approachable through the scattered woodland that extends for several miles to the east, and there are several roads that an intruder could take that would provide cover almost all the way to that hill.

"Provided the intruders keep their heads down and stay out of sight of our aircraft, they can watch without detection as long as we are unaware. However since we are aware we have used our infra-red equipment from the regular CAP patrols." He nodded to Sergeant Talbot, who pressed the switch on his magic box once more.

The screen of the TV now showed a view of the eastern side of the fence and then the camera rose up in the air revealing the far side of the hill. The screen lit up with a scatter of red highlights each of which represented a warm body.

"We counted forty-seven," Sergeant Harry Talbot volunteered. "In addition we located three vehicles on the track at the foot of the hill." His laser focussed on faint red smears at the foot of the hill among the trees there. "We believe there are more, sufficient for the entire group, the others were not recently used. We have also detected high power transmissions from the site though as yet we have not managed to match the sequences to eavesdrop. We are working on it."

"Thanks, Sergeant, I'll take it from here." Chuck swung round to the others in the office.

"Comments?"

Lieutenant General Mike Summers stirred in his chair and smiled bleakly. "Have we any idea who is behind this?"

Colonel Peter Hamilton, Base Commander said "We have at least one, possibly two or even three suspects. Iran, Russia, and Mr Rankin, who needs to keep his Mafia friends happy. All have an interest in neutralising this base."

Hedi Kashani, now acting as liaison between Ali Baranka and the US Base, spoke for the first time. "I do not think this is the Iranians. They are, as you are aware, working on their own scheme which they anticipate will result in the obliteration of the base and all personnel here. We are keeping a close eye on their progress and it seems that they are keeping to their schedule for an attack in ten days' time. This is not their style, the priority for them is the air assault which has the benefit of being poetic justice as far as they are concerned. We bombed them, they retaliate by bombing us."

Katerina said, "My guess is Rankin. These men are Chechen mercenaries. The Russians are working long term on regaining Georgia with their own program. They are unlikely to use Chechens, after the problems they have had recently with that part of the world, although that could be the very reason they would use them. I would vote for Rankin as the culprit, it is in line with the complete ruthlessness of the character of the Mafia and typical of their willingness to spend serious money in the cause of revenge."

Chuck looked round at the others present, each was nodding in agreement with Katerina.

"Right. Working on that assumption, it is in our own interest to sort this out fast, before they get a chance to import heavy artillery.

Chapter twenty

Attack!

Rocco and his remaining men returned to Danek's camp. He approached Danek warily, the hand in his pocket held a cocked automatic. He need not have worried. Danek was angry at the report he had received from the heavy weapons group who were still travelling across country, half a day away.

Danek knew he needed the heavy weapons urgently. If the base reacted fast, they could be in trouble, so the sooner they moved out the better. He turned to Rocco when he returned, "We are going to have to move fast. The heavy gear should be with us by this evening, so we need to set up and be ready by dawn. Can you see any problem?"

"Sounds good to me boss, I'll get my boys fed and we'll make sure we have the weapons pits ready for when the others get here."

The surveillance team of Special Forces watched the interaction between Danek and Rocco, their directional sound equipment picked up most of the conversation between them. The report back to Chuck at the base caused him to update action to the evening of the same day. In the main hanger the Special Forces units and the Airfield protection unit were preparing weapons and equipment for the night attack scheduled. Chuck's re-worked schedule was accepted and the preparations speeded up. At 16.40 that afternoon in the gathering dusk, the 70-member strong party under the command of Captains Saunders and McCoy slipped out of the hanger in small groups. The two commanders separated the group in two sections, each took command of the own section.

On the south side Captain McCoy sent her Special Forces squad of six, to recce the route and cover the sentries posted by Danek.

She kept contact with Richard Saunders on her quiet mike, waiting until he and his party were in position to the north, before starting the attack. The arrival of the first of the Weapon carriers in the Chechen camp made the opening attack more effective, as the Chechens were involved with the welcoming of the vehicles when the attackers opened fire. Whatever else they were the Chechens were skilled soldiers and they reacted fast to the unsuspected attack, scattering and bringing their weapons into action, finding cover, and returning fire.

The weapons carriers were targeted by the attacking party and all four vehicles were reduced to smoking wrecks with missile strikes from the hand-held launchers brought by both sections of the NATO force.

Danek Abramov had broken away from the group as soon as the first shots were fired, he had managed to reach the track at the foot of the slope which had not been specifically targeted. He called Rocco over the personal communication net. "Where are you?"

Rocco replied, "I'm at the rim of the hill, in cover but the opposition is keeping our heads down. This is no good so I am extracting the men down the face of the slope as best I can. If you have a chance get the vehicles there, away on to the main road. The men in the area around the weapons carriers are holding them at the moment but they have had it. I can do nothing for them and they will be out of ammunition soon."

Danek got the Freelander moving collecting a spray of bullets as he did so. Behind him the 2.5 ton pick-up got moving and made it out of range of the attack party. The troop carrier did not make it. It blew up with a spectacular bang following a direct hit on the cargo still waiting stacked between the seats in the truck. The missile caused the mortar bombs in the boxes, to blow and the entire truck disintegrated scattering its bits in lethal shrapnel, over the area around it, causing the only casualties experienced by the attacking force.

Rocco managed to extract 22 men and a further eight got away before the two teams of NATO troops closed in. The last of the defenders ran out of ammunition and after calling back and forth for a few moments the first man rose to his feet waving a dirty once-white handkerchief on the end of his empty AK47. The firing ceased entirely and the other survivors rose to their feet and were rounded up, the medics with the attackers attended to the wounded

A total of 28 men straggled in to meet at the roadside. Rocco had connected up with Danek and the two surviving vehicles. An unfortunate Armenian trader lost his 4ton Ford truck, and was lucky to escape with his life, to provide the survivors with transport.

Without hesitation the small convoy headed for Kars. Danek decided that there were matters that needed clarifying with Avo Rankin that could only be addressed face to face. Rocco redirected the remainder of their heavy equipment, still en-route, to Kars Airfield.

***

The two captains returned to base with the 19 prisoners including five with various wounds, and their own two wounded from the truck explosion. At the base General Gregor Volkov was in conference with General Summers. The situation in Georgia was becoming increasingly unstable with the persistent intervention of Russian agitators. The pressure on the Georgian army was becoming more intense by the day. A strong section of the community was in favour of a firm suppression of the parties lobbying for a return to Russian rule.

***

To Volkov there were many problems with a return to Russian rule, not the least being that the defection of his force to Georgia had been from the Russian army and in the face of the orders of Putin himself. Like the Chechen mercenaries he was facing the prospect of arrest and imprisonment if the Russian takeover was successful.

The prisoners were faced with the prospect of Turkish justice, apart from the prison conditions in Turkey, as Ali Baranka pointed out, there was also the possibility of punitive sentences being handed out. The problem of the prisoners was solved in the short term by the simple expedient of returning them over the border to Georgia, from whence they had entered Turkey. In the custody of General Volkov's men the Chechens were offered the choice of repatriation to Russia's hands or enlistment into the Georgian army with the issue of a Georgian passport after one year.

The 100% acceptance of this offer was not much of a surprise, return to official Russian hands meant almost certain death to the Chechens and they knew it.

The two wounded from Captain Patsy McCoy's section were admitted to the base hospital, but in fact in view of the imminent departure of the Deployed Guard unit, they were returned to the United States the following day for surgery.

***

In Teheran, General Arin Corman rang for Major Reza Gilani. The interview was short for there was little to say. "What is the situation with the Chinese fighters?"

"They are assembled and undergoing test at the moment."

"We have ten days only!"

"They will be ready within three days, the weapons have been selected, sadly we have no nuclear warheads but we do have extremely powerful conventional warheads that we can enhance with nerve gas to mop up survivors. We will have three missiles for each aircraft."

The General sat considering the report. We must give the operation a suitable name, and I suppose we will have to issue pensions to the surviving families of the pilots and crew."

He leaned forward and looked the Major in the eye. "The assembly and servicing crew?"

"All will be involved in the act of sabotage by the Israeli Mossad criminals. There are no survivors from the destruction of the entire airfield resource. We have three Israeli's under wraps ready to stand trial as soon as the operation is completed."

"Good!" The General smiled, "You seem to be better organised than you were with the Hedi Kashani business. As for name I think Khomeini Wind had a fine ring to it, don't you agree?"

Reza shrugged, "It sounds excellent, of course I was let down in the business of Kashani I missed her by seconds. I am still working on it, though since I believe she is with the

Americans anyway, that matter should soon be arranged with no further action on my part."

"For your sake I do hope so, I hate to think that she has 'got away with it' as our American enemies put it."

Major Reza Gilani rose to his feet and donned his cap. He saluted immaculately and left the office. He was inwardly boiling, that stupid apology for a man, sitting in his chair giving his orders and threats out. He made his way to the staff car and ordered the driver to take him to the quiet airfield where the Chinese fighters were being tested.

In the office he maintained at the airfield he called for the three pilots. When they were all present he said immediately " I have arranged that on completion of this mission you will all receive $100.000. If you don't make it back, your families will be looked after for life." He considered for a moment, then "I will tell you now that you are not supposed to return from this mission."

The three men in front of him looked shocked at this.

"I am not talking about enemy action, I refer to self-destruct charges in the aircraft that would normally only be used after a crash landing being adapted to operate after the discharge of the three missiles you carry." He held up his hand to stem their shocked protests. "Gentlemen, I have told you of the plan, I have also made sure that it does not happen, In fact, after the raid, I have arranged for an alternative destination for the aircraft, which I am sure you are aware are worth millions. You will take them over the border to the Ukraine where they will be delivered to a military airfield that I will designate in your final briefing. Do you all understand?" All three, now comfortable with a situation they were accustomed to, had relaxed nodding. Money made all things equal.

"So unofficially the bonus payable will be a minimum of $2 million dollars each. You will of course need to stay out of this country as a result. Is that all clear?"

The three men nodded once more in unison, well pleased with the arrangement. As they filed out of the office Reza marvelled at the stupidity and greed that had delivered the three willing men into his hands.

In the hanger the servicing crew were completing their work on the recently tested aircraft. Wan Li, a specialist in electronics, closed the panel having checked the circuit boards for the self-destruct system. Making sure he was not seen, he removed a small remote control from his pocket and pressed a switch. The small led glowed red. Satisfied, he switched off and returned the control to his pocket. He had no illusions about his survival prospects if left to the Iranians. His extraction had already been planned and arranged by his CIA masters. He wandered across to the quarters allocated to the Chinese contingent. The Chinese aircrew had already left, their job done, so there was plenty of space left for the remaining servicing personnel. Safe in his own room, he covertly swept the room with a minute bug detector. It was all clear, so he removed the remote from his pocket and on the reverse opened a panel and pressed a button, holding the remote to his ear he said, "All the aircraft are ready." There was a brief acknowledgement, He then said, "The building has been rigged to blow. The planes will fly Friday."

The voice said "Pick-up 30 minutes after take-off."

Wan Li closed the flap and put the remote in his pocket. He thought for a moment, of his wife, Su Lee, in their San Francisco apartment. He checked his watch, she would be in bed he thought, though he was not really sure, he was still confused by time zones involved, the entire operation had been last minute. His addition to the team had been arranged by inserting him as a replacement for a man who had been injured. The man he was supposed to be was currently in a US Federal prison.

***

Avo Rankin was feeling uncomfortable. There had been no news from Danek Abramov and his Chechens and he had anticipated that he would know something by now.

Fedor, up to now his right hand, was beginning to bother him also. He seemed to be getting restive and less willing of late. As he sat at his desk he wondered if his disagreement with Hazel had anything to do with things. Perhaps Fedor thought he was getting soft? If that was the case it was time to replace him, sooner rather than later. He reached for the telephone.

***

Fedor took a final look round his room. There was little to love about it, but it had been home for the past seven years. He had his passport and his personal iPad with all his account records. A change of clothing and his spare automatic and ammo clips. With no real regret he left the room and went out to his Audi A4 and climbed in. His quiet departure at 0300 was only observed by the night security guard at the gate, who saluted him in passing as Fedor abandoned his long-time boss forever. He was confident that Avo Rankin would not send out a search party for him. He would be aware that Fedor was in the position to put him away for life at least, if he released what he knew.

***

It was with some trepidation that Avo faced Danek Abramov. It did not show. When Danek burst into his office to confront him, he looked up and coolly said, "So have you carried out your instructions?"

The furious Danek was stopped in his tracks, only too aware that the man before him was the tip of a long tentacle that reached all the way back to Moscow, and maybe to God knows where. Whatever he said now could result in a midnight visit from professional assassins, who would not take no for an answer. With an effort he suppressed his anger and unclutched the butt of his hand gun. Before he could speak, Rankin said, "Have you brought your deputy with you?"

Danek nodded.

"Call him!" The calm voice commanded.

"Rocco, in here!"

Rankin spoke to Rocco, "Are the men with you under your control?"

Bemused, Rocco nodded.

Rankin shot Danek twice, once in the stomach once in the head, the silenced automatic making little noise.

"You have just taken over command. Have your men find accommodation in the warehouse for now, tell them Abramov tripped and broke his neck, or whatever you think best. When you're settled, come back and we'll discuss plans for future operations." He settled back in the chair placing the automatic on the desk in front of him. "Any question?"

"None that won't wait till later." Rocco sketched a salute and left the room to get the men settled in.

***

In Ciranu Base Hedi was in discussion with Hazel Cantrell who had come in response to a call from Chuck Hartog. Leaving Hedi to talk with Hazel about the situation of the premises at Kars, Chuck had gone to assemble a group from the Special Forces contingent. Chuck returned with Lieutenant Jerry Peters SAS whom he introduced to the two women. At 5ft 11in Peters was 29 years old hazel eyes and light brown hair, cut to suit his age. Dressed in casual shirt chinos and trainers he looked like any other young man of his era. Perhaps a climber or sportsman with a smooth innocent-looking face. Hedi looked at him wonderingly, Hazel with interest. Chuck introduced them and sat down to go over the drawings of the headquarters occupied by Rankin's company. He then mentioned that the survivors of the Chechen force had been observed entering the warehouse on the premises.

Hedi said "I thought it would be someone other than the Iranians that had mounted the attack on the base. This Rankin, you say he is Mafia?"

Hazel answered, "I discovered that he was when I started to enquire into the explosion of one of the convoy vehicles in a mercy run to Iran. He was using the convoy to transport a stolen atom bomb to the Iranians. It was a shock, he had been my guardian since the death of my parents, twenty years ago. I now have reason to believe that he murdered my parents. He was my father's business partner at the time.

"There are no formal defences at the premises?" Hedi commented.

"None at all." Hazel answered, "Apart from the fact that the place is on the outskirts of town beside the airport road. There is little to cause anyone to take an interest in his activities."

"The isolation could be to our advantage." Jerry Peters suggested. "There will be security defences in the form of motion sensors and trip wires, I would think?"

"Au contraire, Lieutenant, you forget where we are. Here in Turkey there is no real need for such things, mainly because there is a security group that operates on the premises. They are armed, as are most groups of that type in Turkey. The authorities here have little tolerance for thieves and vandals. Sentences are savage by Western Europe standards, and intruders shot by security patrols get scant sympathy."

Jerry Peters looked keenly at Hazel, aware she looked up and met his eye. They maintained eye contact for several seconds, while Hedi looked on with a smile, thinking either sparks will fly, or something will start between them.

Chuck broke the silence. "In the circumstances there are things we need to know. We cannot presume it is all over."

"What about the Iranians?" Hedi said.

"That must be a problem for Colonel Hamilton. We concentrate on this particular situation. So let us get on with it."

Chapter twenty-one

...Khomeini Wind

Major Reza Gilani was feeling angry, it was not an unusual feeling, more and more he was suffering from the sarcastic comments of General Corman. The general was upset at the defection of Hedi Kashani and blamed the major for her loss. It was true he had failed to detain her in time, but as far as he was concerned the general was not aware of the surveillance that Reza had been conducting. Now he was not so sure. The new secretary was pretty enough but not in the same league, in Reza's estimation.

More important, the assembly of the Chinese fighters was progressing well, all should be tested before the weekend. Once that was accomplished the raid could go ahead. He turned his jeep through the gates of the airbase and noticed with fury that there was one of the aircraft out on the apron in front of the hanger. There was a group of people around it, several he was appalled to note were personnel from the Air Force unit stationed at the base.

He pulled up beside the group and noticed the security chief of the project standing to one side. Stepping out of the vehicle he went to the security man, who was standing watching, looking most unhappy.

"What is going on?" Reza asked in a restrained voice.

"The general came here this morning, the first of the planes was ready to fly. he ordered the flight to take place and the aircraft to be wheeled out. The pilots were all in the International Hotel in Teheran. They had all been drinking and none was fit to fly. The aircraft was out and of course all the spare people in the area came to look. No one dared order the aircraft to be returned to the hanger, so it has been out here all morning, waiting for a test flight this afternoon when a pilot will be available."

Major Reza Gilani stood thinking for several minutes. It was obviously crunch time, the general must go. He walked into the hanger and lifted the wall mounted telephone inside the door. Connected to the supervisor he barked down the telephone,

"Get that aircraft inside the hanger now!" He broke the connection and rang the number for the SAVAK Director. He was connected to the desk of Marshal Pitta, the legendary creator of the security service in its present form.

"Yes?" The crisp voice answered.

"This is Major Reza Gilani, aide to General Arin Corman, project Khomeini Wind has been compromised by my general, sir."

"Explain?" The voice did not alter.

"Sir, he had the first of the aircraft wheeled out onto the open apron when there was no pilot available to fly it. He failed to have it returned to the hanger, and when I arrived to check on progress I found it surrounded by Air Force personnel who were not authorised on the need to know basis."

"Can they be rounded up?"

"The aircraft has been outside for 5 hours. I would presume that there were many people out there looking that have since gone back to their work, also photographs of the aircraft have been taken by many of the onlookers. I do not think we have a chance of getting all people involved, or all photographs either. I think there has been a press reporter here also."

"Shoot him!" There was a pause, "Make it look like suicide, overwork, you know what to do."

"Very good, sir. I will arrange it immediately."

When the conversation ended, the Director lifted his other telephone and spoke to someone. The conversation was short and to the point. "Major Reza Gilani. SAVAK, he is about to kill General Arin Corman, his Chief. The killing is supposed to look like suicide. Clear up, please, they can fight over the woman in the office. She can go, too. See to it." The cold man put the phone down and stepped over to the cabinet beside the desk. Opening the door he removed the holstered automatic, a suppressed Glock, and belted it round his waist. As he went through the door he picked up his hat and settled it firmly on his head. The elevator took him down the three floors to the office of General Arin Corman. In the outer office the secretary was sitting cleaning her nails.

"He's out to a launch ceremony." She said with a smile. The officer was good looking.

The cold man smiled, "It is a lucky man who can have the company of a girl as pretty as you, I envy your general."

The girl grimaced, "He's alright I suppose, but not really my choice."

"So there would be hope for me then?"

"Possibly." The girl said with a small smile, "I might consider it if the circumstances were right."

He leaned forward and kissed the girl, taking her chin in his hand and caressing her neck.

"You are a bad boy." The girls said with a giggle.

He stood up, "Please, a bad man, at least!"

She looked pointedly at his groin, "Ah I think I see what you mean." She ran her tongue around her lips. She said softly, "The general will not return for nearly two hours, would you like to see his office?"

"That would be interesting, I'm sure."

Taking his hand she led him through the door into the general's empty office with the ottoman along the wall opposite the desk.

"Now you were saying that you were a bad man, I believe. Show me what you mean by that."

The general's office door closed quietly.

***

Major Reza Gilani returned to the office first. He noticed that the office door was closed and at first drew the conclusion that the general had returned before him. In view of his orders he shrugged, 'Why not?'

Drawing his automatic he cocked it and went to the door, turning the handle quietly as expected he heard the noise of the coupling that he guessed he would hear. Reassured he opened the door wide and stepped in. The couple on the ottoman did not notice at first, but the cold man realised from the draft that someone had entered. His gun was on the floor just under the ottoman and he took it up in the nearest hand and turned to see who had entered saying "Please a little privacy at least." The astonished Reza was just too slow to react. The cold man's silenced bullet took him between the eyes, dropping him on the spot. The girl underneath him stirred, not aware of what had just happened. "Please don't stop now!"

"Of course not." He whispered and continued to conclude the exercise they had started. He waited until she cried out in her satisfaction before he shot her dead.

Uncoupled once more he used the en suite bathroom to clean up and fully dressed once more, sat at the general's desk to await victim number three.

***

Before leaving the office finally, the cold man took the guns of the general and the major and using the rather plush overstuffed cushion from the ottoman, he fired two shots through the opened window overlooking the arid landscape, from the general's gun, followed by one from the major's and placed the guns in the hands of the two men. He ripped the cushion apart, watching the feathers scatter in the wind, then he wrapped the cloth cover into a small roll and took out with him in his hand. He locked both inner and outer doors, before taking the elevator three floors up to his own office.

***

There was a report from the watchers that they had intercepted radio traffic between the Chechen survivors and a convoy of heavy vehicles on their way south through Georgia. Chuck spoke to Jerry Peters, in charge of the surveillance team. Jerry had no idea what the convoy contained, but he suspected that it was bringing heavy weapons for the Chechen assault on the base. A man called Rocco had spoken in English to the convoy asking for their ETA. The reply had been in Russian, they were speaking of no more than two days.

General Mike Summers contacted General Grigor Volkov by secure telephone. Volkov was back in Batumi Base after touring and speaking, in an effort to get elected to the Georgian Parliament. Katerina Shukov was with him, helping with the campaign.

General Summers congratulated Volkov, then he gave the reason for his call. "Grigor my friend, we have a problem. The Chechen mercenaries you have accepted into your force; can you find out if there is a convoy bringing heavy weapons for the attack on the base here?"

"Katerina will find out." He spoke to Katerina and came back on the phone. "So how are you getting on, any more threats to the base?"

"We have discovered that the Iranians are preparing three Chinese new super fighters for an attack before we leave here. I understand they are superior in performance to anything NATO can provide. We are taking precautions."

"That is not the best news, Michael, it could be real trouble. But surely the Iranians will be inviting the response of NATO?"

"We believe that Putin will be blamed."

Volkov paused and Mike heard voices at the other end of the line then Katerina came on. "Sir, the men here say that there were missiles and launchers loaded and despatched by road when they set out by air to make the latest attack. They believe that is the only convoy that Abramov, their leader, arranged."

"That sounds definite enough for me. Thank you. Katerina."

The voice of Volkov returned to the phone. "Michael if you need us we are here. Katerina is returning by air today, do not hesitate to call, I will put my people on standby."

"Thanks, Gregor. I would like to know when the convoy is due to cross the border."

"It will be done, my friend, it will be done. If you need back-up let me know, I have a lot of happy men here who could do with the exercise."

"Thanks but no thanks for now. I will keep in touch, though you do realise that we will be returning to the USA in 8 days?"

"I will come and make sure you actually leave Europe, you keep causing trouble while you are here."

The laugh that followed took any sting out of the words, and the call closed on that note.

Chuck heard the news and called Jerry Peters, "There is a convoy of five heavy vehicles on its way loaded with goodies for the Chechens. I am considering stopping them before they reach you."

"With respect sir, it would be better to allow them to reach here, and take them out when they arrive. It will also allow us to inflict collateral damage on the property of our mafia friend Rankin. It would expose his activities to the authorities, and make Colonel Baranka's job a little easier."

***

Hedi arranged reinforcements for Lieutenant Peter's small surveillance group for the forthcoming action.

For Hedi life had become interesting, the temporary persona adopted for the travel period when she left Iran had now been dropped and she was now employed under her own name by the USAF. The State Department had arranged a temporary passport and visa so that she could travel with the unit when they returned to the United States. The situation with Chuck Hartog was as yet unresolved both willing to wait until they reached Michigan before taking things further. Their relationship was otherwise moving along nicely in a sort of old fashioned romantic way. Because of her agent training, Hedi found it difficult settling into an exclusive administration position consequently she had suggested that she would be better employed as part of Jerry Peter's team, providing alternative surveillance to the otherwise exclusively male group. Having arranged the on-call re-enforcement unit, she packed a case and set off in a locally registered land-cruiser, for the town of Kars, and attachment to Lieutenant Peter's surveillance unit.

The uniform that was packed in her case carried the rank of Lieutenant, though she was travelling in plain clothes and would operate in them until the actual action against Rankin and the Chechens commenced. Apart from the Walther in her purse, there was a Glock plastic pistol and Kevlar knife at hand. In uniform her weapon of choice was a Colt Bullpup, that weapon would come with the re-enforcements. A woman travelling alone in Turkey in the eastern part of the country was an unusual sight, Hedi took the precaution of bringing trooper David Bowman SAS as driver and team partner. The standing order for all Special Operation's personnel was, that all active units operated on the buddy system. No exceptions were allowed. Patsy McCoy was leading the re-enforcement company the following day, the day before the convoy was expected.

Hedi drove up the road D957, with David Bowman sprawled in the seat next to her listening to an MP3 player. Both had tourist visas as US visitors, friends travelling together.

There were roadblocks at some points, but Ali Baranka had people in most places, ready enough to step in if needed. There was no need, and when they reached Kars, they checked into adjoining rooms in the Kars Hotel, located in the centre of town. The airport and location of Rankin's headquarters was to the south of the town but within easy reach. Hedi had a working knowledge of Turkish which she did not disclose. As a holidaymaker from USA nobody expected her to know Turkish and people spoke freely in front of her. She soon learned that Rankin was not liked in the town. His links with the Mafia were recognised and despised by most of the people she was in contact with in her excursions into the culture in the local area.

The convoy arrived the second day of the visit. Hedi and David connected with Jerry Peters at the first indication that the convoy was in the area. At the hired warehouse in the Airport freight area, Hedi met up with Patsy McCoy. Having changed into uniform, there was little to link her with the light hearted tourist of the day before.

***

For Rankin the arrival of the heavy weapons could have been an embarrassment. In fact, his arrogance was his undoing. When the convoy drew up in his compound a police car pulled in to check the origin of the goods carried.

Rankin sent his current deputy out with a wad of money to shut the man up. This time the man refused the money and demanded Bills of Lading, since the goods had crossed the border into Turkey.

When it was clear that there were no Bills with the cargo, the policeman called for back-up.

With the arrival of the local armed response unit, all hell broke loose. The police were all in Kevlar gear but suffered injuries despite their protective clothing. That was where the unit standing-by were called in. Since the convoy was carrying military equipment the NATO unit were tasked to act in concert with local law and order forces. Since they happened to be in place on exercise, Captain

McCoy and her company entered the premises in support of the armed police.

Hedi took her squad and ensured that the convoy vehicles could not be moved. The Chechens were billeted in Rankin's warehouse and they became involved with the police shootout with Rankin's men. The warehouse was targeted by McCoy's people who used rocket grenades and shoulder mounted missiles to reduce the building to a smoking wreck.

Hedi's unit broke into the big trucks and found wheeled AA(SAM) missile launchers with missiles, ground attack missiles with launchers, and two armoured cars armed with twenty mm cannon, and machine guns.

When the racket died down and the prisoners disarmed, Rankin came out of his office where he had sheltered during the entire operation. He was accompanied by his deputy armed with an UZI smg. As soon as he appeared he was disarmed and both were handcuffed. His arrest was accompanied by loud claims of innocence that fell on deaf ears. The bribe money was produced and despite all his denials he was taken to the police station where he was placed in a cell along with others of his men were present at the time. Assisted by Hedi, the police searched the premises and found records of enough illegal operations to ensure Rankin would be unlikely to see the light of day as a free man ever again.

By arrangement Hazel Cantrell appeared and gave evidence that mercy convoys were being used by Rankin to transport arms and ammunition into Iran. Against the protests of his lawyers, Avo Rankin was placed in prison to await trial. The conditions in the prison were not good and Rankin's demands for special treatment were successful, money talked. His death followed closely after. Suspicion arose that he was passing information to the authorities in return for favourable treatment. True or not, it was enough for his Mafia colleagues to act. He was found hanging in his cell. His passing was not mourned. He never went to trial.

***

Four days before the movement order for the return to America of the National Guard wing to its base on the shores of Lake Michigan, three Chinese jet fighters were wheeled out onto the apron of the military airfield on the outskirts of Teheran. Marshal Pitta was present to watch the departure of the aircraft. At a ceremony prior to their departure all three pilots and their crewmen were personally decorated with Iran's highest award.

In the transient staff quarters Wan Li took the remote control out of his pocket and looked at it carefully. He then took his cell phone out and as he heard the three planes spooling their engines up for the take-off, he pressed a speed dial button. The pre-arranged message was sent to warn the NATO base in Turkey that the enemy had taken off.

In the Teheran base, Wan Li pressed the remote control button, and the light changed from red to green. On all three aircraft, under the inspection panel LED lights glowed into life waiting for the half hour deadline before the self-destruct program shut down the engines and operated the ejector seat system before it destroyed the three raiders.

Chapter Twenty-two

...Two from three makes one!

Whatever it was that warned him he could never after-wards recall. Something made him look out of the window, across the open area beside the hanger containing the visit-ing air mechanics and aircrews. He could hear the other members of the group celebrating the completion of their task. He had come to his room to carry out his own pro-gram to ensure the aircraft never made it to their destina-tion. What he saw confirmed his own worst fears. The overalled and masked group of heavily armed men were debussing from two vehicles. They were all looking toward the hanger. They began to move forward as he watched.

Wan Li picked up his gunbelt and grabbed the AK47 with the vest holding the spare magazines and ran through the door into the main recreation room. As he ran through the room he called out. his warning.

"Masked armed men are coming for us, arm your-selves and get out of here." He made it through the far door into the main hanger. The two armed guards who were about to lock the door were taken by surprise, as the door slammed open in their face. The AK 47 in Wan Li's hand spat bullets in a short burst. Both men went down, but Wan Li was not waiting. Still running, he made it to the door on the other side of the hanger. He knew that outside was the car park and the private aircraft tie down area. As he dived through the door the first of the other member of the visiting Chinese party were bursting into the hanger.

Outside he avoided the parked cars and made for the private aircraft area. The twin Cherokee was sitting with engines running and the door open. By the reception centre a limousine was standing the occupants were being seen off by a group of senior officers and officials. The faint popping of gunfire was now interrupting the peace of the morning though the VIP party could not hear it over the noise of the engines.

Wan Li slowed and walked casually over to the waiting aircraft, the AK47 hanging down beside his right leg out of easy sight of the party. At the door of the aircraft he climbed the small ladder and looked along the cabin. The hostess turned surprised and seeing the gun checked the warning she was going to shout. Wan Li said "Out!" She ran down the steps and exited the aircraft. Wan Li hauled the door shut, the steps folded flat as the door rose into place. The pilot yelled something from his place at the controls. Wan Li went forward and showed the pilot the gun, "Now take off!" he ordered.

Without a word the pilot opened the throttles and the aircraft began to roll forward. Wan Li seated himself in the co-pilot's seat. He sat as the pilot opened the throttles wide and the Cessna left the ground smoothly.

"Where is the other pilot?"

"He was filing the flight plan." The pilot replied. He was quite calm, as if being hi-jacked was an everyday occurrence in his busy life, a Pakistani, in immaculate white shirt, black slacks, and four gold bands on his shoulder boards. "Where to?" He asked.

"Any suggestions?" Wan Li asked.

Startled the pilot looked at Wan Li. "Are you serious?" he asked.

"They will send up a fighter or two to find us and shoot us down I would think, Yes I am serious."

The cool expression warmed up at this comment.

"In that case may I suggest down as soon as possible to find some other form of transport." He pushed the control column forward and the aircraft started to descend from the 2500 ft it had gained since take off. The private landing strip was only just long enough for the Cherokee, and the pilot pulled it up just short of the barn that was obviously used as the hanger for whatever aircraft lived there. The afternoon sun was casting long shadows as it descended in its regular journey into night. The aircraft was within the shadow as it stood cooling off, engines quiet. The two men got out of the plane and looked around the barn. There was no house near, and it did not surprise Wan Li that the barn was locked. He kicked the side door open and they entered the building, the pilot leading. The De Havilland Chipmunk stood just inside the closed double doors. Wan Li checked the fuel levels in the wing tanks. The tanks indicated full.

Turning to the pilot he said, "What has happened so far will already be enough to get you shot if they catch you, or can you be sure your boss will defend you?"

The pilot thought for a moment. "I was hired for this trip. My boss is back in Karachi, and I would not trust him as far as I can spit. What are you saying please?"

Wan Li considered in turn. "What I am saying is that we put the Cherokee in here, and take the Chipmunk. You can stay with me until we are across the border into Georgia or Turkey. I am American, I need to get to a NATO Base as soon as possible. If we help each other it will probably save your life as well as mine."

The pilot shrugged and the hint of a smile crossed his face as he reached for the door control and started it opening. "My name is Raj, what do I call you?"

"Wan Li! OK let's get this plane out and the other in, it will be a tight squeeze through the doorway but there is plenty of room in here."

Between them they rolled out the Chipmunk, there was no sound of aircraft as with some difficulty they manoeuvred the other aircraft through the barn door.

Before the door was lowered Raj yelled "Wait One!" And he ran to the back of the barn where there was a refrigerator and sink with cupboards. From the Frig he brought out bottles of water, and from a cupboard he got a packet of crackers and some energy bars. Clutching his booty he came out and dumped the lot on the wing root. "Right. You can close it now."

When Wan Li had the door closed, Raj said "I thought it made sense, just in case."

Wan Li nodded thoughtfully. " I'll drive," he said. "Split the loot into two and take the forward seat." The pair climbed into the tandem seats of the Chipmunk and Wan Li started up, checked the magnetos and when they were both settled in their seats he opened the throttle of the single Gipsy 8 engine and took off along the single runway, into a slight breeze. He switched on the radio, but left the level low, and from habit switched on the navigation lights. At 3000 feet he levelled off and turned onto a north westerly heading. He checked the carburettor setting and moved the throttle to the economic cruising level and sat back with a sigh.

***

657 miles on the way to their destination, the junior pilot of the trio of Khamenei Wind aircraft was astonished to

see the cockpit canopies of his two companions fly off closely followed by the ejector seated pilots of the two aircraft. Both aircraft slowed and their engines flamed out. As their noses dropped the planes exploded. The astonished surviving pilot looked at his dashboard in panic. The small LED in one corner was flashing intermittently red green, red green. The cover over the self-destruct button was firmly in place. Otherwise there was no other sign of trouble. He had gone into a circle when the others had been destroyed and was able to see that the parachutes had deployed for both pilots, re-assured he shrugged and returned to his base course. Orders forbade the use of the radio under any circumstances. He pressed on to carry out his orders. He dropped the wingtip fuel tanks before he reached the Turkish border. The GPS tracker was set for his destination. But as he watched it suddenly went off. He tapped it "Fucking Chinese crap!" It did not occur to him that it was nothing to do with the Chinese. More to do with the electronic countermeasures transmitted from the target. It flickered, and started up once more. Suddenly his radio came alive. A voice spoke in Farsi.

"Unknown jet aircraft, identify yourself?"

He ignored the transmission. His dashboard lit up once more and the deedle deedle warning of a radar locked missile flashed up on the small screen before him.

"Shit!" he said and slammed on full right rudder causing the aircraft to swerve violently. The Iranian SAM missile flashed past. He straightened the aircraft. returned to his mean course. Immediately another missile was signalled, he swore again and slammed the throttles wide. The afterburners kicked-in, punching him back in his seat. As the G-force increased the relentless pressure grew and the speed increased to 2500 mph. He was aware that this meant there was no going back, there would not be sufficient fuel.

***

Group Captain David Sheldon lifted off the runway at Ciranu in the Typhoon, the Euro-fighter felt alive under his practiced hands. In a gentle spiral he climbed up to a height of 30.000 ft, with radar off. He listened carefully to the radar operators from the Boeing E-3 Sentry. The AWAC reported three fast movers, it then corrected itself, one fast mover circling over the Iranian border. The fast mover identified as hostile, resumed course for Ciranu.

Missile attack from Iran Border protection, evaded by fast mover now moving at 2500 mph. Eta Ciranu 5 minutes-now extended-15 minutes-aircraft slowed down to 500 mph-vector co-ordinates thus. They appeared on the attack screen before him. "Sector patrol 3, have you got that?" The other two Typhoons both acknowledged.

David called Ciranu Base. "Bandit discovered and identified, am challenging." Ciranu acknowledged.

Pushing the control column forward David moved to intercept the incoming aircraft.

In the remaining attacker Zem Parvis did his final attack checks, pulled the straps of his harness tight and clicked open the covers of the missile launch buttons. In the instructions there were nominated targets based on three two or one aircraft. Discarding the other sets he concentrated on the single air attack.

Parvis was shocked at the impact of a scatter of bullets on the wing of his aircraft. The Tornado with the RAF insignia swept past rocking the Iranian aircraft in the turbulence.

The radio came alive and the voice speaking English called on him to land his aircraft immediately, or be shot down.

Parvis was taken aback, he had never anticipated anything like this. As he considered two other Typhoons appeared and took up station along both sides, the third appeared directly overhead. Whatever else Zem Parvis was, he was not stupid. He lowered the undercarriage and landed as instructed on the long runway of Ciranu. He taxied as instructed to the parking area.

After opening the canopy he unstrapped himself and leaving his parachute in place, he stepped onto the wing. He leaned back into the cockpit and unclipping the cover to the self-destruct button. He pressed the button and jumped down from the wing.

The security team hustled him into their Humvee and took him off to the admin building.

The three Typhoons landed in turn and parked. The call from Wan Li was a surprise. He used a code word which got their attention, and asked for pickup.

The Chinese fighter was left untouched and under guard, awaiting a specialist avionics expert who could disable the self-destruct system.

When Wan Li arrived with his new friend Raj, he looked at the Chinese fighter in amazement.

"How did that get here?" He asked. His escort explained that it had been forced down when it arrived.

"The pilot set the self-destruct and it didn't go off now they are waiting for an expert to come and make it safe."

Wan Li nodded gravely. "I see, that could be a problem. I happen to be an avionics technician, perhaps I could take a look?"

The base aero engineers were all over the Chinese fighter after Wan Li had performed his magic in defusing the threat of explosion. The dust of the airfield at Teheran had been the reason for the failure of the booby trap on the aircraft. Wan Li merely had to open the small access panel, remove the additional board he had inserted, and manually disable the self-destruct circuit.

He apologised to General Summers for failing to eliminate the third fighter before it came into range.

"You have given my engineers an opportunity they would never have had in other circumstances. They are re-assured that the vaunted Chinese fighter is no better that the Typhoon and in some ways not as well made or designed. You may be interested to know that the fighter will be returned to the Iranians after our Georgian friends have studied it.

***

Wan Li departed Ciranu base to return to the United States, via Istanbul the next day. His term with CIA as a technical agent was strictly based on their need for an avionics expert. He would be returning to his regular employment with the USAF research unit. The National Guard unit collected its people together, for the final time at Ciranu.

The Turkish Ministry of War had decided that the military use of the airport would be ceased, and Commercial Operations commenced.

***

The unit gathered for a parting celebration in the main hanger. As farewell parties go it was regarded as up to standard. The final separation from the unit of Lieutenant General Mike Summers was properly recognised and his departure with Colonel Mrs. Sarah Summers, marked with a full honour parade and march past.

At the air steps of the Lear jet, Colonel Peter Hamilton, and Colonel Jessica Browning saluted their friends and shook hands, both kissed Sarah. Colonel Chuck Hartog, impassive as ever was part of the farewell party, Hedi Kashani and Hazel Cantrell, stood back. Both recognised the debt they owed to the quiet man who had refused to stand by and watch injustice done.

For Grigor Volkov and Katerina Sheldon, Nee Shukov, it was an emotional moment. They had said their private farewells along with Group Captain David Sheldon and Colonel Ali Baranka, earlier that morning. General Volkov faced an uncertain future in Georgia. But as he said with great good humour, at least he still had a future.

The Lear jet was escorted after take-off, for the entire flight to Istanbul, by the Typhoons of the RAF led by Group Captain David Sheldon.

In Teheran a funeral cortege passed through the City carrying the remains of Marshal Pitta, former Chief of the Government security agency Sazeman-e Ettela'at va Amniyat-e Keshvar (SAVAK) who had died of a heart attack two days before.

The Chinese Ambassador was presented with the bodies of almost the entire contingent of experts who had brought a Chinese fighter for evaluation, to Iran. The unprovoked attack by Kurdish insurgents had resulted in the deaths of 47 men and women. The Iran nation was in mourning over the disaster and the arrest of those responsible was imminent.

The End

Meet our author

David O'Neil

Artist and Photographer David O'Neil started writing seriously with a series of Highland guide books. His boyhood ambitions were to fly an aeroplane, and sail a boat. As a boy he and his family were bombed out of their home in London. He learned to fly with the RAF during his National Service. He started sailing boats while serving in the Colonial Police, in Nyasaland (Malawi). He spent 8 years there, before returning to UK. Since then he lived in southern England where he became a management consultant, for over twenty years. He returned to live in Scotland in 1980, and became a tour guide in1986. He started writing in 2006, the first guide book being published in 2007. A further two have been published since He started writing fiction in 2007 and has now written eleven full length novels. He has a collection of short stories in publication at present.

Also by David O'Neil

Action/Adventure/Thriller series
Counterstroke # 1

Exciting, Isn't It?

O'Neil's initial entry into the world of action adventure romance thriller is filled with mystery and suspense, thrills and chills as *Counterstroke* finds it seeds of Genesis, and springs full blown onto the scene with action, adventure and romance galore.

John Murray, ex-Police, ex-MI6, ex management consultant, 49 and widowed, is ready to make a new start. Having sold off everything, he sets out on a lazy journey by barge through the waterways of France to collect his yacht at a yard in Grasse. En route he will decide what to do with the rest of his life

He picks up a female hitch-hiker Gabrielle, a frustrated author running from Paris after a confrontation with a lascivious would-be publisher Mathieu. She had unknowingly picked up some of Mathieu's secret documents with her manuscript. Although not looking for action, adventure or romance, still a connection is made.

An encounter with Pierre, an unpleasant former acquaintance from Paris who is chasing Gabrielle, is followed by a series of events that make John call on all his old skills of survival to keep them both alive over the next few days. Mystery and suspense shroud the secret documents that disclose the real background of the so called publisher who is in fact a high level international crook.

To survive, the pair become convinced they must take the fight to the enemy but they have no illusions; their chances of survival are slim. But with the help of some of John's old contacts, things start to become... exciting.

Counterstroke # 2....

Market Forces

Market Forces, Volume Two of the Counterstroke action adventure romance thriller series by David O'Neil introduces Katherine (Katt) Percival, tasked with the assassination of Mark Parnell in a hurried, last-minute attempt to stop his interference with the success of the Organization in Europe. As a skilled terminator for the CIA, Katt is accustomed to proper briefing. On this occasion she disobeys her orders, convinced it's a mistake. She joins forces with Mark to foil an attempt on his life.

Parnell works for John Murray, who created Secure Inc that caused the collapse of an International US criminal organisation's operation in Europe, forcing the disbanding of the US Company COMCO. Set up as a cover for money-laundering and other operations designed to control from within the political and financial administration, they had already been partially successful. Especially within the administrative sectors of the EU.

Katt goes on the run, she has been targeted and her Director sidelined by rogue interests in the CIA. She finds proof of conspiracy. She passes it on to Secure Inc who can use it to attack the Organization. She joins forces with Mark Parnell and Secure Inc. Mark and Katt and their colleagues risk their lives as they set out to foil the Organization once again.

Counterstroke # 3....

When Needs Must...

The latest action adventure thriller in the Counterstroke series opens with a new character Major Teddy Robertson–Steel fighting for survival in Africa. Mark Parnell and Katt Percival now working together for Secure Inc. are joined by Captain Libby 'Carter' Barr, now in plain clothes, well mostly, and her new partner James Wallace. They are tasked with locating and thwarting the efforts of three separate menaces from the European scene that threaten the separation of the United Kingdom from the political clutches of Brussels, by using terrorism to create wealth by a group of billionaires, and the continuing presence of the Mob, bankrolled from USA. An action adventure thriller filled with romance, mystery and suspense. With the appearance of a much needed new team, Dan and Reba, and the welcome return of Peter Maddox, Dublo Bond and Tiny Lewis, there is action and adventure throughout. Change will happen, it just takes the right people, at the right time, in the right place.

Counterstroke # 4....

When Needs Must

The latest action adventure thriller in the Counterstroke series opens with a new character Major Teddy Robertson–Steel fighting for survival in Africa. Mark Parnell and Katt

Percival now working together for Secure Inc. are joined by Captain Libby 'Carter' Barr, now in plain clothes, well mostly, and her new partner James Wallace. They are tasked with locating and thwarting the efforts of three separate threats to the European scene that threatens the separation of the United Kingdom from the political clutches of Brussels, by using terrorism to create wealth by a group of billionaires, and the continuing presence of the Mob, bankrolled from USA. An action adventure thriller filled with romance, mystery and suspense. With the appearance of a new team, Dan and Reba, and the return of Peter Maddox, Dublo Bond and Tiny Lewis, there is action and adventure, mystery and suspense, romance and surprises throughout. Change will happen, it just takes the right people, at the right time, in the right place.

Young adult action/adventure/ romance thriller series
Donny Weston & Abby Marshall # 1

Fatal Meeting

A captivating new series of young adult action, romance, adventure and mystery.

For two young teens, Donny and Abby, who have just found each other, sailing the 40 ft ketch across the English Channel to Cherbourg is supposed to be a light-hearted adventure.

The third member of the crew turns out to be a smuggler, and he attempts to kill them both before they reach France. The romance adventure. now filled with action, mystery and suspense, suddenly becomes deadly serious when the man's employers try to recover smuggled items from the boat. The action gets more and more hectic as the motive becomes personal

Donny and Abby are plunged into a series of events that force them to protect themselves. Donny's parents become involved so with the help of a friend of the family, Jonathon Glynn, they take the offensive against the gang who are trying to kill them.

The action adventure thriller ranges from the Mediterranean to Paris and the final scene is played out in the shadow of the Eiffel Tower in the city of romance and lights; Paris France..

Donny Weston & Abby Marshall # 2

Lethal Complications

Eighteen year olds Donny and Abby take a year out from their studies to clear up problems that had escalated over the past three years. They succeed in closing the book on the past during the first months of the year, now they are looking forward to nine months relaxation, romance and fun, when old friend of the family, mystery man Jonathon Glynn, drops in to visit as they moor at Boulogne, bringing action and adventure into their lives once again.

Jonathon was followed and an attempt to kill them happens immediately after his visit. They leave their boat and pick up the RV they have left in France, hoping to avoid further conflict. They are attacked in the Camargue, but fast and accurate shooting keeps them alive. They find themselves mixed up in a treacherous scheme by a rogue

Chinese gang to defame a Chinese moderate, in an attempt to stall the Democratic process in China.

The two young lovers, becoming addicted to action and adventure, link up with Isobel, a person of mystery who has acquired a reputation without earning it. Between them they manage to keep the Chinese target and his girlfriend out of the rogue Chinese group's hands.

Tired of reacting to attack, and now looking for action and adventure, they set up an ambush of their own, effectively checkmating the rogue Chinese plans. The leader of the rogues, having lost face and position in the Chinese hierarchy, plans a personal coup using former Spetsnaz mercenaries. With the help of a former SBS man Adam, who had worked with and against Spetsnaz forces, the friends survive and Lin Hang the Chinese leader suffers defeat.

Donny Weston & Abby Marshall # 3....

A Thrill A Minute

They are back! Fresh from their drama-filled action adventure excursion to the United States, Abby Marshall and Donny Weston look forward to once again taking up their studies at the University. Each of them is looking forward to the calm life of a University student without the threat of being murdered. Ah, the serene life.... that is the thing. But that doesn't last long. It is only a few weeks before our adventuresome young lovers find that the calm, quiet routine of University life is boring beyond belief and both are filled with yearning for the fast-paced action adventure of their prior experiences. It isn't long before trouble finds the couple and they welcome it with open arms, but perhaps this time they have underestimated the opposition. Feeling excitement once again, the two youths arm themselves and leapt into the fray. The fight was on and no holds barred!

Once again O'Neil takes us into the action filled world of mystery and suspense, action and adventure, romance and peril.

Donny Weston & Abby Marshall # 4....

It's Just One Thing After Another

Fresh from their victory over the European Mafia, our two young adults in love, Abby Marshall and Donny Weston, are rewarded with an all-expense-paid trip to the United States. But, as our young couple discover, there is no free lunch and the price they will have to pay for their "free" tour may be more than they can afford to pay, in this action adventure thriller. Even so, with the help of a few friends and some former enemies, the valiant young duo face danger once again with firm resolve and iron spirit, but will that be sufficient in face of the odds that are stacked against them?

And is their friend and benefactor actually a friend or is he on the other side? The two young adults look at this man of mystery and suspense with a bit of caution. Action, adventure and romance abound in this, the latest escapades of Britain's dynamic young couple.

Donny Weston & Abby Marshall # 5

What Goes Around...

Just when it seems that our two young heroes, Donny Weston and Abby Marshall are able to return to the University to complete their studies, fate decides to play another turn as once again the two young lovers come under attack, this time from a most unsuspected source. It appears that not even the majestic powers of the British Intelligence Service will be enough to rescue the beleaguered duo and they will have to survive through their own skills. In the continuing action adventure thriller, two young adults must solve the mystery that faces them to determine who is trying to kill them. The suspense is chilling, the action and adventure stimulating. Finding togetherness even among the onslaughts, Donny and Abby also find remarkable friends who offer their assistance; but will even that be enough to overcome the determined enemy?

Sea Adventures

Better The Day

From the W.E.B. Griffin of the United Kingdom, David O'Neil, a exciting saga of romance, action, adventure, mystery and suspense as Peter Murray and his brother officers in Coastal Forces face overwhelming odds fighting German E-boats, the German Navy and the Luftwaffe in action in the Channel, the Mediterranean, Norway and the Baltic – where there is conflict with the Soviet Allies. This action-packed story of daring and adventure finally follows Peter Murray to the Pacific where he faces Kamikaze action with the U.S. Fleet.

Distant Gunfire

"Border s Away!" Serving as an officer on a British frigate at the time of the French Emperor Napoleon is not the safest occupation, but could be a most profitable one. Robert Graham, rising from the ranks to become the Captain of a British battleship by virtue of his dauntless leadership, displayed under enemy fire, finds himself a wealthy man as the capture of enemy ships resulted in rich rewards. Action and adventure is the word of the day, as battle after battle rages across the turbulent waters and seas as the valiant British Royal Navy fights to stem the onslaught of the mighty French Army and Navy. Mystery and suspense abound as inserting and collecting spy agent after spy agent is executed. The threat of imminent death makes romance and romantic interludes all the sweeter, and the suspense of waiting for a love one to return even more traumatic. Captain Graham, with his loyal following of sailors and marines, takes prize ship after prize ship, thwart plot after diabolical plot, and finds romance when he least expects it. To his amazement and joy, he finds himself being knighted by the King of England. The good life is his, now all he has to do is to live long enough to enjoy it. A rollicking good tale of sea action and swashbuckling adventures.

Sailing Orders

For those awaiting another naval story of the 18/19th century, then this is it. Following the life of an abandoned 13 year old who by chance is instrumental in saving a family from robbery and worse. Taken in by the naval Captain Bowers he is placed as a midshipman in his benefactor's ship. From that time onward with the increasing demands of the conflict with France, Martin Forrest grows up fast. The relationship with his benefactors family is formalised when he is adopted by them and has a home once more. Romance with Jennifer the Captains ward links him ever closer to the family.

Meanwhile he serves in the West Indies where good fortune results in his gaining considerable wealth personally. With promotion and command he is able to marry and reclaim his birth-right, stolen from him by his step-mother and her lover.

The mysterious (call me merely Mr Smith) involves Martin in more activity in the shadowy world of the secret agents. Mainly a question of lifting and placing of people, his involvement becomes more complex as time goes on. A cruise to India consolidates his position and rank with the successful capture of prizes when returning convoying East-Indiamen. His rise to Post rank is followed by a series of events, that sadly culminate in family tragedy.

While still young Martin Forrest-Bowers faces and empty future, though merely Mr Smith has requested his services????

Adventure thrillers

Minding the Store

O'Neil scores again! Often favourably compared to America's W.E.B. Griffin and to U.K.'s Ian Fleming, and fresh from his best-selling action adventure, "Distant Gunfire," O'Neil finds excitement and action in the New York garment district. The department store industry becomes the target of take-over by organized crime in their quest for money-laundering outlets. It would seem that no department store executive is a match for vicious criminals, however, David Freemantle, heir to the Freemantle fortune and Managing Director of America's most prestigious department store is no ordinary department store executive and the team of ex-military specialists he has assembled contains no ordinary store security personnel. Armed invasions are met with swift retaliation; kidnapping and rape attempts are met with fatal consequences as the Mafia and their foreign cohorts learn that not all ordinary citizens are helpless, and that evil force can be met with superior force in O'Neil's latest thriller of adventure and action, romance and suspense, mystery and mayhem that will have the reader on the edge of his seat until the last breath-taking word.

The Hunted

David O'Neal, UK's answer to W.E.B. Griffin and Dean Koontz strikes again with his newest suspense thriller filled with action, adventure, romance and danger. When the Russian Mafia joins forces with other European and Asian gangsters to take over a noted world-wide charity organization to smuggle guns and drugs into unsuspecting nations and begins to kill innocent people, one man – Tarquin Gilmore – Quin to his friends – declares war on the Mafia. To achieve his goal of total destruction of the criminal gangs, he surrounds himself with a few dangerous men and beautiful women. But don't be fooled by their beauty, the girls are easily as deadly as any man. On the other hand, there are a lot more gangsters than Quin and his friends and it's a battle to the finish. A stirring tale of crime and murder, mystery and suspense, passion and romance, guns and drugs... but that is war!

The Mercy Run

O'Neil's thrilling action adventure saga of Africa: the story of Tom Merrick, Charlie Hammond and Brenda Cox; a man and two women who fight and risk their lives to keep supplies rolling into the U.N. refugee camps in Ethiopia. Their adversaries: the scorching heat, the dirt roads and the ever present hazards of bandit gangs and corrupt government officials. Despite tragedy and treachery, mystery and suspense while combating the efforts of Colonel Gonbera, who hopes to turn the province into his personal domain, Merrick and his friends manage to block the diabolical Colonel at every turn.

Frustrated by Merrick's success against him, there seems to be no depths to which the Colonel would not descend to achieve his aim. The prospect of a lucrative diamond strike comes into the game, and so do the Russians and Chinese. But, as Merrick knows, there will be no peace while the Colonel remains the greatest threat to success and peace.

*****

New Dynamic Series with Jonathan Penroc

The Raptors
Book One, Sarah Paige Chronicles

A New World Order?

A one government world?

The United States with a weak president and a divided government. The world in chaos and turmoil. Happenstance or a diabolical scheme? Emerging from the dark shadows are "The Raptors," human birds of prey seeking to establish a new one-world government under their iron rule. For more than a century, no one has been able to stop this mysterious force from altering entire governments, forcing resignations and where necessary, assassinations. No one is safe, not the President of the United States, not the Shah of Iran, not the Russian Premier. No one has even been able to slow down the onslaught that is gradually, nation by nation, acquiring control of the entire world. Resistance is met with overpowering force and nothing has stemmed their advance as they annihilate one obstacle after another. Then they made a mistake. They killed the wrong person and now they are faced with an infuriated woman out to revenge the killing of her one true love. Having finally found romance only to have it rift away by terrorist fanatics under the control of "The Raptors," Sarah has only one goal: vengeance or death. Can one distraught and determined female take on a clandestine world power? There is a saying, "Hell has no fury...."

~*~

Available from:

WEB Publishers Inc
www.a-argusbooks.com